SANDRA MARTON
SARAH MAYBERRY
EMILIE ROSE

HOT CITY NIGHTS

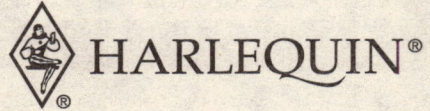

TORONTO • NEW YORK • LONDON
AMSTERDAM • PARIS • SYDNEY • HAMBURG
STOCKHOLM • ATHENS • TOKYO • MILAN • MADRID
PRAGUE • WARSAW • BUDAPEST • AUCKLAND

If you purchased this book without a cover you should be aware that this book is stolen property. It was reported as "unsold and destroyed" to the publisher, and neither the author nor the publisher has received any payment for this "stripped book."

ISBN-13: 978-0-373-83726-7
ISBN-10: 0-373-83726-7

HOT CITY NIGHTS

Copyright © 2008 by Harlequin Books S.A.

The publisher acknowledges the copyright holders of the individual works as follows:

SUMMER IN THE CITY
Copyright © 2008 by Sandra Myles.

BACK TO YOU
Copyright © 2008 by Sarah Mayberry.

FORGOTTEN LOVER
Copyright © 2008 by Emilie Rose Cunningham.

All rights reserved. Except for use in any review, the reproduction or utilization of this work in whole or in part in any form by any electronic, mechanical or other means, now known or hereafter invented, including xerography, photocopying and recording, or in any information storage or retrieval system, is forbidden without the written permission of the publisher, Harlequin Enterprises Limited, 225 Duncan Mill Road, Don Mills, Ontario M3B 3K9, Canada.

This is a work of fiction. Names, characters, places and incidents are either the product of the author's imagination or are used fictitiously, and any resemblance to actual persons, living or dead, business establishments, events or locales is entirely coincidental.

This edition published by arrangement with Harlequin Books S.A.

® and ™ are trademarks of the publisher. Trademarks indicated with ® are registered in the United States Patent and Trademark Office, the Canadian Trade Marks Office and in other countries.

www.eHarlequin.com

Printed in U.S.A.

Praise for our authors and their work

SANDRA MARTON

"Sandra Marton writes with an emotional intensity that will sear your heart and leave you breathless! *The Italian Prince's Pregnant Bride* is a highly emotional tale laden with sizzling sensuality, pulse-racing drama and poignant romance."
—*CataRomance.com*

"*The Desert Virgin,* the first book of Sandra Marton's Knight Brothers trilogy, sizzles.... Marton delivers a novel with suspense, intense emotion, steamy scenes and fantastic dialogue."
—*Romantic Times BOOKreviews*

SARAH MAYBERRY

"Unexpected twists, sympathetic characters and sizzling sex make Sarah Mayberry's *Take on Me* a wonderful book."
—*Romantic Times BOOKreviews*

"*All Over You,* by Sarah Mayberry, is another great book.... Very funny characters, great dialogue and sensual details make this a winner."
—*Romantic Times BOOKreviews*

EMILIE ROSE

"By turns witty and charming, Emilie Rose's characters are attractive, intelligent and strong in this excellent installment of the Monte Carlo Affairs series."
—*Romantic Times BOOKreviews* on *The Prince's Ultimate Deception*

"Hot, sexy and witty, *The Playboy's Passionate Pursuit* is definitely the right way to wrap up the Monte Carlo series. Emilie Rose has written a real keeper of a story."
—*Romantic Times BOOKreviews*

ABOUT THE AUTHORS

Sandra Marton wrote her first novel in elementary school. Her doting parents told her she'd be a writer someday. In high school and college she wrote dark poetry only her boyfriend understood. At last Sandra realized she wanted to write books about what all women want: love with that one special man. She sold her first novel to Harlequin Presents and has since written more than seventy books. A four-time RITA® Award finalist, she's also received numerous *Romantic Times BOOKreviews* Reviewers' Choice Awards for Best Harlequin Presents of the Year, and has been honored with a *Romantic Times BOOKreviews* Career Achievement Award for Series Romance. Sandra lives with her very own hero in a sun-filled house on a country lane in northern Connecticut.

Sarah Mayberry is an Australian who currently lives in New Zealand. Sarah has dreamed of being a writer since she was a little girl, and has worked as a journalist, scriptwriter and magazine editor before being published with Harlequin Books. When she's not writing and reading romance, she loves cooking, going to the movies, shopping for shoes and avoiding exercise.

Bestselling Silhouette Desire author and RITA® Award finalist **Emilie Rose** has sold twenty-four projects to Harlequin/Silhouette since her first sale in 2001, and her books have been released in more than twenty countries. Emilie lives in North Carolina with her four sons and two adopted mutts. Writing is her third—and hopefully last—career. She's managed a medical office and run a home day care, but neither compare to plotting happy endings. Her hobbies include gardening and cooking. Her favorite TV shows include *Grey's Anatomy, ER, CSI, Dancing with the Stars, American Idol* and Discovery Channel's medical programs. Emilie is a rabid country music fan because she can find an entire book in almost any song.

CONTENTS

SUMMER IN THE CITY 9
Sandra Marton

BACK TO YOU 149
Sarah Mayberry

FORGOTTEN LOVER 237
Emilie Rose

SUMMER IN THE CITY

Sandra Marton

For my husband: hot city nights, cool country mornings... Whatever the place, season or time, you will always be my hero.

CHAPTER ONE

Rio de Janeiro, April

CARNAVAL had ended almost two months ago, but Rio didn't seem to know it.

Lincoln Aldridge wasn't surprised. He'd been to Rio before. The city could be an endless party, especially for a man with money, rugged good looks and connections.

Linc had all three but he wasn't in a partying mood. He'd been on the go for almost two weeks, first flying to Argentina, then Colombia, then Brazil. His business meetings had gone well, but he had a more important matter on his mind.

Too much time had gone by since he'd heard from his sister. Kathryn and her husband, married five months, were on what she'd called a belated honeymoon, seeing the world.

New York City was part of the world, Linc had said wryly, and he damned well expected that Kath and the husband he'd never met intended to make it part of their trip.

"Absolutely," she'd answered, sounding almost like

the kid he still thought of her as being. "We're going to stop there last so we can spend some time with you. And, Linc? Get ready for a wonderful surprise!"

The best surprise would be seeing her again. Kath was twenty-two and he'd all but raised her. Now she lived in L.A., where she'd met Mark and eloped to Vegas. Linc, ten years her senior, would have felt better if he'd laid eyes on the guy before the wedding, but at least he would meet him soon.

It was why he was eager to get home.

First, though, he had to finalize the deal he'd made with entrepreneur Hernando Marques. They'd shaken hands on it but Marques wanted to sign the contract at his home. An odd request, maybe, but when a man was about to spend twenty-five million bucks a year giving Aldridge Inc. full responsibility for the security of all his residential and commercial properties, an odd request was okay.

"This is my poker night, Lincoln," Marques had said. "I spend it with a few old friends whose company I am sure you would enjoy. Please. Join us."

So Linc had smiled and said he looked forward to it.

A little before eight, his taxi glided through the massive iron gates that guarded the Marques estate.

Force of habit made Linc check the perimeter. One of his teams had installed the latest security systems a couple of weeks ago. Electric eyes. Hidden cameras. Sensors. He couldn't spot them all, which was as it should be, but what he saw looked perfect.

The taxi stopped at the foot of wide stone steps. His host flung the door open before Linc could ring the bell.

"Lincoln!" Marques grinned and extended his hand. "I was afraid you might have forgotten my invitation, *meo amigo*."

"Traffic," Linc said with a quick smile, even as he wondered at his host's reaction. Brazilians were a friendly people but Marques seemed to be taking things to a new level.

Marques led him to a leather-walled game room where a dozen or so men stood chatting in small groups near an expansive buffet laid out on a mile-long table.

"Come and meet my friends, Lincoln."

Linc shook hands, smiled, said hello and how are you to men he'd met before and others he knew by reputation. This was a gathering of some of the wealthiest men in South America. Eight years ago, when he'd started Aldridge Inc. with nothing but guts and his Special Forces experience, he'd have given anything to have been invited to an evening like this.

Now, it was Marques's guests who expressed pleasure at meeting him.

He moved from group to group, eating a little, drinking hardly at all, wondering when he could get away. No one seemed in a hurry to play cards.

At last, Marques sought him out again. He was smiling but tiny drops of sweat stood out on his forehead. Something was wrong. Had the man decided against the deal despite the binding handshake?

"Hernando," he said pleasantly. "I was just going to look for you. This is great but—"

"But you have had a long day and you wish for an early night."

"I'm glad you understand."

"I do. So perhaps—perhaps, now, we might adjourn to the library to—to—"

"To sign the contract," Linc said, his eyes on the other man's.

"Certainly. To sign the contract." Marques hesitated. "And to talk."

The library was big and leather-paneled like the game room. A pair of French doors graced the far end; a fire blazed on the hearth of a stone fireplace to ward off the faint chill of the night.

Marques offered brandy. A cigar. Coffee. Linc said no to all three.

"Something's on your mind, Hernando." Linc's tone was polite but cool. "I'd appreciate it if you'd just get to it."

His host nodded. Licked his lips. Fussed at the logs on the hearth with a poker before finally looking at Linc.

"This is difficult for me, Lincoln."

"But?"

"But there is something I must ask." A quick laugh. "I am not good at asking for favors. Not that this is a favor, exactly. I mean, it is something that will surely benefit you, as well as me."

Here it comes, Linc thought, folding his arms over his chest. A request to change the terms of their agreement? To renegotiate the price? What else could it be?

"And what is it you must ask?"

Marques cleared his throat. "You are unmarried Lincoln. That is correct, yes?"

"Excuse me?"

"I said, you are single. Am I right?"

Linc frowned. What did his marital status have to do with anything? "Uh, yes. Yes, I'm single."

"No children, then?"

"Marques. What is this about?"

"Because, you see, it is possible only a man with a child—with a daughter—would understand my feelings on this matter."

"What matter?"

Marques looked at him, then away. "I have a daughter. She is young—but," he added quickly, "mature for her age."

"I'm afraid I don't see what—"

"She is also bright and well-educated. Obedient and well-mannered. And—"

And, Linc thought in horror, as the truth began to sink in, Marques wanted to marry her off. To him?

"I am a modern man, Lincoln. Still, when it comes to my daughter, I have some old-fashioned ways."

Hell. Absolutely to him. He'd heard about this kind of thing, of course, arranged marriages, especially in wealthy families in Europe and South America…

"…would never hand her off to a man I didn't trust and respect…"

They did this back home, too. Not quite this openly but he'd been the target of a couple of attempts at marriage brokering. He was in his thirties, he was single, he was well-off…

Why think in polite euphemisms? He was rich and that was fine because he'd gotten that way strictly on his own. Nobody had given him anything in this life, which made what he'd acquired—the homes, the cars, the private plane—all the more enjoyable.

And his looks were acceptable.

Okay. Most women made it clear his looks were more than acceptable. He'd always had his pick of women, even back in the days he'd never had more than ten bucks in his pocket. So, yeah, he'd been here before. Approached, you could call it, by some of New York's best-known *grands dames*. They had daughters and he was, by their reckoning, eligible, and so what if his blood wasn't as blue as theirs?

You'd love my Emma, they said. Or, *Why don't you come out to our place in Easthampton this weekend? Glenna will be there. You do remember Glenna, don't you?*

Yes, but nobody had ever come straight out and said, *Here's my daughter. I'd like you to marry her.*

"...a charming young woman, Lincoln, polite and very willing to accommodate. If you'd simply agree to meet her—"

"Hernando." Linc took a deep breath. "I—I want you to know I appreciate how—how direct you're being. This can't be easy for you."

Marques gave a little laugh. "It's one of the most difficult things I've ever done."

"I'm sure it is but the thing is—the thing is—"

A polite knock sounded at the door. A servant popped his head in, smiled apologetically and said something in rapid Portuguese.

Marques sighed. "My wife is on the phone, Lincoln. I'll take the call in my office. She is visiting her sister, but you know how it is with women."

Linc didn't. Not with wives, at any rate, and he had every intention of keeping it that way.

"I'll only be a minute. Help yourself to some brandy while you consider my proposition."

Linc waited until the door closed. Then he muttered an oath and decided brandy was a fine idea.

How did a man turn down what Marques called a proposition? Grimly, he poured an inch of amber liquid into a snifter. He didn't want to insult him. He didn't want to lose this account, either, but if that was what it took to get out of here…

What was that?

Had something stirred outside the French doors? Clouds had moved in to obscure the moon; the light was poor, but… Yes. There it was again. He had a better look now, enough to be sure what was out in the darkness wasn't a something.

It was a someone.

Linc put down the brandy glass. He moved slowly, instinctively falling back into survival tactics honed to a fine edge years ago. Adrenaline pulsing through him, breathing steady, he felt himself come alive as he always had in moments like this.

The handles to the French doors were almost within reach. One more step…

He exploded into action, yanked the doors open, threw himself into the night and wrapped his arms around the intruder.

Wrapped his arms around a woman.

Definitely a woman. Her long hair swept across his face. Her breasts filled his hands. Her rounded bottom pressed against his groin. She fought him with all her strength, which was considerable, but it was no match for his.

A cry rose in her throat. Linc sensed it coming and clapped his hand over her mouth. For all he knew, she had an accomplice.

The feel of his hand increased her frenzy. She twisted like a wild thing caught in a trap. Linc lifted her off the ground and drew her, hard, against his body. She grunted. Her elbows slammed into his belly. Her heels rapped his shins.

He put his mouth to her ear.

"Stop it," he hissed.

She fought harder. Deliberately, he spread his hand over not just her mouth but her nose.

"I said, stop!"

Another jab. Another kick. His hand pressed more insistently. After a few seconds she sagged against him but he wasn't fooled. The fight had gone out of her too fast. She was faking it.

He put his mouth to her ear again. She smelled of roses or maybe lily of the valley. He wasn't much on flowers or scents. All he knew was that she fought like a man, but she sure as hell smelled like a woman.

"Behave, or it's lights out. You hear me?"

A second passed. Then she nodded. Slowly, carefully, he eased his hand from her face and swung her toward him.

"Who are you?" he demanded. "What are you doing here?"

"Let go of me!"

It was too dark to see her features, but he could hear the fury in her voice, sharp with command and condescension. It was almost enough to make him laugh, but laughing when your best security system had been breached didn't quite cut it.

"I asked you a question, lady. What's your name? How'd you get past the gate?"

"You asked two questions. And I gave you an order. Let go of me. Now!"

He did laugh then; how could he help it? The woman, who had been speaking in lightly accented English, spat out a phrase in Portuguese he was pretty sure women didn't generally use.

Right then, the moon decided to put in an appearance. It was only a quarter moon but it gave enough light for him to see her.

His breath caught.

She was, in a word, spectacular. Long blond hair. Big blue eyes. Razor-sharp cheekbones, an elegant nose, lush mouth and a body made for sin, poured into a black one-piece thing that lovingly molded every feminine curve.

"How dare you look at me that way?"

He'd seen a lot of thieves in his life but never one who looked like this.

"Damn you," she said, "are you deaf? I said—"

"I heard what you said."

Was that really his voice? So low? So hoarse? Better still, was this really happening? Was he holding an intruder in his arms who looked like every man's dream?

She began to struggle. He drew her closer. Her breasts, her belly, pressed against his. Was it the sense of danger?

Was it the feel of her? Whatever the cause, his body responded in a heartbeat.

He froze. So did she.

"Let go," she said, her voice suddenly trembling. "If you don't, I swear, you'll pay for this."

She was right, he would. Once he dragged her into the house, told Marques, the contract they'd yet to sign would go down the drain...

In which case, wasn't he entitled to some compensation?

The thought was cold; the swift rise of heat in his blood was not. He wasn't a man to take what had not been offered, but suddenly that didn't matter. Nothing did, except the feel of the woman in his arms.

Deliberately, he cupped her face with one hand. Tilted it up to his. She read what was coming and gasped, beat her fists against his shoulders.

He didn't give a damn. Slowly, he bent his head to hers and kissed her.

She made a sound of protest. Tried to twist her head away. He wouldn't let it happen. He thrust his fingers into her hair, felt it slide like silk through his hand and went on kissing her.

Kissing her. Kissing her...

She ignited like dry tinder under the flame of a match. Her hands slid up his chest. Her mouth softened. She gave a sexy little moan...

A light came on just outside the house.

The woman stiffened. Linc, lost in the moment, started to draw her into the shadows.

"No!" she gasped, and sank her teeth into his bottom lip.

Startled, he loosened his grip. One lithe twist and she disappeared into the darkness.

"Lincoln?"

It was Marques. Linc shuddered. He drew his handkerchief from his pocket and dabbed it to his bloody lip. He was a man who lived by rigid rules of self-control; there was no way to explain what he'd just done. He could only tell his host that an intruder was on the grounds and he had lost her.

No need to supply the humiliating details.

Marques smiled when he saw him. "There you are. I thought perhaps you'd…" His smile faded. "What happened to your lip?"

"It's nothing. An insect bite."

"One of the maids will get you some antiseptic."

"No. No, thanks. I…" Linc cleared his throat. "I'm fine."

"Nonsense. Small wounds can become a problem in this climate. Come inside, Lincoln. I'll ring for—"

"Hernando, listen to me. That security system my people installed?"

"It is excellent," Marques said, smiling broadly. "The best, just as you promised."

"It isn't. I mean, it is but—"

"Papa?"

A girl—obviously Marques's daughter—stood silhouetted in the hallway just outside the room. Marques held out his hand.

"Ana. Come in, child."

Linc smothered a groan. Damn, what a mess! Bad enough he had to tell Marques his high-tech security system had been compromised and he'd let the intruder slip away. Now he had to top that off by saying no, he wasn't interested in marrying a sweet, well-bred innocent young woman while she stood by, listening.

Oh, yeah, this was definitely turning into a fun night, Linc thought glumly…and felt his jaw slide to his shoe tops as Marques's daughter entered the well-lit room.

The sweet, well-bred innocent was the woman he'd just kissed.

The sexy black outfit had been subtly altered by the addition of a pale pink jacket, long and loose enough to hide all those feminine curves. The silky tousle of golden hair was drawn back in a severe knot. But it was she, and one look at her face told him she was as stunned as he was.

"Ana," Marques said, "this is the man I've been telling you about. Lincoln, this is my beloved daughter, Ana Maria."

For the first time in his life, Linc found himself struggling for words. What did you say to a man whose "beloved daughter" had been in your arms moments ago? Whose innocence was obviously a ruse only her father was foolish enough to believe?

His cell phone rang. Ordinarily, he'd have ignored it. Now, he yanked it from his pocket like a lifeline.

"Aldridge," he barked.

"Lincoln," he heard his lawyer say solemnly, "I'm afraid I've had word about your sister."

Somehow, in that instant, he knew what was coming. He turned his back to the room, to Marques, to Marques's daughter. The lawyer was hemming and hawing, stalling for time. Linc interrupted with a sharp command.

"Spit it out, man. What's happened?"

A chartered plane had gone down in a mountain pass. The pilot, the passengers...all of them, gone.

Linc felt the blood drain from his head. Dimly, he heard Marques say something, but he ignored him and stepped blindly into the night.

"No," he said sharply. "Not Kath."

"I'm sorry, Lincoln. Your sister and her husband both. But, miraculously, there was a survivor."

One survivor. A baby. A two-month-old little girl.

A little girl who was Lincoln Aldridge's niece.

CHAPTER TWO

New York City, two months later

IT TURNED out that some clichés were true.

Tragedy fell on a man without warning, but life went on. It changed, but it went on.

Somehow, you kept going. Somehow, you adapted.

You adapted, Linc thought groggily, as the piercing wail of the gorgeous, brilliant, impossible four-month-old hellion who now ruled his life shot him from sleep.

He threw out a hand, searched on the bedside table for his watch and peered blearily at the luminescent dial.

Oh, God!

It was five-oh-five. Five-oh-five in the a.m. He had a meeting at eight-thirty with his own people, another at eleven with the European clients he'd taken to dinner last night. He had to be sharp and focused and how could a man be either when he hadn't had a solid night's sleep?

He never had a solid night's sleep anymore. And he rarely had a full day to devote to his work.

First there'd been the awful, sad details of Kath's death to handle. When that was over, the baby—Kath's secret—had taken center stage.

At first, he'd wondered why his sister had kept the child a secret, but simple math had explained it. Kath had reversed the usual order of things. She'd gotten pregnant first, then married. Maybe she'd worried he'd have thought less of her for that reversal, which damned near broke his heart. Or maybe she just hadn't known how to break the news to him long-distance.

Whatever the reason, all that mattered now was the baby's welfare.

He had met with his attorney and, of course, immediately agreed to provide the baby a proper home. He didn't know a damned thing about babies—how could he? But he hadn't known a thing about running a business, either, when he'd started out.

No problem.

You didn't know how to do something, you learned. Or, if it was more expedient, you hired people who did. That was what he'd done, what he'd assured the social worker whose job it was to make sure the baby was properly cared for he would do.

And he had.

He'd sent his PA shopping for baby clothes, a crib, a high chair, bottles, formula, diapers and the thousand other things an infant required. He'd had the interior designer who'd done his Fifth Avenue triplex turn the guest suite into a nursery. He'd contacted a nanny agency and interviewed more women eager to clean baby bottoms than he'd have imagined existed in the world, let alone New York.

And, last week, Kath's mother-in-law had suddenly

come on the scene. Nobody had even known she existed until then.

Would she ask for custody? If she did, should he fight her for it? Or would his niece be better off in her care?

Linc couldn't come to a decision. On the one hand, women knew more about kids than he ever could. Wasn't it in their DNA? On the other, the child was his blood. She was his only remaining connection to Kathryn.

What would Kath have wanted? She'd loved him the way he'd loved her. The circumstances of their lives—no father, a mother who drank and forgot they existed most of the time—had made them unusually close. Still, there was no way to know if she'd have wanted her baby raised by him or her mother-in-law. His attorney was checking things out.

The bottom line was that Kath was gone and a small, squalling stranger had dropped into his life. He'd had to leave increasing responsibility for running Aldridge Inc. in the hands of his people. They were all excellent managers, hand selected by him, but Aldridge had grown into a multimillion-dollar company and he was integral to that growth.

He knew it was time to put the turmoil of the past months behind him and get back to the work he loved and maybe to some kind of social life, but you had to sleep nights to do that.

Right now, the baby's screams were reaching a crescendo, carrying all the way from the guest-suite-turned-nursery on the second floor of the penthouse to his bedroom on the third.

Where in hell was the nanny?

Linc threw back the duvet and started to the door.

Halfway there, he remembered he was wearing boxers, his usual sleeping apparel, but not what you'd choose for an appearance before Nanny Crispin.

She was the fifth woman he'd hired and the first that seemed to be working out.

The first hadn't lasted a week. Linc had come home an hour early one night and found her rolling on the Aubusson rug in the great room with a guy with studs in his ears, nose and lip and other places he'd glimpsed and tried to forget.

He'd thrown them both out.

Nanny Two had lasted ten days. Day eleven, she'd reeked of pot.

Nanny Three had simply vanished. Her replacement, Nanny Four, had seemed okay until the evening she'd greeted him at the door wearing one of his Thomas Pink handmade shirts, spiked heels and a smile.

Then the agency sent him Nanny Crispin.

She was sixtyish, tall and skinny. Her hair was steel-gray, her small, wire-framed eyeglasses sat squarely on the bridge of a high, narrow nose. Linc doubted if she knew how to smile, but she'd come highly recommended and, he supposed, whether or not she ever smiled was immaterial.

It couldn't possibly matter to a four-month-old infant. A baby's needs were purely physical. Food. Warmth. Cleanliness. This baby was getting all that. He'd made sure of it by hiring Nanny Crispin.

Sighing, Linc grabbed the trousers he'd worn last night. The baby's howls had reached earsplitting proportions. Nanny Crispin would have to endure the sight of his bare chest—and what the hell was she doing, anyway, letting the kid scream?

He marched down the hall and went down the steel and oiled teak spiral staircase.

The door to the nursery stood open. All the lights were on, illuminating the crib where the baby was screeching like a wind-up toy gone berserk. Nanny Crispin, wrapped like a mummy in a flannel robe the same color as her hair, sat in a straight-backed chair beside the crib, arms folded over her flat chest.

Linc cleared his throat. Pointless. Nobody could have heard the roar of a jet engine over the wails of the baby.

"Nanny Crispin?"

As always, he felt like an idiot addressing a woman twice his age that way, but she'd made it clear that she expected his housekeeper, his driver and him to call her by her title.

He walked to the crib and waited for her to notice him. When she didn't, he tapped her on the shoulder. She reacted as if she'd been scalded, leaping to her feet, spinning to face him, her mouth forming a perfect O.

"I didn't meant to startle you."

Nanny Crispin stared at his chest.

"I said, I didn't mean to—" Hell. He took a breath, fought back the urge to grab something to cover his naked chest and decided to get to the point. "What's wrong with the baby?"

"Do you not own a robe, Mr. Aldridge?"

"Do I not...?" Linc flushed. Suddenly, he was six years old. "Well, sure, but I heard the baby and—"

"Your attire is inappropriate. I am a single woman and you are a man."

"Yes, but—"

But one of them was crazy. He was indeed a man. She was about as sexually appealing as a stick, never mind the age difference or the fact that she was his employee. If she'd looked like the reincarnation of Marilyn Monroe, that last fact would have been enough to keep him at arm's length.

Linc jerked his chin toward the crib. "I'm not worried about decorum right now, Nanny Crispin. I want to know why the baby is screaming."

"She is screaming because she is undisciplined."

"Undisciplined. Well, then, of course she…"

His voice faded away. Undisciplined? He frowned. True, he knew nothing about babies, but did four-month-old infants cry because they were undisciplined?

"Are you sure?"

"I have been taking care of babies for forty years, Mr. Aldridge. I know an undisciplined child when I see one."

Linc looked at the baby. Her face was purple. Her arms and legs were pumping. His frown deepened.

"Maybe she's hungry."

"I gave her eight ounces of formula four hours ago. Eight ounces is the proper amount."

"What about her diaper? Does it need changing?"

"No."

"Well, is she too warm? Too cold? Could something be hurting her?"

Nanny Crispin's thin mouth narrowed until it all but disappeared. "She is simply in need of discipline, as I said."

"And that means?"

"It means I shall outlast her temper tantrum. Good night, sir."

Linc nodded. "Okay. Sure. Good night."

He turned, walked away, got halfway up the stairs and paused. The baby was still crying, but her screams had become sobs. Somehow, that was even worse.

Would Kath have let her daughter weep? Would she have called this a temper tantrum?

He swung around, went back to the nursery, ignored the scowl of disapproval and the pursed lips.

"How about picking her up?" Nanny Crispin looked at him as if he'd spoken in Urdu. "You know, take her out of the crib. Hold her, walk around with her."

"One does not reward poor behavior."

"No. Of course not. I mean…"

What in hell did he mean? Suddenly, Linc plunged back in time. He remembered coming home from football practice, finding Kath sobbing her heart out in the corner of the kitchen that had been her bedroom. He'd been maybe seventeen, so she'd have been seven. She'd been crying because some kid had made fun of her, the way she'd looked in the too-big winter coat he'd gotten her at the Salvation Army, and she hadn't stopped weeping until he'd scooped her up, rocked her, told her everything would be all right.

Linc walked slowly to the crib. Looked in. Hesitated. Then he reached down and picked up the baby. It was the first time he'd held her since the day a social worker had placed her in his arms.

This is your sister's daughter, she'd said.

Those simple words, the unfamiliar feel of the kid in his arms, and he'd finally had to accept that Kath was gone.

Now, he stared at the red, unhappy face of Kath's child. His niece. Funny how he never thought of her that way. Awkwardly, he cupped her head with one hand, her bottom with the other, and rocked her back and forth.

A little bubble of spit appeared in the corner of her mouth.

The kid was cute, he thought grudgingly. He hadn't really noticed before, but she was.

"Mr. Aldridge, I must protest. You are undermining my authority in front of the child."

He looked at the baby, then at Nanny Crispin. The look on her face said he was committing a capitol offense.

"She has a name," he heard himself say.

"What has that to do with anything?"

"She has a name. Jennifer. I've never heard you use it."

"Her name is irrelevant."

It wasn't irrelevant, nor was the fact that he never used the baby's name, either. He knew that, deep where it counted.

"Mr. Aldridge. The child needs to be taught a lesson. Either you put her back in her crib or I'm afraid I will have to tender my resignation."

Linc looked down at his niece. Her sobs had stopped. She was staring up at him, her expression solemn.

"Did you hear me, sir? I said—"

"I heard you. Consider your resignation accepted."

Nanny Crispin gasped. Linc almost did, too. What in hell had he done?

"Wait a minute," he started to say, but his cell phone, still in his trouser pocket, beeped. He shifted the baby to the crook of one arm and dug out the phone.

It was his attorney. At—what was it now?—at six in the damned a.m.?

"I couldn't reach you last night, Lincoln."

"Well, you've reached me now, Charles. This better be good."

Kath's mother-in-law had filed for custody. Linc wondered whether he felt relief or maybe something else.

"Yeah, well, we kind of figured—"

"What we didn't figure," his lawyer said briskly, "was that the lady basically abandoned her own son—Kathryn's husband—when he was three. Now she's claiming to have been a devoted mother who had problems."

"Do you buy her story?"

"What I buy is that she just found out about the trust fund you set up for your sister, and that the money in it now transfers to the baby."

Linc's mouth thinned. "Great."

"Indeed."

They made an appointment to meet later in the day. Oh, the lawyer added, the social worker wanted a meeting, too. This afternoon, with him and Linc and the baby.

"She wants to see how the child is doing."

"Sir?"

Linc turned and saw Nanny Crispin, dressed and with her suitcase in her hand.

"I'll see you later, Charles," he said, and ended the call.

"I phoned for a taxi, Mr. Aldridge. Unless, of course, you've changed your mind?"

Two meetings this morning. Two meetings this afternoon. Linc had always been a logical man. There was still time for a logical man to say he'd changed his mind.

"I will reconsider my departure if you are prepared to acknowledge my authority."

Linc's jaw tightened. "Send me the bill for the cab."

He waited as Nanny Crispin stalked from the room. Then he looked down at his niece.

"Well, kid, it looks like it's just you and me."

Jennifer gave a huge yawn. Her eyelids drooped. A second later, she was asleep.

An excellent idea, Linc thought, but there wasn't much point in going back to bed, not anymore.

Okay, then. Time for a plan. When his housekeeper showed up, he'd ask her to do him a favor and watch the baby for the day. He'd go to his office, hold his meetings, contact the nanny agency—again. This time tomorrow he'd have nanny number six and life could return to whatever level of normalcy was possible.

Carefully, he lowered the sleeping baby into the crib.

"Waaaah!"

Linc hoisted her up. She screamed. He rocked her. She roared. Finally, gingerly, he brought her against his chest. Hot drool fell against his naked flesh. The baby gave a shuddering sigh and promptly fell asleep.

Linc waited. Then, very slowly, he sank into the straight-backed chair Nanny Crispin had vacated.

The baby slept on.

Half an hour later, he heard his housekeeper in the

kitchen. He rose stiffly from a chair that had surely been designed by a sadist, lowered the baby inch by slow inch into her crib, hobbled to the shower and stepped gratefully under a blast of hot water.

MRS. HOLLOWELL couldn't babysit.

Her daughter was in the city for the day and she was taking the afternoon off to spend with her. Had Mr. Aldridge forgotten?

Mr. Aldridge had. He'd come close to forgetting his own name. Three hours of sleep could do that to a man.

He told her not to worry.

At eight, he strode into his office. His PA's eyes widened at the sight of Jennifer in his arms.

"I fired the nanny," he said brusquely. "Phone the agency, please. And take care of the kid for the next hour."

Another nod, but when he tried to hand the baby over those tiny lungs contracted and the baby began to scream. Linc rolled his eyes and reached for her. His PA started to grin, but one glance put an end to that.

Frowning, Linc plunked Jennifer against his shoulder again and vanished into his office.

He took his eight-thirty meeting with Jennifer still plastered against him. His people pretended not to notice.

By nine-thirty, she'd drifted off to sleep. After a quick survey of the Italian leather, smoked glass and cherrywood furnishings of his office, Linc sent his PA on another shopping expedition. In short order a thing that looked kind of like a tilted basket stood on the conference table along with diapers, baby bottles and formula.

The basket thing was pink and padded. Linc put the

baby into it and breathed a sigh of relief when she didn't object.

His PA had phoned his European clients at the Waldorf. They were not in their rooms but, at Linc's direction, she'd left a message changing the location of their meeting to Peacock Alley, the hotel's posh dining venue.

The trouble with messages was they didn't always get where they were meant to go.

Midmorning, just as Linc was getting ready to leave for the Waldorf, his clients walked in. So sorry, they said, they knew they were early, but…

The baby chose that moment to wake up.

Her face turned pink. Her rosebud mouth pursed. Linc snatched her from her sleeping place before she could shriek.

She smiled, drooled, and—there was a God after all—his clients melted. The meeting went on, the baby gurgled and smiled. Finally, mercifully, his clients left.

Linc started to put the baby in the crib. She began to whimper.

"She's hungry," his PA said helpfully.

Linc looked at her. Looked at the baby. Then he handed the kid over.

"Feed her," he commanded.

His PA started to say something, thought better of it, turned away, opened the door…

Someone brushed by her and walked in. Strode in, was more like it.

A blonde. Tall. Slender. Wearing a black suit, black spiked heels and with a sleek black leather attaché case hanging from a strap across her shoulder. The look on her face meant trouble as she marched toward him, stopped a foot from his desk and slapped her hands on her hips.

Linc's green eyes narrowed. His temper was hot, his patience shredded, his exhaustion a black cloud waiting to burst loose with thunder and lightning…

Holy hell!

The blonde was Ana Maria Marques.

Linc scraped back his chair and jumped to his feet. "What are you doing here?"

"You made my father a promise, Senhor Aldridge. I do not think he will be pleased when he hears that you intend to renege on it."

The baby let out a cry. Linc let out a groan. And assumed, as any intelligent man would, that he had somehow fallen through a wormhole in space and emerged in a nightmare.

CHAPTER THREE

As a boy, Lincoln had taught himself Tai Chi.

Well, maybe not Tai Chi, precisely. The classes had been held after school; they'd cost money and no way would his mother have been able to afford them. Hell, there was no way she'd have paid for something he'd wanted even if she'd been able to afford it.

But he'd spied on the class by cracking open the locker-room door, and he'd learned. Not the finer points, perhaps, but enough to find Tai Chi useful.

The ancient Chinese martial art was as much about self-control as it was about physical strength.

Eventually, he'd figured out that was something you could apply to life in general. He'd used that realization over the years and he thought of it now as he fought the growing tension inside him.

Too bad you didn't think about Tai Chi when you first met this babe, a smug voice inside him said.

Linc ignored it. He'd made a fool of himself with her once. It wouldn't happen again. Besides, Ana Maria Marques looked as furious as he felt.

She also looked spectacular, every man's dream of a

dressed-for-success female, the black suit elegant and proper, yet somehow hinting at the rounded contours of her body, the black pumps discreet until you took a look at the height of those heels and what they did for her long, lean legs.

His PA had stepped back into the room, the baby pressed to her shoulder, a bewildered look on her face.

"Sir? My apologies. I don't know why Reception let this woman—"

"It's all right, Sarah."

"If the lady has an appointment, I don't have anything in my calendar about it."

"If you think you are going to throw me out because I don't have an appointment," Ana said hotly, "I assure you, Senhor Aldridge, you are not!"

A muscle flexed in Linc's jaw but his tone was calm.

"Thank you, Sarah. Shut the door, please. I'll ring if I need you."

The door swung shut. Ana didn't blink. She simply glared at him.

Linc folded his arms. "Explain yourself."

"You have it wrong, *senhor.* You are the one who must do the explaining. To me. Or, if you prefer, to my father."

What in hell was she talking about? Better still, what was she doing here? The last he'd seen, she'd been pretending to be a dutiful daughter while her old man worked up the courage to offer her as a bride. In fact, Marques had been so caught up in the offer that he'd gone on talking even as Linc ran out the door that night.

His gut knotted. Had he missed something? Agreed to something? Was that night about to bite him in the tail?

"Because if you think I will not tell him how you have treated me—"

"Sit down, Miss Marques."

He spoke sharply, his words slicing across hers. It worked. Not that she sat down. He hadn't really expected that. But at least she shut up.

Linc took the chair behind his desk, folded his hands on its glass surface and looked at her. How many Ana Marias were there? Three, so far. The sexy night-stalker. The demure innocent. And now this gorgeous sophisticate.

Which was the real woman?

"When you're done mentally undressing me," she said coldly, "perhaps we can get down to business."

Linc raised one dark eyebrow.

"Trust me, Miss Marques. If I wanted to undress you, I wouldn't be satisfied with doing it mentally." He paused. "And neither would you."

A flush rose in her cheeks. "Would you force yourself on me again, *senhor?* As you did the night we met?"

"Is that why you returned my kiss? Because I 'forced' myself on you?"

"I did not return it. And I am not about to be drawn away from the topic at hand."

"What were you doing in that garden?"

"I just said—"

"Among other things, you blew past my best security system."

She smiled the way a cat might when confronted with a delectable mouse. "Indeed, I did."

Time to change direction. "Do you make it a habit to sneak around at night?"

"Do you make it a habit to force yourself on women?"

Back to the beginning. Linc sighed. "Let's move on, Miss Marques. What are you doing here?"

"I am here because of the promise you made my father. Have you conveniently forgotten? Or did you hope I would not wish to follow through on it? Is that the game?"

Calmer now, Linc decided this couldn't concern a marriage proposal. Her father would be with her if it were. Still, he had no idea what she was talking about, but only a fool would have admitted it. Instead, he sat back and flashed a cool smile.

"Why don't you tell me, Miss Marques? You seem to have all the answers."

He was afraid it sounded like a desperate ploy but it worked. A moment's hesitation and then she marched to one of the chairs in front of his desk, sat down, crossed her legs and propped the attaché case in her lap. The pencil-slim skirt of her black suit rode up her golden thighs.

"My father asked a favor of you."

Linc dragged his gaze to her face.

"Funny. I don't remember him asking anything—but then," he said, his tone hardening, "*you* seem to have forgotten that I left your home in a rush that night."

Another splash of color swept across her high cheekbones. "About that." She cleared her throat. "I should have offered you my sympathy on the loss of your sister."

"Thank you."

Ana narrowed her eyes. The words were polite, but she knew what this arrogant *bastardo* really meant was, *Go away.* Anyone viewing the scene would have thought she'd materialized out of the air instead of taking the elevator from Human Resources, two floors below.

Was he playing dumb? Could he really not know why she was so angry? He knew. He had to. He also knew damned well that he'd lied. That he'd said yes to her father only to placate him and had never, not in a million years, expected her to show up in New York.

If only Papa had never asked him.

She'd considered telling him not to, once she'd realized the man who'd forced his kisses on her that night was the man he was going to entrust her to, but how could she?

She'd worked a minor miracle, convinced Papa to let her take a stab at a career in New York, the city where all things were possible. She could have gone off without his approval, yes, but she knew her desire for independence pained him. She wanted to do it without hurting him, and she had.

After months of talk, Papa had finally agreed to let her go, but only if he hand-picked her employer.

"A good man," he had said. "An honorable one with a successful business."

Papa knew lots of good, honorable men who were successful. They were also middle-aged, overweight and balding. That was the kind of man she'd expected.

Instead, Papa's selection had turned out to be Lincoln Aldridge. Tall. Dark. Not middle-aged, not overweight, not balding.

Lincoln Aldridge was a magnificent male specimen.

He was also a sexist pig who'd overpowered her, forced her into his arms, forced his kisses on her, forced her to melt against him and yearn, plead, burn for him to do more, more, more...

Nonsense.

It hadn't been like that. She had been offended by his behavior and she would have told Papa the ugly truth about the good, honorable Senhor Aldridge, but Aldridge had gotten that terrible phone call about his sister.

After that, Ana had assumed Papa's plan was done with. Then, last week, he'd showed her the letter he'd written and Aldridge's response...

"Miss Marques?"

He was watching her through amazingly green eyes, looking at her as if she were little more than an annoyance. The hell with that, she thought coldly, and lifted her chin.

"Yes, *senhor*."

"I am a busy man, Miss Marques. I don't have time for nonsense."

"A promise is not nonsense."

"I promised your father nothing," he said briskly.

"Not then, no. But he sent you a letter."

A scowl crossed Aldridge's too-handsome-for-his-own-good face.

"A letter?"

"A proposal, to which you replied."

He turned pale. Proof, as if she'd needed any, that he had been lying.

"Your father made no proposal," he said. "And if he had, I surely would not have said—"

"You said yes."

"Impossible."

"You said that you would give me a try."

"I beg your pardon?"

"You said you could promise nothing, but that if I showed any talent, you would personally help cultivate it."

He turned even paler. Good. This was what happened when you trapped a liar with his own lies.

"Miss Marques. I could never have said any such thing about—about your talent. And I cannot imagine your father would have agreed to—to such an arrangement."

"He didn't want to, but I explained that a—what do you call it?—a period of trial is not North American, it is universal. Should my performance not prove adequate—"

"For God's sake, Miss Marques—"

"Should it not, I would not expect you to keep me on. But I can assure you, *senhor,* I am a quick student. I have a degree in business."

He was looking at her as if one of them had gone crazy. Ana frowned. Was it possible Lincoln Aldridge wasn't lying? Could he really know nothing of the employment offer he'd made in response to Papa's request?

No. It was not possible. He had sent that letter. Of course. The letter! Ana opened her attaché case and plucked two sheets of paper from its depths.

"What's that?"

"Something to refresh your memory."

She leaned forward and sent both pages sailing across the expanse of glass that separated them. He stopped their progress with his hand and stared at her for what seemed forever. She was almost out of patience when he finally began to read.

And laugh.

Laugh! This horrible man was laughing at her.

Ana wanted to fling herself across the desk and claw at his eyes. She had come almost five thousand miles. Her plane had landed late so that she'd barely had time to drop her luggage at the hotel and change her clothes before coming here. She'd gone straight to Human Resources, pinned on her best smile, tried to ignore the way her knees kept threatening to knock together…

And found nobody expecting her.

Not the receptionist. Not the manager she'd demanded to see. Not anyone, including this—this oaf sitting across from her, laughing as if he were at the funniest show in the world.

To hell with wanting to claw his eyes. Ana sprang to her feet with every intention of doing it.

"You—you—"

He looked up, not just laughing but guffawing.

"*Tu es um porco,*" she snarled as she flew around the desk. He shot from his chair, caught her wrists as she went for him…

His laughter died. What he wanted now burned flame-bright in his eyes.

"No," she said. "Damn you, no!"

He pulled her hard against him and kissed her.

The kiss scalded her; his heart thudded against hers. He swept his hand down her spine, cupped her bottom, brought her body tightly to his. His tongue penetrated her mouth.

It was a macho display of power, of arrogance, of all the things Ana despised…and none of that mattered. She heard herself making little cries. Soft, desperate sounds of desire. Her arms wound around his neck; her hair tumbled free as he tore the pins from it.

His hands molded her hips.

He lifted her. Something crashed to the floor as he sat her on the edge of the desk. Her thighs parted in welcome as he stepped between them. She was hot. Burning hot. And she wanted—she wanted...

"Mr. Aldridge?"

He spun around, blocking her from view, but it was too late. His PA had already seen them.

"Oh. Oh, good grief, Mr. Aldridge!"

The PA's shocked face vanished. The door closed. And Ana wanted to die.

She slipped down from the desk, pushed her hair away from her face with trembling hands. Smoothed down her jacket. Her skirt. Somehow, she'd lost one shoe. Oh, God, she'd lost a shoe...

"Here."

She looked up at the gruff sound of Aldridge's voice. Her shoe was in his hand. She grabbed it, thrust it on her foot.

She was a shaken mess. And he—he looked as if nothing had happened. Every strand of his dark, close-cropped hair was in place. His tie was neatly aligned. His suit jacket was uncreased. Only a glitter in his eyes suggested anything out of the ordinary had happened, though she doubted if this was out of the ordinary.

Lincoln Aldridge was a man who surely had many women in his life and took pleasure when and where he pleased.

She knew all about men like him. You couldn't grow up in Brazil, no matter how sheltered your existence, and not know. It was a man's world. Now she knew it was like that in the States, too.

Just as well Aldridge had decided to pretend ignorance of why she was here. Even if he'd offered her a job, she wouldn't take it.

Ana stepped back. Carefully, she picked up her attaché case. The letters—one from her father, thanking Aldridge for his generosity in offering her a position with his firm, the other Aldridge's response, requesting she show up for an interview today—were still on his desk.

Let them stay there. She never wanted to see them again.

She would give up the foolish idea of the career for which she had been trained, go home, let her father do what he'd wanted all along and find her a suitable husband—

"Miss Marques."

The hell she would. Ana straightened her shoulders and strode to the door. She would not let this one man defeat her. She'd stay in New York, take any job she could get and prove, once and for all, that a woman could succeed without becoming a man's property.

"Miss Marques! Ana. Wait."

She had her hand on the knob but she paused. She would not let this—this idiot write her off as a coward. She would make her exit with dignity.

His hand fell lightly on her shoulder.

She jerked away and spun toward him. At least he had stopped laughing.

"I am happy to have provided you with so much amusement."

Her English had lost the fluidity she'd worked so hard to achieve, but so what? There was no reason to impress Lincoln Aldridge with anything except the fact that he could not rattle her.

"Ana."

He ran a hand through his hair. He looked—what was the word? *Contrite*. She didn't believe it, not for a moment.

"Ana." He drew a deep breath, slowly expelled it. "There's been a mistake."

"There most certainly has."

Her voice could have turned water to ice. Linc couldn't blame her. She'd been right about why she was here and he'd been wrong. As for the kiss...a moment of hubris, that was all. He'd never kissed a woman in anger before, but there was a first time for everything. Anyway, the kiss didn't require an explanation.

The rest of it did.

"That letter your father sent—" He paused. "I never saw it. It's true," he added quickly, when her eyes narrowed. "Because of what happened to my sister, I had to turn some things over to others the last couple of months. Somehow, that letter ended up on the wrong desk."

"You replied to it."

Linc shook his head. "One of my people did. Obviously he recognized your father's name and assumed we'd grant his request as a courtesy."

"Whatever," she said, as if it didn't matter when it surely did. "My father should not have requested a favor from you. I do not need favors."

A lie, big-time. Linc knew it. "Really?"

"Really."

"Then why did you come here?"

"I came for a job. I certainly did not come here to be laughed at."

"I wasn't laughing at you, *senhora*. I was laughing because I misunderstood what your father…" No, Linc decided. Better not to go there. What he needed was a way out of this mess, one that wouldn't insult her or her father. "You say you have a degree in business?"

"That is correct."

"Can you, uh, can you type?"

She drilled him with a look.

"Okay. I know that sounds sexist but entry-level jobs…" He paused. "We don't have anything here, but let me call around. Maybe I can find something."

"I told you, I want no favors from you. I will find a position elsewhere."

"This is New York. Good jobs are tight. If I can come up with something—"

"Goodbye, Senhor Aldridge."

Linc's mouth thinned. Fine. Let the lady take her expensive outfit, her attaché case and her attitude and hit the streets with the thousands of other well-dressed, well-educated hopefuls dreaming of careers.

With luck, she'd end up waiting on tables—which might do wonders for her overblown ego.

He folded his arms as she yanked the door open… and raised his eyebrows as his PA almost fell through it, holding a squalling Jennifer in her arms.

"I'm sorry, sir," she said desperately, "but the baby—"

She held the baby toward him. Linc looked around, as

if he hoped Mary Poppins might suddenly materialize. Then he took the baby and held her as if she were an alien life form.

The baby's screams increased.

"Did you phone the nanny agency?" he said, raising his voice over the din.

"They said maybe tomorrow."

Shock sent his eyebrows climbing again. "Tomorrow?"

"Or Monday. They weren't hopeful. They said nobody ever seems to suit you and—"

Ana Maria Marques clucked her tongue and held out her arms. "Give the poor *bébe* to me!"

It was a command, not a request. Linc didn't argue. He handed his niece over.

"Whose child is this?"

"She's my niece. My sister's child."

Ana looked down at the squalling bundle. Her expression softened. "Ah, *pobre bébe*! Where is her papa?"

"He died with my sister."

"How sad," Ana said gently. She cooed at the baby. Whispered something in Portuguese. The child's screams became sobs; the sobs became whimpers. And, to everyone's amazement, the tiny rosebud mouth curved in a smile.

"She likes you," Linc said.

Ana threw him a sharp look. "What a shock."

"I only meant—"

"I have a dozen little cousins. They all like me. What is her name?"

"Jennifer."

"Jenny," Ana crooned, touching the tip of her finger to the baby's chin. "Such a lovely name for a lovely little girl."

Jennifer—Jenny—smiled giddily and blew a bubble.

Linc watched in fascination and upped the count. There weren't three Anas, there were four. Sexy siren. Demure innocent. Tailored cosmopolitan and now earth mother.

He thought of what it would be like to find out which of the Anas was real. To kiss that soft mouth until she melted against him and revealed herself. To him. To his hands, his mouth, his body. Revealed all the rich layers that waited for discovery...

Hell, he thought, and cleared his throat. "Sarah?" he said briskly to his PA. "Take the baby, please."

His PA looked him straight in the eye. "I have work to do, sir," she said, and walked out of the room.

Linc wanted to call her back, but she was right. What was he supposed to do now? No nanny until tomorrow. Or Monday. Or maybe never, the way things were going. He had an afternoon full of meetings. His lawyer. The social worker, who'd probably just love to watch as his niece screamed her displeasure to the world.

The baby grabbed Ana's hand and smiled. Ana gave a soft laugh. And an idea so ridiculous any sane man would have dismissed it sprang to life in Linc's brain.

"So, Ana," he said, trying to sound casual, "what will you do now that the job thing hasn't panned out?"

Her shoulders straightened. "That is not your problem."

"Yes, you made that clear. But, ah, but I feel somewhat responsible. That letter did go out on my letterhead." He paused. "Actually, I've thought of something that might suit you."

"Thank you," she said, though her tone made a mockery of the words, "but I do not want charity. I have already said that it was wrong to let my father ask you for a favor." She looked quickly at the baby, then held her toward Linc. "You may take her now, *senhor*."

Linc dug his hands into his pockets.

"No charity. This is a real job, but I warn you it doesn't require that degree in business."

"It doesn't?"

"You wouldn't be working for my company, you'd be working for me."

Color flooded her face. "If you think I would take money to—to—"

"I need a nanny for my niece."

Her jaw dropped. Obviously she couldn't believe what he'd just said. Well, dammit, neither could he, but he was desperate.

"Are you up to some honest work?" His tone hardened. "Or would you rather hurry home to Papa and admit that your first foray into the world turned out to be too much reality to handle?"

CHAPTER FOUR

Wasn't there a North American expression? Something about being caught between a boulder and a hard surface?

There was, Ana was sure, though maybe she had the syntax wrong. She'd studied English since childhood and she spoke it well, but when she was under pressure her command of the language sometimes faltered.

Besides, language was fluid. And if you lived a medieval existence, if you were sheltered, all but smothered by a well-meaning father and a doting mother, you couldn't possibly keep up with its ebb and flow.

There was, however, no way to misunderstand what Lincoln Aldridge had just said. This was the real world. He lived in it. She did not.

Never mind the college degree. She had one, yes, but the truth was that most of what she'd learned about business she'd learned through her own reading. The college she'd attended was a nice place, but it demanded little of the wealthy young women who were its students.

Papa had sent her there to placate her, just as he'd done by sending her north. To Lincoln. First he'd given her a safe education at a school he could trust. Then he'd sent her to New York for a safe job with a man he could trust.

What irony!

Why would anyone trust Lincoln Aldridge? Obviously he lived by his own rules. He'd kissed her because it had pleased him to do so. Now he was offering her a job for similar reasons.

"Well?"

Aldridge's eyes were locked on hers. He looked impatient and arrogant. And beautiful.

A sweet fire engulfed her.

She'd never seen a man you'd describe that way, but it suited him. That hard masculine face. The long body. The musculature of it that not even an expensive suit could disguise.

Ana dragged her gaze from his. There was a baby seat in the middle of an enormous conference table. She carried the contented baby to it and took her time securing the safety harness, grateful for the chance to regain her composure.

Of course she would not accept his offer. Why would she even contemplate saying yes? She wasn't a nanny. She adored children but she had not come to New York to burp babies.

"Never mind." A patronizing little smile lifted one corner of his mouth. "That look on your face says it all. You expected me to make you second in command at Aldridge. Instead, I'm offering you good wages to do an honest job—"

"What do you call 'good wages'?"

She could see the question surprised him. Well, it surprised her, too, but what harm was there in asking?

He named a figure. Another surprise. It was a lot of money. Ana did some fast mental calculations.

"Plus, of course, room and board."

"Room and board? You mean, I'd be expected to live in your home?"

"Unless you'd rather get calls from me in the middle of the night if my niece needs tending."

His tone was so flat it took her a second to realize he was being sarcastic. But he was right. You couldn't care for a baby at a distance.

Still, she would not do it. She could not do it. Even if it meant returning home and admitting failure...

"I'll take it."

His dark eyebrows rose. What a pleasure, she thought coldly, to have taken him by surprise again.

"With one caveat."

He sighed. "Health insurance? Paid holidays? Mondays and alternate Saturdays off?"

"Insurance, naturally. As for the rest, when I want time off, I will ask for it."

"Then what's the caveat?"

"You will keep looking within your organization for something for me."

"I just told you—"

"I know how large corporations work," Ana said, lying with aplomb. "People come, people go. When you find a position for which I am suited, you will offer it to me."

Linc's body tightened. He had a damned good idea of what position would suit Ana Maria Marques.

He thought back to how she'd just responded to his kiss. It had been the same way that very first night.

"That night," he said, "in the garden... Were you going to meet a man?"

Her face colored. For an instant she was tempted to tell him the truth, that she'd been doing what she always did when the constraints of her life became unbearable. For years, she'd slipped out of the beautiful house that was her prison, slipped away from the grounds and wandered the hilly streets in blissful solitude.

A faceless entity named Aldridge Inc. had changed all that.

She'd memorized the master code that bypassed the alarm system, come up with a way to dress that would ensure she'd blend into the darkness. And the very first time she'd tried it...

"Answer the question, Ana. Were you going to meet someone? Or were you coming from a liaison with your lover?" His tone roughened. "Was I the lucky recipient of leftover lust?"

For the second time today, she wanted to hit him. Ball up her fist and smack it right into his jaw. If only he knew how many times she'd relived what had happened, the hours she'd wasted trying to figure out why she'd kissed a stranger...

"Yes," she said with a careless toss of her head, "that's it, exactly. I had just left my lover and you took advantage of what he'd made me feel."

His face darkened; his big body tensed. She wanted to call back the outrageous lie but it was too late. Aldridge had already pulled her into his arms.

His kiss was hard. Merciless. And, oh, God, exciting!

Men had kissed her, but not like this, as if the planets and stars were nothing but an illusion and the only thing real was their passion. She told herself not to react, but even as she did she was twisting her hands into Lincoln's jacket, letting herself lean into him—

He let go of her and she stumbled back.

"The truth, *senhora*," he said calmly, "is that your lover left you unsatisfied."

Ana spat a word at him, one she'd heard but never dreamed she'd use. To her fury, it made him laugh.

"What a charming choice of words, Ana. Yes, I know what you called me. I've spent some time in Rio, remember?" His mouth twisted. "Now, do you want the job or don't you?"

"Do you really think I would accept employment in your home after what you just did?"

"What I think," Linc said, "is that you're hardly the trembling innocent your father thinks you are."

"What *I* think," Ana said, "is that you are a—"

"I also think that you're not a fool. You want to stay in New York. That means you need a job. I'm offering you one. Good pay, a roof over your head and food in your belly." His eyes narrowed. "I can assure you, there won't be any other benefits. I've never tolerated personal relationships between management and employees in the office and I'm not about to tolerate them in my home." He shot back his cuff and frowned at his watch. "I have a busy schedule this afternoon. I need an immediate answer. Do you want this job or don't you?"

Was he crazy? Did he really think she would work for him?

He looked up, impatience etched into every hard feature. "Well? Yes or no?"

Ana swallowed drily. And said yes.

THE MEETING with the social worker seemed to go well.

Linc met with her alone and then had Ana bring in the baby. Fresh from a bottle, a nap and a diaper change, Jenny glowed with contentment in her new nanny's arms. A few minutes of polite chitchat about babies and then the social worker changed topics.

"That's a great suit, Miss Marques," she said pleasantly. "Armani? Oh, and I love your shoes. Gucci, right?"

The new direction puzzled Linc. Not Ana.

"Yes to both and thank you." Her smile was woman-to-woman. "Of course, I have only just arrived in the city. When you see me again, I am afraid I will be dressed more conventionally. You know, for spit-ups and diapering."

Both women laughed politely. Then Ana leaned forward.

"I hope Senhor Aldridge told you how grateful my father and I are to him for giving me this opportunity."

It was the social worker's turn to look puzzled. "Your father?"

"It is common practice in my country," Ana said demurely, "for young ladies of a certain class to go north, if they wish, and try their hand at genteel employment. Under the close supervision of an old family friend, naturally."

Linc looked at her. Amazing. Nobody would suspect she was lying through her teeth.

"Fortunately for me, Senhor Aldridge is just such an old, trusted friend. When we heard he needed help caring for Jennifer, Papa saw it as the perfect chance for me to do something useful."

The social worker looked as if Ana had just explained the mysteries of the universe.

"Excellent," she said briskly. "Thank you for your time, Mr. Aldridge. I'll see you in another few weeks."

Linc waited until the woman was gone. Then he scratched his head.

"What the hell was that all about?"

"You are a man," Ana said briskly. "I am a woman."

"Really? I'd never have known."

"She was trying to figure me out."

"Tell her to join the club."

"She could tell my clothes are expensive."

"So?"

Ana rolled her eyes. "So, it crossed her mind that you might have bought my things for me. That I am your mistress."

He wanted to say she was crazy, except she wasn't. His lawyer had warned him that his life would come under the closest scrutiny.

"So I told her a story about practices in my country." She smiled sweetly. "You'd be amazed how naive some people are about South America. The taxi driver asked me where I was from. Then he wanted to know all about my encounters with jaguars and head-hunters." Her smile faded. "Satisfied?"

Linc nodded. Who wouldn't be satisfied? His niece was happy. The social worker was happy.

Unfortunately, when his attorney showed up a couple of hours later, he wasn't.

Linc called Ana in and introduced them. She was the perfect nanny: polite, respectful, almost deferential. Charles smiled, said all the right things, but as soon as he and Linc were alone, he shook his head.

"She's a liability, Lincoln."

Linc sat back in his chair. "Since when is a nanny a liability?"

"When she's young, stunning and somebody's spent a million bucks on her clothes."

Linc sighed. "Her old man's loaded."

"The Social Services people won't know that."

"Yeah. They will. They already do."

He told Charles what had happened. The lawyer nodded.

"Young, stunning—and bright. That's one hell of a combo."

"The baby's putty in her hands."

"And you?"

"What, you think I'm gonna make a move on my nanny? Give me a break, Charles. Except for the last one, all Jenny's nannies were young and attractive, too."

"This girl's not attractive, she's spectacular."

Linc sat straight in his chair. "I hadn't noticed."

"Maybe not, but Social Services—"

"I just told you, Ana took care of that."

"For the moment."

"Meaning?"

"Meaning, until they decide you're a fit guardian for your niece—well, just don't underestimate their power, all right? Especially with Kathryn's mother-in-law hovering in the background."

"You have to be kidding. The woman was a failure as a mother to her son. She's only interested in custody of Jenny because of the money I'd put in trust for Kath. No court would—"

"You're male, Kathryn's mother-in-law is female. You're an uncle. She's a grandmother." The attorney held up his hand when Linc would have spoken. "I know it sounds crazy, but I've seen judges make decisions that defy logic. We don't want that to happen here."

"No," Linc said grimly, "we don't."

The men rose to their feet and walked slowly to the door.

"All I'm saying is, remember Caesar's wife."

"Meaning?"

"Meaning," the lawyer said, clapping Linc on the back, "remain above suspicion."

"You're serious, aren't you?"

"Dead serious. One wrong move, one blurring of the line between you and Ana, and you'll leave yourself open to losing Jennifer. Unless you've changed your mind about wanting to raise her…?"

Changed his mind?

Forget Kath's greedy mother-in-law. He'd never let someone like her raise Jenny… But there was more to it than that. Early this morning, he'd lifted a tiny stranger from her crib and sat down with her in his arms. Somewhere during the next hour, that tiny stranger had turned into a child he loved.

It defied logic, and Linc was a logical man. But…

"Lincoln? Have you changed your mind?"

Linc held out his hand. Charles took it.

"The only thing that's changed," he said, "is that I'm more convinced than ever I want to raise Jenny. And I'll do whatever it takes to make that happen."

The lawyer smiled. "In that case, just remember to treat Miss Marques like the employee she is and things will..." he hesitated "...and things should be fine."

FINE WASN'T exactly the word Linc would have chosen.

Not for the first couple of weeks. Ana's arrival in his life was like a tornado touching down.

First, there was her luggage.

She'd left it at her hotel. He'd sent his driver for it. The guy was a body builder, long on muscle and stamina, but he'd come back looking stunned.

No wonder.

Six suitcases, each the size of a small truck, were lined up behind him in the marble foyer of Linc's penthouse.

"Oh, hell," Linc said softly.

"Yeah," his driver said, just as softly.

Together, they wrestled the stuff up the spiral staircase and into the nursery. Ana left the baby with the housekeeper and followed them, snapping out directions. When the luggage was placed where she wanted it, Linc cleared his throat.

"I don't suppose you have anything suitable for, uh, for nannying in those bags?"

"Such a typically male attitude," she said with a cluck of her tongue.

Linc brightened. "Good. For a minute there, I was afraid you owned nothing but—"

She opened one suitcase. Then another. And another.

He saw suits, silky blouses, more of those pumps that looked so demure until you noticed the sky-high heels.

"I thought you said—"

"What I said was that your attitude was typical."

And right on the mark, Linc thought, but he wasn't foolish enough to say it.

"I will shop tomorrow and buy what is required."

She swung toward him. Strands of golden hair had come loose from the neat chignon at the nape of her neck and lay against her cheek. What if he went to her and tucked those errant strands behind her ear?

"Do you know what would be appropriate?"

He blinked. "Sorry. Appropriate for…?"

"For me to wear."

Lace. Black lace against her creamy skin. Or maybe pale pink. The shade you'd see inside a seashell on a Caribbean beach. Yes. Definitely. Soft, delicate pink against that soft, lovely body.

Was he losing his mind?

"Of course not," he snapped. "How would I know what you should wear?"

"You have employed a nanny before this, have you not?"

He thought of the long line of useless females who'd filed through his life the last months, flashed on the one who'd worn his shirt and that thong…

"Just buy regular clothes. Casual stuff. Jeans. Cotton tees. Whatever you'd wear to care for a baby, like other nannies."

"I am not like other nannies."

He knew that. Oh, he knew that…

Linc yanked his wallet from his pocket. Tossed a credit card on the bed.

"Leave Jenny with Mrs. Hollowell in the morning," he said gruffly. "Go to the park. Look around. You're bound to see other nannies. See what they're wearing and then go shopping."

"I do not need you to buy my clothes."

He ground his teeth together with enough force to have sent his dentist running from the room.

"And I," he said, "do not need you to argue over everything. Besides, this isn't a gift. I'll take the money out of your pay."

"That will be acceptable."

"Damned right, it will," Linc said, and then, because he wanted to cross the room, haul his impossible, intractable, infuriating new nanny into his arms and kiss her until that look of superiority gave way to one of passion, he turned on his heel and strode away.

LINC HAD ALWAYS worked late, played hard, spent little time at home.

He saw no need to change that.

His days were long. So were his evenings. Longer than usual. With things under control at home, he was giving his little black book one hell of a workout, even though he found himself ending his evenings by giving his dates chaste kisses on their upturned faces and pretending he didn't notice their looks of surprise and disappointment.

Well, hell, that was what happened when a man worked hard. It had nothing to do with the fact that Ana was living under his roof. Why would it? He hardly ever saw her, and when he did they spent a couple of minutes discussing Jenny and then each of them moved on.

He was pleased.

He'd made a wise move, hiring her. Mrs. Hollowell said she was a lovely young woman. Jenny cooed and smiled and squealed with delight. He could hear her in the mornings, could hear Ana laughing with her.

Ana had a terrific laugh. Husky. Sexy.

Not that he cared.

What mattered was that the baby was thriving and nights were peaceful again. No sobs, no screams, no shrieks. Just blessed silence.

What woke him, instead, were his dreams, hot and disturbing and, dammit, ridiculously adolescent. Well, he was human. Having a good-looking woman sleeping one floor down was a little distracting. Once he'd figured that out, he worked his little black book even harder—and left another half dozen puzzled, unhappy women in his wake.

The first weeks of her employment rushed by. She hadn't even asked for a day off. She seemed content, spending all her time with Jenny, who loved her. His housekeeper loved her. The doormen and the concierge loved her. Ana was Mary Poppins come to life.

Impossible, a voice inside Linc whispered slyly.

She was, as his lawyer had so succinctly put it, spectacular. And she was filled with passion. That kiss in the garden. The kiss in his office. When would she show her true colors? He kept waiting for the other shoe to drop.

One morning during the third week, Linc picked up

the phone to make a quick call before he left for his office. He heard Ana's voice, speaking in Portuguese, and then her low, sexy laugh.

"Oh," he said, "sorry," and hung up the phone.

Who had she been talking to? He frowned, adjusted his tie, grabbed his wallet and went briskly down the stairs and out the door.

That was her business, not his.

BY NOON, it was driving him crazy.

Who did she know in New York? Better still, who did she know who spoke Portuguese? He knew she hadn't been calling home. She'd bought a cell phone expressly for calls to and from Brazil, and made a point of telling him her father didn't know about her job as Jenny's nanny.

"And you are not to say anything of it, should you speak to him, *senhor*," she'd added in a tone of voice that made him want to point out that he did not take orders from her...except he wanted to do it by hauling her into his arms and showing her exactly who was boss.

And he wasn't like that.

Certainly he wasn't.

By midafternoon, he was pacing his office. Enough, he thought, reached for the phone and dialed home.

The phone rang a long time. Then Ana answered, sounded rushed. "Hello?"

"It's me," Linc said.

"Yes. What is it, please, Senhor Aldridge? We are in the middle of something. I am very busy."

Not rushed. Breathless. And there was a hint of suppressed laughter in her voice.

Linc tapped a pencil against the edge of his desk. "Very busy with what?"

"I have a visitor."

"A visitor?"

"I am permitted visitors, am I not?"

"Where is Mrs. Hollowell?"

"She left early. She had a dental appointment. *Senhor,* if you are done, I am—"

"Busy. Yeah. So you said." Linc's voice roughened. "Who is this visitor? And where is my niece?"

"The visitor is a friend. And Jenny is, of course, right here with us."

Linc hung up the phone. He thought about who might visit a woman who knew nobody in New York. He thought about that phone call. He thought about Jenny, right there with…

Us.

Twenty minutes later, he stepped out of his private elevator, marched through the foyer and heard his nanny's soft, uninhibited laughter coming from the great room.

"Oh," she said, "*bébe,* you are incredible! When did you learn to do that?"

Linc tossed his briefcase in the general direction of a table and ran.

"What in hell do you think you're—"

Ana, seated cross-legged on the carpet, looked up in surprise. But mostly the surprise was Linc's.

His nanny did, indeed, have a visitor. Another young woman—dark-haired, in jeans and sneakers and cotton shirt. And another baby, sitting in the vee of the girl's legs, just as his niece was seated in the vee of Ana's, grinning and clapping her chubby hands.

"—doing?" Linc finished lamely, and felt his face burn.

Ana's blue eyes narrowed as if the scene he'd expected to find was painted in garish detail across his forehead. The other girl looked from one face to the other, then scrambled to her feet with her charge in her arms.

"Thanks for the coffee, Ana," she said in heavily accented English.

"You are welcome," Ana said, her gaze never leaving Linc's.

"See you tomorrow, at the playground?"

Ana didn't answer for a long minute. Then she shrugged. "Perhaps."

Linc ran his hand through his hair. "Listen," he said, "Ana, your friend doesn't have to leave. I mean, I didn't intend to—"

He was talking to an empty room. Ana's visitor and her charge were gone, and Ana and Jenny were halfway up the stairs.

"Ana. Ana! Dammit, wait!" Linc called as he hurried after her. "Okay. So I was wrong. I'm sorry, all right?"

The nursery door slammed shut in his face. He thought about kicking it open, then decided he'd done enough stupid things for one day.

Ana would get over it.

Besides, what was there to apologize for? She lived under his roof. She took care of his niece. He had the absolute right to hold her responsible for her actions.

She'd taken a lover in Rio.

Why, sooner or later, wouldn't she take one here?

CHAPTER FIVE

ANA avoided him.

She spoke when spoken to, answered questions about Jenny and saw to it their paths hardly crossed.

Why would he want anything more?

Because, he decided after another couple of weeks, because this woman was his employee. He didn't like her attitude. Her behavior was insolent. It was time to put an end to the nonsense.

Friday afternoon, he told his PA to cancel a three o'clock meeting, phone his dinner date and tell her he might be a little late.

Then he headed home.

Ana was in the great room with Jenny. They were sitting on the carpet, playing a game that seemed to involve Jenny giggling while Ana gently tugged her to a sitting position.

"Good girl," Ana crooned. "That's my *pequena preciosa.*"

Jenny spotted him first. "Baa baa baa," she said, and shot him a huge grin.

Ana looked up and stopped smiling. "You're early, *senhor,*" she said coolly, and rose to her feet.

She was wearing one of what he supposed she'd call her nanny outfits, suitable for a midsummer day. Cropped trousers, a loose-fitting T-shirt, sandals. Her hair was pulled back in a ponytail; her face was makeup free.

She looked about as sexy as a stick. Then why this sudden knot in his gut?

"Jenny and I will be out of your way as soon as I've collected her toys."

"Ana." Linc hesitated. He'd come home angry, wanting a confrontation. Now he knew what he wanted was to offer what she deserved. An apology. "Ana," he said, "I'm sorry."

"There is no need to apologize. You are, of course, free to come into your own home whenever you wish. I should not have brought Jenny in here."

"No! I mean, it's fine that you're here with Jenny." Linc took a breath. "What I'm saying is that I'm sorry about what happened that day you—you had your friend here."

"There is no reason to apologize for that, either."

What she meant was, it was too late.

"Yeah, there is." Linc took a step toward her. "See, I had some, ah, some unfortunate experiences with a couple of the nannies who took care of Jenny before you came along."

"I am sorry to hear it."

Her accent was growing heavier. It made him smile. He'd noticed that about her, that her perfect English always became a shade too perfect when she was angry.

"I have said something amusing?"

"No," Linc said quickly, "not at all."

"Whatever your experiences with the others, you had no reason to distrust me."

You had a lover, he almost said. But so what? Her personal life was none of his affair. Besides, she was right. He had no reason to distrust her. He had no reason to keep remembering the way she felt in his arms, either, the warmth of her body, the sweetness of her mouth.

"You're right," he said quietly.

"I would never bring a man here. How could you think I would?"

"That's why I'm apologizing. I know you wouldn't get involved with a man."

Her eyes became as cold as the Arctic. "I did not say that."

"Sure you did. You said—"

"I said I would never bring a man here, but my life is my own, *senhor*. I did not come thousands of miles to let you take over where my father left off."

"Is that why you left Rio? Because your father found out about your lover and wanted you to stop seeing him?"

She looked at him as if he'd lost his sanity. Hell, maybe he had. Hadn't he just told himself her personal life was none of his business?

"Are you dissatisfied with my work?"

"What? No. No, not at all. I just—"

"Then I see no reason for this conversation."

Ana picked up the baby, turned her back to him and started briskly from the room. Dammit, he'd started to tell her he was sorry for how he'd behaved. Instead, he'd insulted her all over again.

"Ana!"

She stood still, though she kept her back to him.

"Yes, *senhor?*"

"I really am sorry. For what happened last time. For now. For screwing up every time I open my mouth."

Would she respond? Or would she walk away? He didn't realize he was holding his breath until she swung toward him.

"I am sorry, too. Perhaps I am—what is the word?—stubbly?"

"Stub…" Linc grinned. "Prickly."

"Prickly," she said, nodding in agreement. "So, I accept your apology."

"Good." He hesitated. "The thing is, we might get along better if we knew more about each other."

"Certainly. I can give you a copy of my résumé."

"I didn't mean…" He hesitated again. "Are you, uh, are you satisfied, being here? I mean, I know you didn't come to New York to become a nanny."

"I'm happy being with Jenny."

And are you happy being with me? The words were on the tip of his tongue. Hell, maybe he really was crazy.

"Good," he said briskly. "She's certainly happy with you. You're wonderful with her."

Ana smiled. "She's a joy. Did you know she can roll over?"

"No," Linc said, following her lead, carefully stepping back from the thin ice that had appeared under his feet moments ago. "Really?"

"If I put her on her tummy in her play yard, she rolls onto her back." She paused. "If you want to come upstairs with us, she'll show you."

Turn away an olive branch? He might be nuts but he wasn't stupid.

"Great idea," he said. "Lead the way."

He followed her up the stairs. Ana put Jenny in the play yard and the baby rolled right onto her back.

"*Baa baa baa,*" she chortled.

Linc grinned. "*Baa baa baa* to you, too, kid."

"She's a very special little girl," Ana said, smiling.

"Yeah. She's really something. Kathryn would be..." He frowned, swallowed past the lump that had suddenly risen in his throat and turned to the door. "Well. I don't want to keep you guys from your routine, so—"

"It must be terrible," Ana said softly. "Losing someone you loved as you loved your sister."

Linc nodded. "Kath was one in a million."

A light hand fell on his shoulder. "So is her daughter." Ana hesitated. "Lincoln? It's Jenny's bathtime. Would you like to stay and help?"

Lincoln. She'd called him Lincoln for the very first time. Linc cleared his throat.

"You sure I won't be in the way?"

She smiled. "You won't be in the way if I put you to work."

He smiled back. "Just point me in the right direction and step back."

CLEARLY, he was going to be second in command.

Linc took off his jacket. Rolled back his sleeves. Held Jenny while Ana put on an oversized apron and filled the baby tub.

She did the actual bathing, though he got as wet as if he'd been part of the procedure. Jenny, it seemed, was great at slapping at the water and giggling.

"All done," Ana said, and that was his clue to wrap the baby in a big towel and dry her during an improvised game of peekaboo that sent her into fits of laughter.

"She loves to play," Ana said proudly, and it occurred to him that he didn't know as much as he should about his niece.

It was definitely time to change that.

Ana dressed Jenny in a pair of pajamas with little yellow ducks all over them. Then she looked up at Linc.

"Thank you for your help."

"I enjoyed it."

She smiled. "You're soaked, Lincoln. I should have offered you an apron."

"No problem."

"Well—"

"So," he said briskly, "what's next?"

"Next? Oh." Her face pinkened. "With Jenny, you mean? Well, I'm going to take her down to the kitchen and feed her."

"Fine. Give me five minutes to get out of this wet stuff and I'll meet you there."

"Oh, but that isn't—"

"I think it is," Linc said quietly. "It only just hit me that I don't know a lot about my niece, and I should."

JENNY WAS EATING something noxious-looking when he came down.

"Mashed banana and Pablum," Ana said, trying not to laugh at his expression. "And be careful, Lincoln. Babies are very good at reading faces."

"Yum-yum," he said bravely.

Jenny flashed him a gummy smile.

When the banana-and-whatever was all gone, Linc took the baby in his arms and fed her her bottle. Her eyelids were drooping by the time she'd reached the final inch.

Ana held out her arms. "I'll put her to bed," she whispered.

Linc nodded. He followed Ana into the hall, watched as she started up the steps. The evening was at an end. He was grateful it had worked out well. After all, it was easier to get along with an employee than not to get along with her...

"Ana?"

Ana turned. His heart seemed to rise into his throat. How beautiful she was. How right she looked, with the baby asleep against her breast.

"Ana." He cleared his throat. "Mrs. Hollowell's sure to have left something for supper."

"Oh, she did. There's cold chicken and a salad, and—"

"How about having supper with me?"

An eternity seemed to pass. Ana touched the tip of her tongue to her lips. "Don't you have dinner plans?"

"None," he said blithely, and made a mental note to have his PA send his would-be date a couple of dozen long-stemmed roses in the morning.

"Still, Lincoln—"

"I figured you could bring me up to speed on what's new with Jenny."

"Oh. Of course. I'll be right down."

Linc hurried back into the kitchen. Should they eat

here or in the dining room? Summer still gripped the city so building a fire on the hearth in the great room's massive stone fireplace would be—

For God's sake, Aldridge!

"Just get out the chicken," he muttered, "and the salad, set the kitchen counter and remember this is a meal, nothing more."

Still, by the time Ana reappeared he'd set a table on the terrace. Hey, it made sense. It was a warm night; the trees in the park were an intense green. Why have a terrace if you didn't use it?

He opened a chilled bottle of Sauvignon Blanc for the same reason. Why not? Didn't a meal deserve some *vino?*

They chatted easily while they ate. Ana had a dozen Jenny stories and Linc smiled at all of them. Then they fell silent.

He cleared his throat. "So," he said, "what do you think of New York?"

"Well, I haven't seen much of it, but what I have seen seems wonderful."

He almost winced. As brilliant conversation starters went, his had just fizzled. Ana was being polite. She couldn't have had more than glimpses of the city, and whose fault was that?

His.

She'd come to the States for a nine-to-five job and he'd pushed her into a 24/7 arrangement she'd never have considered under normal circumstances.

"Well," he said, "you should take a day off. I'm sure Mrs. Hollowell can watch Jenny."

"That's all right, Lincoln. I don't—"

"The Empire State Building. The Statue of Liberty. The museums." What in hell was the matter with him? He sounded like a travel brochure. "There's a lot to see."

"I know, but—"

"I'd like to show the city to you."

Their eyes met. He could have sworn he felt electricity sizzle across the table.

"Thank you, Lincoln, but—"

"I like that, too," he said. "The way you say my name."

"What?"

He reached for her hand, enfolded it in his. "Lin-cone. As if it were two separate words."

"My English," she said, her voice a little breathless, "isn't always per—"

"Yes, it is. Perfect. Everything about you—"

Ana wrenched her hand from his and shot to her feet. "I—I have to check on Jenny."

Linc pushed back his chair and stood up. "Ana—"

"Don't," she whispered.

All he had to do was reach out and take her in his arms. He knew what would happen. So did she. He could see awareness in her eyes. But he'd done enough to this woman already. He'd crushed her dream of coming north and getting a job with his company. Worse, he'd taken that dream and used it for his own purposes.

Only a true SOB would want more from her. Except, God help him, more was exactly what he wanted.

He took a step toward her. Saw the pupils of her eyes enlarge and darken. One kiss. Just one kiss—

The baby's tentative cry trailed down the stairs.

"Jenny," Ana said in a rush.

Linc nodded. Jenny. And reality. Just in time.

"Sure." He forced a smile. "Go on. I'll clean up here."

Then, before he could weigh the consequences, before she could protest, he cupped Ana's face in his hands, lowered his head and brushed his mouth lightly over hers.

Her eyes closed. She swayed toward him. For a moment, nothing existed but the magic of their kiss.

Linc dropped his hands to his sides. And Ana fled.

SO MUCH FOR quiet, friendly dinners.

At least things were peaceful. No more sniping cold looks and turned backs. But there were also no more smiles from Ana. No more easy conversation, either, not even when he gave Jenny her bottle or went to the nursery to tuck her in. He was doing those things now, coming home earlier, not going out at night, working hard at getting to know his niece.

The baby made it easy. She beamed whenever she saw him.

He just wished Ana would beam. Or at least smile. She was unfailingly polite, doling out *Yes, senhors* and *No, thank you, senhors* as if they were part of the job requirement—which, he supposed, they were.

But he kept remembering that for one evening, at least, she had not behaved as if this were a job. He knew, deep inside, that was wrong. She worked for him; he had rules about that. Okay. So he shouldn't have kissed her. But that didn't mean she had to stop talking to him, did it?

Saturday, he decided to find out.

He waited until he knew she had Jenny in the stroller. Then he ambled into the foyer.

"You going to the park?" he said, as casually as if they chatted like this all the time.

He'd caught her by surprise. He could tell by the way she looked up from adjusting Jenny's harness.

"Yes."

"Great." He smiled. "I've been cooped up in the office all week. A walk in the park sounds great."

Ana didn't miss a beat. "Jenny will love having you with her," she said pleasantly. "And I can have a little time for myself."

"To do what?" he said, before he could stop himself.

"Go shopping. Wash my hair. You know."

What he knew, he thought grimly as he pushed the stroller through Central Park, was that those were things women offered as excuses when they didn't want to see a man. When they didn't like a guy.

Well, that wasn't what was happening here.

Okay, it was. But not because Ana didn't like him. She liked him, all right. That evening they'd spent together, the way she'd slipped into using his first name, her easy laughter…

It made him angry. At her, for not admitting she'd wanted to kiss him as much as he'd wanted to kiss her. At himself, for doing something stupid.

At the entire situation, because he couldn't seem to find a remedy.

So, as time passed, he did his best not to think about it. He had other things on his mind. Meetings. Appointments. Business.

And there was this thing with the social worker.

The woman had paid two home visits. He'd been there

for both. They'd seemed to go smoothly, but he'd caught her giving Ana what could only be called suspicious looks.

"Your nanny is such an attractive woman, Mr. Aldridge," she'd said the last time, when Ana took Jenny from the room to change her diaper.

Linc, remembering his lawyer's initial warnings, had felt something cold tap-dance along his spine.

"I guess she is," he'd said with lazy ease, "but what matters to me is that she's wonderful with Jenny."

He knew it was almost decision time. The social worker asked him more and more questions about the future. Had he thought about Jenny's schooling? About her possible need, as she got older, for a female figure in her life?

Was she measuring him against Kathryn's mother-in-law? What he knew for certain was that the mother-in-law was turning up the pressure.

She had the right to visit Jenny. She never came when Linc was there, and at first her visits had been cursory. Hello, goodbye. Ana had told him they'd lasted maybe five minutes.

Lately, though, she said, the visits were lengthier and more frequent.

"She doesn't hold Jenny or anything, but she brings a toy each visit, and she makes a point of asking me the time when she arrives and when she leaves."

His lawyer grew solemn at the news.

"She's building her case, Lincoln. Little presents. Longer visits. It's a way of showing she's interested in Jennifer's welfare."

"But Ana says she never goes near Jenny."

The attorney shrugged. "Trust me, she will if she's there at the same time as the social worker. She's a clever woman, working at looking like Mother of the Year even though we know she isn't."

"Then why hasn't Child Protective Services kicked her out on her butt and given me formal custody? This woman is only after Jenny's inheritance, Charles. Surely they can see that?"

"Be patient, Lincoln. We're gathering information."

Linc had been patient. And finally his lawyer called to say it was paying off.

"The detective we hired came by this morning," he said. "He gave me a folder two inches thick. The woman has a long history of men and addiction. Give me a week and I'll be ready to move ahead."

Linc sighed with relief. "That's great news, Charles."

"This should all be resolved in your favor pretty quickly. Well, assuming the social worker doesn't pop in for a visit and find you and the nanny in, shall we say, a compromising situation."

Both men laughed.

"Speaking of things going well, how is she working out?"

She's so polite she makes my head ache, Linc thought. "She's working out fine," he said.

He hung up the phone and pushed back from his desk. Why think about that now? Except for Charles's phone call, the day had been rough. A hush-hush security system his people were installing in a Dallas museum was causing problems. A fire had crippled production of a new computer chip.

Add Ana's attitude to that mix and his head might just explode.

He thought about taking a couple of aspirin, glanced at his watch, saw that it was almost five. Ana would be bathing Jenny. Mrs. Hollowell would be getting ready to leave. His home would be quiet. He could shower, get into jeans and a T-shirt, sit on the terrace with a cold beer for company and watch twilight overtake the park.

It was, he decided, an excellent plan.

DEFINITELY EXCELLENT.

By the time Linc stepped out of his private elevator, the ache in his head was easing. And he'd figured right. The place was as silent as a tomb. Ana and the baby were undoubtedly in the nursery. Mrs. Hollowell was still here—he could hear her humming softly in the kitchen—but she'd be leaving soon.

He headed for the stairs. He'd take those aspirin now, then a long shower...

"Whoa!"

He saw the tracks and the gaily colored wooden trains, but by then it was too late. He only had time for a couple of frantic dance steps, a pirouette over the tracks that would have delighted Baryshnikov...

Then he went down on his ass.

The resultant crash was impressive. He heard his housekeeper call out. Ana shouted something, too, and then he heard both women running toward him.

"Mr. Aldridge," Mrs. Hollowell gasped, "are you all right?"

"Lincoln, ohmygod," Ana said, and followed that with a lot of other things he couldn't understand.

He told himself it was because she was saying them in Portuguese. It couldn't be because she was kneeling beside him, wearing nothing but a frantic look and a bath towel.

Venus, Linc thought, *rising from the sea.*

Venus making a fool of him the last weeks, treating him as if they hadn't had that quiet meal together, as if she hadn't sighed when he kissed her. Did he have to break his neck before she deigned to notice him?

"Lincoln. Please, do you need a doctor?"

Linc glared and got to his feet. His tailbone hurt, but he'd sooner have said he was Bobo the Clown than admit to that.

"What I need," he said coldly, "is a no-toy zone in this place!"

She turned pale. Who gave a damn? How much crap was a man supposed to take from a woman?

"There's a closet in the nursery. And a big toy box. That's where these trains belong."

"Yes. You are right." Ana rose to her feet, one hand clutching the edges of the towel together. "I apologize, but—"

"But what? If the nursery needs more storage space, tell me and I'll arrange for a carpenter to build some shelves."

He knew his voice was rising but he was done with tolerating disrespect in his own home, and to hell with anyone who didn't see Ana's avoidance of him as that.

"Uh...uh..." Mrs. Hollowell, wise soul that she was,

began backing out of the room. "I'll—I'll just—it's late, sir, and—"

Linc nodded and turned his attention back to Ana.

"If you needed shelves," he snapped, "you had only to say so, but how could you do that without talking to me?"

She was trembling. Good. Let her remember her place here. She was his employee. When had she lost sight of that?

"And what is Jenny doing that you thought you could leave her alone?"

"Jenny is asleep. I would never—"

"People take showers in the morning. They take them at night. They don't take them in the middle of the day."

Her eyes narrowed. "It is not the middle of the day, and I do not need your permission to shower."

"Walking around like that. In a towel. Where's your sense of decorum?"

Where was his sanity? was a better question. She hadn't been walking around, she'd been in her room until he took that stupid fall, but how could a man be logical when a woman as beautiful as this, as impossible as this, stood before him wearing nothing but a towel?

"Stop yelling at me!"

"I am not yelling," he roared. "And never mind crying. Tears will get you nowhere."

"You think I weep because of you?" Ana jerked her chin up. "Hah! I cry for myself. For ever agreeing to work for a—for a—"

She spat out a word. He took a step toward her.

"What did you call me?"

"Trust me, *senhor*. You do not want to know."

Linc grabbed her by the shoulders. "I've had enough of your attitude!"

"And I have had enough of your dictatorialness. I quit."

"There is no such word," Linc snarled. "And you can't quit. You're fired!"

"You are a horrible, arrogant man."

"You are an insolent, ungrateful woman."

"You—you—"

"That's right, baby." Linc jabbed a thumb into the center of his chest. "Me. *I* set the rules. *I* am in charge. And you are—you are—"

He cursed, hauled Ana into his arms and kissed her.

Ana gasped.

The pig! The no-good, despicable brute. The insolence of him. The audacity. The impudence…

Oh, God, Ana thought, and she dug her hands into Lincoln's dark, silky hair, dragged his head down to hers and kissed him back.

He groaned and gathered her closer.

She sighed and rose toward him.

Wrong, her fevered brain shouted, this was all wrong. Lincoln was her employer. There were rules. There was propriety.

And there was this.

This, Ana thought, and opened her mouth to his.

Lincoln said her name. Cupped her face. Tilted back her head and took his mouth from hers just long enough to nip at her throat.

Ana shuddered with excitement. "Lincoln," she whispered.

"Yes," he whispered back. "God, yes—"

His hands slid under the towel and cupped her bottom, lifting her into him. His body was all hard, powerful muscle; his erection, pressing against her belly, made her moan with need.

Another minute and surely her heart would burst. Nothing she'd ever imagined had prepared her for this.

His kiss deepened. Ana felt the sweep of his tongue against hers; delicately she sucked on the tip, and he made a sound deep in his throat that sent heat racing from her breasts to her groin.

His hand moved. Moved again. Slid between her thighs, where she was hot and wet. So hot. So wet. So—so—

Ana cried out. She tore at Lincoln's shirt. Buttons popped and then her palms were against his hot, silky, hair-roughened skin. He lifted her; her legs wrapped around his waist as backed her against the wall...

"What in heaven's name do you people think you're doing?"

The voice cracked through the room with the force of a whip. Linc and Ana sprang apart, just as they had that day in his office, only this was worse.

A thousand times worse, Linc thought in horror.

Ana, damned near naked, was twined around him. His shirt was in tatters, his hands were all over her. And the woman who'd barked those words, who stood staring at them with revulsion, was the social worker.

CHAPTER SIX

LINC swept Ana behind him.

Think, he told himself furiously. Disaster loomed but there had to be a way to avoid it. He'd made presentations that turned hostile CEOs into allies; once, in Colombia, he'd even fast-talked his way out of what associates said would have been a kidnapping.

Surely he could talk his way out of this?

"Miss Harper," he said calmly.

Mrs. Hollowell stepped into view, took in the scene and went white. Hey, why not? A man might as well have an audience for a performance like this.

"I'm so sorry, sir," she said, clasping her hands over her bosom. "The doorman rang and he said this lady wanted to come up and he knew she'd been here before and I said to wait until I spoke with you but you—but you were occupied, sir, and—and—"

"I understand, Mrs. Hollowell. Perhaps you'd make some coffee? I'm sure our—guest—would appreciate it."

His housekeeper shot him a look of gratitude and fled, but the social worker's expression grew even more frigid.

"I am not your guest, Mr. Aldridge. I am here on official business. What we call an unannounced visit."

Linc thought of the joke his lawyer had made about being caught in a compromising position. Damn, damn, damn. Behind him, Ana was trying to tug her hand free of his. He tightened his grasp. The last thing he needed was her racing across the room in that towel.

"We find such visits most illuminating." The woman's smile could have curdled cream.

Ana gave a soft moan of despair and buried her face in his shoulder. Despite everything, this disastrous encounter, his unconscionable loss of control, he wished he could draw her into his arms to comfort her.

What he had to do was think. Hadn't Charles said they had almost everything they needed to push Jenny's money-hungry grandmother out of the picture? To lose the baby now...

And in that instant Linc saw the path to salvation.

"Miss Harper," he said carefully, "I know how this appears—"

"*Appears,* Mr. Aldridge?"

"I can explain."

"I don't think you can. What I have just observed... I must say, Jennifer's grandmother warned us that you had, shall we say, quite a reputation as a bachelor, and now—"

"And now," Linc said briskly, turning to Ana, shielding her still as he shrugged off his suit coat, wrapped her in it and then drew her to his side, "and now those days are over." He smiled for the social worker, but tightened his arm around Ana in what he hoped she'd recognize as a warning.

"Over?" The contempt in Miss Harper's voice was almost palpable. "Not from what I just observed."

Linc beamed at Ana, who was looking up at him in confusion. *You don't know the half of it, sweetheart,* he thought, and drew a steadying breath. "What you just saw was a celebration. You see, Senhora Marques has done me the honor of agreeing to become my wife."

Silence fell over the room. Linc figured it was the calm that might precede a tornado.

"Ana?" he said softly, but she was already shaking her head.

"No! Miss Harper. What Senhor Aldridge just said—"

"What I said is not for publication," Linc said pleasantly. He smiled at Ana, though his eyes flashed a warning. "I'm sure you can understand our wish for privacy."

"Lincoln—"

"Darling, surely you can see that we have to let Miss Harper in on our secret? Otherwise she'd reach the wrong conclusion, and that would not be good for Jenny."

Ana blinked. "Not good for—"

"Exactly."

"Oh." He could almost see her figuring it out. Then she flashed him a dazzling smile and sent another to the social worker. "We would not want you to think Lincoln and I— That we were—" She blushed. "We are, of course, engaged. Otherwise this would never have happened."

The social worker looked dazed. Welcome to the club, Linc thought.

"You're getting married?"

He nodded. "Ana's done me the honor of agreeing to become my wife."

The social worker folded her lips in. "Still, what happened here—"

"We thought my housekeeper had left for the evening. We knew Jenny was in her crib, asleep. And—" He chuckled. "And I guess we just got carried away."

"I see."

"Good. I hoped you would, because—"

"When will this marriage take place, Mr. Aldridge? I wouldn't want Jennifer in this sort of, um, this sort of situation any longer than necessary."

"Nor do we—which is why we've decided to get married at the end of the week."

Ana jerked as if she'd touched a live wire.

"Lincoln," she said, "I told you, it takes time to arrange a wedding."

"I know, sweetheart." Linc tightened his hold on her and gazed down into her eyes. "Which is why I told *you* that I don't care about fancy weddings." He smiled, bent his head, gave her a light kiss and considered himself lucky she didn't snarl and bite him. "Being husband and wife, making a home for our Jenny...that's all that matters. Isn't that right?"

He knew Ana wanted to kill him, but Miss Harper was buying the performance. Moments ago she'd looked as if she'd stumbled into an orgy. Now she was beaming.

"Well, that's just wonderful news, because—well, let me be candid. We've run into some difficulties concerning Jennifer's grandmother."

"Really?" Linc said carefully.

"That's one of the reasons we decided to step up our visits here." Miss Harper dropped her voice. "I have to admit, after what I saw this evening, I'd have been faced with a dilemma. Would it be better to leave Jennifer in a, uh, a morally questionable situation with you, or place her in foster care while we tried to sort things out?"

"No foster care," Ana said sharply. "Not for our little girl."

"Well, no. Not now. Everything else about Mr. Aldridge checked out well. And now that you and he are getting married...I have noted how much Jennifer's bonded with you, Miss Marques. There's no harm in telling you both that I'm going to file a very positive report." She laughed gaily. "That's a secret, of course, but then, you've already shared *your* secret with me!"

They made small talk for another minute or two. Then Linc pressed a tender kiss to Ana's hair.

"Darling, I'll just see Miss Harper out..."

"You do that, *darling*," Ana said, with another of those dazzling smiles.

It was too dazzling. When he came back, she was gone.

Linc sighed, went up the stairs to the nursery and knocked on the door.

"Ana?" No answer. He knocked again. "Ana. We have to talk."

"We have nothing to talk about."

"You know damned well we do. Come on. Open the door." He waited. Then he cursed under his breath and tried to open it but it was locked. "Dammit, Ana—"

The door swung open a couple of inches, just enough to let him see a quadrant of her face.

"You will wake the baby!"

"Get some clothes on and come downstairs so we can discuss this like rational human beings."

"I told you, we have nothing to talk about. Lying to that woman was stupid. Telling her we were getting married in a couple of days was even stupider. How long do you think she'll believe that ridiculous story? And what about me?"

"Look, Ana—"

"This is twice you used me, Lincoln. First when you forced me to take this job, and now you've forced me to lie about getting married."

"I didn't force you. I offered you employment when you needed it. As for tonight, what did you want me to do? What I told that woman was all I could think of to keep my niece! I love the kid. I thought you loved her, too, but I guess I was wrong."

"You really are a horrible man! How can you say such a thing? Of course I love her."

"Then we're on the same page."

"The same...? What does that mean?"

He considered telling her in detail, but why ruin things so quickly?

"Just get dressed and come downstairs so we can work this thing out."

"We have nothing to work out," she said with frost in her voice. "The lie was yours. So is dealing with it."

"Okay. You're right. Now, please, get dressed and come down."

She stared at him. Then she gave a reluctant nod and closed the door. He heard the lock fall into place. For some crazy reason, that definitive *click* infuriated him. He wanted to kick the door down, sweep Ana into his arms...

"Ana!"

The door opened again, this time barely an inch. "What now?"

"I'm going to ask Mrs. Hollowell to stay for a couple of hours."

"Excellent," Ana said coolly. "She can play referee."

Linc decided to ignore the gibe. "Put on something suitable for going out."

She looked at him as if he'd lost his mind. Well, maybe he had.

"Nothing fancy. Just what you'd wear for dinner at any little restaurant." Hell, he sounded like a maniac. "Look, we can't talk here. We need a place that's private."

"This is a huge apartment, Lincoln. It has, what? Ten, fifteen rooms?"

"I know how many rooms it has, dammit!"

"Then why—?"

"Because I say so. Because I'm your boss. Because that's how it's going to be. Any more questions?"

He felt it again, the almost overwhelming desire to sweep her into his arms... Jenny, he reminded himself. Jenny was in the very next room.

It was the only reason he was able to walk away.

Dinner. Dinner out, with Lincoln.

Ana bit her lip as she stared into the mirror. She had to be crazy even to consider it.

But what choice did she have? He was right, he was her boss. More to the point, that look in his eyes... Heaven only knew what he'd have done if she'd said no. He wanted to talk, he said, but what was the point? He'd told a lie so enormous it still made her breath catch.

Now what?

He would not actually ask her to marry him any more than he would expect her to agree to it. He didn't want a wife. She didn't want a husband. He was a bachelor, in the prime of his life. She was a woman just finding her way in the world. Each of them was committed to the idea of freedom—and even if they hadn't been, they weren't in love. Her father, people like him, might not believe love had to exist before a man and a woman wed, but she did.

If she ever chose to marry, in the distant future, she would marry for love. For passion. For all the reasons her father didn't understand, like—like feeling your heart lift at the simple sight of your beloved, or wanting to throw yourself into his arms when you saw him, or smiling at the sound of his voice...

Ana's throat constricted.

All right. Yes, she felt those things about Lincoln, which only proved she knew nothing about love. All those emotions had to do with infatuation, not any deeper emotion. And, yes, she was a little infatuated with him. What woman wouldn't be? Lincoln was handsome. He was smart. He was funny and easy to talk to, and when he wasn't barking out orders he was charming.

And—*truth time, Ana*—and what had almost happened a little while ago was what she dreamed of every night.

Lincoln's kisses. His caresses. She wanted them. Wanted him. If the Harper woman hadn't walked in, she would have given herself to him right there, against the wall…

Thank God she hadn't.

What mattered was that he had told a monumental lie, and even though she'd said it was his problem, she would do her best to help him get out of it, for Jenny's sake.

Okay.

She took a deep breath. How did she look? Her hair hung loose to her shoulders; she'd put on a simple silk dress that barely grazed her knees and was the color of rich cream. Her shoes were shiny black leather, the heels spiked. She carried a small black leather purse.

She hadn't worn any of these things since she'd come to work for Lincoln. He was accustomed to seeing her in jeans. What would he think when he saw her tonight?

Her heart thundered.

Who cared what he thought? They were going out to discuss strategy. Dress for dinner at a casual restaurant, he'd said. And she had.

Ana shut off the light, went into the baby's room for one last check, then headed down the stairs.

WOULD SHE SHOW UP?

Or would she stay in the nursery and lock the door?

Linc paced the foyer, hands in the pockets of his tan chinos.

No. She'd be here. She'd said she would, and Ana

always kept her word. Yes, but what would she say when he told her there was only one way out of this—?

"Lincoln."

He looked up. Ana was at the top of the stairs, standing very still with her hand on the railing.

His mouth went dry.

She was beautiful. God, she was more than that. He just didn't have a word for it. Nobody would. There was no single word that could possibly describe Ana. The elegant bone structure of her face. The slender body that curved in all the places it should. And those long, lovely legs. The shoes that made him imagine her wearing just them and nothing else…

Put your eyes back in your head, Aldridge.

"Ana." His voice sounded rusty. He cleared his throat, cleared his brain, shot a look at his watch as if he could actually read it, then looked at her. "Excellent timing. I made a reservation for eight."

He waited for her to say something. To start down the stairs. When she didn't, he jerked his head toward the door.

"Let's go," he said briskly. "We don't want to be late."

She nodded and descended toward him. Lincoln watched the flash of leg, the sway of hip, until he knew it wouldn't be wise to watch any more. Instead, he grabbed his jacket and busied himself putting it on.

A CASUAL RESTAURANT, he'd said.

As restaurants went in Manhattan, Ana supposed this one was casual.

It was Italian, intimate and quietly elegant. It was also

romantic. The perfect place for a date, had this been a date, which, absolutely, it was not.

The captain obviously knew Lincoln. He greeted them with smiles, then led them to a candlelit table that overlooked a small garden. He and Lincoln had a brief conversation about wines before Lincoln asked her if she preferred white or red.

"Neither," she said, hating herself for sounding so prissy, but, really, what did wine and candlelight and gardens have to do with the reason they were here?

A muscle knotted in Lincoln's jaw. "No wine tonight, thank you, Mario. Just the menus, please."

Ana opened hers, glanced at it, then put it down.

"Have you decided on what you're having so quickly?"

"Actually, I am not very hungry."

Lincoln leaned forward. "Actually," he said, "you don't want to be here. Isn't that right?"

"We are here to discuss the lie you told."

"Is it against the law to eat while we do that?"

Their eyes met. What could she say that wouldn't sound ridiculous? Ana frowned, opened her menu again.

"A green salad," she said crisply. "Chicken Marsala. Coffee." She snapped the menu closed and put it aside. "Satisfied?"

He nodded. "For the moment," he said, and discreetly signaled for their waiter.

THE FOOD WAS probably wonderful, but she couldn't taste any of it.

Lincoln, she kept thinking. She was here with Lincoln.

Weeks of living under his roof, of being polite strangers except for that one incredible night when they'd shared a meal and laughed and talked and he'd kissed her, and now she was here, in this elegant little restaurant, sitting at a table with him.

The meal had begun stiffly, but he hadn't let it continue that way. When their main courses had arrived—the chicken for her, pasta for him—he'd asked if hers was to her liking.

"Fine," she replied politely.

He said he was glad because, for some reason, he'd just flashed back to the first meal he'd ever eaten in a real restaurant.

"I was a senior in college," he said, "and it wasn't fine at all."

"You'd never eaten in a real restaurant?" she said, before she had time to think.

"Not unless you count McD's as fine dining."

She stopped herself from smiling. They weren't supposed to be telling amusing stories, they were supposed to be planning a way out of Lincoln's monumental lie.

"We didn't have the money for it when I was growing up. And what self-respecting university student wastes his hard-earned money on fancy places when there are school cafeterias and Twinkies in the world?"

He'd been poor? It was hard to imagine. He seemed so comfortable in his life... Although, yes, it would go a long way toward explaining the fire and steel she'd seen within him.

Not that she cared.

"Anyway, I was a college senior, interviewing for jobs,

and this guy in a three-piece suit invited me to dinner. I scrounged a sports jacket from my roommate and splurged on a new tie. A good thing, considering he took me to this French place where everything was so expensive I could have lived a week on the cost of one item on the menu."

He forked up a swirl of Pasta Putanesca, put it in his mouth and chewed. Ana waited as long as she could.

"And?"

Lincoln looked up. "Oh. I thought maybe I was boring you."

His eyes glinted with mischief. She wanted to tell him that he was, but how many lies could one evening support?

"Just tell me the story, Lincoln, all right?"

"Well, I didn't recognize anything on the menu, so I decided to order whatever the recruiter ordered."

Ana laughed. "You ended up with snails?"

"Worse. It was Ballotine de Veau Cordon Bleu." Lincoln put down his fork. "Basically, it was—"

"Boiled parts. I don't even want to think about *what* boiled parts," Ana said, with a little shudder.

"You've had it?"

"One summer in Tours. When did you find out?"

"When I couldn't chew through my first mouthful." He smiled. "I asked the guy what we were eating, he told me, and I guess I turned green."

"And he didn't offer you the job?"

Didn't. She'd said didn't *instead of* did not, *which meant she was calming down.*

God, how beautiful she was. And that smile…

"Lincoln? Am I right? You didn't get the job?"

"Oh, he offered it. I turned it down. I knew right then I wasn't cut out for that kind of life."

"But—"

"But I eat in places like this now. And I own that condo." He shrugged his shoulders. "Yeah, but I came to those things my own way, if that makes sense."

It made absolute sense. He was an independent man, her Lincoln. A loner. In another age, he would have been a knight. A warrior.

Her Lincoln? Ana pushed her plate away. "We came here to talk."

"Well, we are talking. You're getting to know me, I'm getting to know you."

"We came to talk about what you told the social worker, and how you can get out from under that monstrous lie."

His smile faded. "Getting out from under it is easy, Ana. I just call her up and tell her there isn't going to be a wedding. The hard part is what happens after." He paused. "Jenny in foster care."

Ana's face whitened.

"Or maybe Grandma will come up with a hotshot lawyer who'll find a way to make her look like Saint Joan. At the very least, there'll be a long court battle. For all I know, they'd take Jenny from me while it goes on."

"From us, Lincoln. I love her. You must know that."

He did. He'd counted on it. Now he leaned forward. The moment of truth had arrived.

"There's one solution," he said softly. "But I'd need your cooperation."

"I would do anything for Jenny. You know that."

He'd counted on that, too.

"In that case…" Linc looked straight into Ana's eyes as he reached for her hand. "Marry me, Ana. And help me guarantee our little girl a happy life."

CHAPTER SEVEN

Was this his idea of a joke?

What did she know of North American humor? A joke would fit with their conversation. He'd told her an amusing story a couple of minutes ago, so this could very well be—

It wasn't. Nobody told jokes when they stared at you as hard as Lincoln was staring at her. Ana dragged her hand from his and sat back.

"Are you *luoco?*"

"You have a better idea?"

His tone was as flat as his eyes. He was serious. Tension made it hard to breathe.

"She knows what she saw, Ana. And she thinks it was dead wrong."

"It was."

His eyes flashed. "The hell it was!"

"I am Jenny's nanny. You are her uncle."

"You're a woman." His voice roughened. "An incredibly desirable woman. And I'm a man. We've been dancing around that since the night we met."

"We have not!"

"This isn't the time to argue about it. I did what I had to do. For all I know, the social worker could have taken Jenny on the spot."

She couldn't argue with that. He had done what he had to do to protect his niece, but marriage...

"I know," he said softly, as if she'd spoken the words aloud. "Marriage isn't at all what you want for yourself. Well, it isn't what I want, either. You know those magazine articles? *One Hundred Things To Do Before You Die?* Trust me, Ana. Getting married wouldn't even make it into my top thousand."

Nor into hers. Then why this sudden ache in her heart?

"Don't look at me that way," he said gruffly. "Do you think I'm happy, asking this of you?"

Did he think *she* was happy, hearing him first suggest the impossible and then describe it as one step up from hell?

"Look, if I could come up with another idea, I would. But I can't, and if you don't marry me, I'll lose Jenny."

Ana reached for her purse. Anger was safer than whatever other emotion was trying to push its way through.

"Just listen to yourself, *senhor*. If *I* do not agree to something *I* do not want, *you* will suffer the consequences."

"That's not what I'm saying and you know it. It's Jenny who'll suffer the consequences."

"You will find a way around it. You always do."

"There *is* no way around it! We get married or Jenny goes into the hands of the state."

Tears burned her eyes. "How can you do this, Lincoln? It is not fair! To make me feel responsible for my baby's future..."

"Did you hear what you just said? You called her your baby."

"A slip of the tongue."

"The hell it was. You say you love her, but you'd let her go into foster care or into the hands of an avaricious woman who sees dollar signs whenever she looks at Jenny?"

He was pushing all the right buttons. She could feel herself weakening. Desperate, she shook her head.

"No. It's insane."

"Because?"

"Because—because of what you said. That neither of us wants to get married."

"I agree. But this wouldn't really be a marriage."

She blinked. "It wouldn't?"

"We'd only have to stay married until my guardianship of Jenny is secure."

Ana stared at him. "You mean, we would have—what do those romance novels call it?—a marriage of convenience?"

"I don't know the term, but, yeah, that's what it would be. My attorney would draw up an agreement. We'd both sign it. You can file for divorce as soon as Jenny's custody is settled." His eyebrows rose. "You didn't think I meant we'd do the until-death-do-us-part thing, did you?"

That was exactly what she had thought. Now she realized how foolish she'd been. Lincoln was not an until-death-do-us-part person. Well, neither was she. Wasn't that what had brought her to New York in the first place?

Then why did his words stab at her heart?

"Ana." He reached for her hands, clasped them lightly in his. "I know I'm asking a lot."

She nodded. It was the understatement of a lifetime.

"If there were another way…"

She nodded again. He was right, there wasn't.

"We both love Jenny."

Ana nodded a third time. All this nodding. Was that the reason for the ache blooming behind her eyes?

"So, we do what we have to do to keep Jenny safe. A civil ceremony. Something quick but legal. And once Jenny's situation is resolved—"

"We end the marriage."

"Right. I'll tell my attorney to find the fastest way to do it."

"A quick marriage, a quick divorce," she said brightly. "Who could ask for anything better?"

"Of course I'll make a generous settlement on you."

Ana's face whitened. She pulled her hands free of Lincoln's. He knew right away he'd made a mistake.

"Do you think I would take your money?"

"Okay. Okay, no settlement."

"If I did this—if I did it—it would not be for payment!"

Her eyes had gone hot with anger. Linc nodded. He'd have to tread carefully.

"A job, then. Don't look at me like that. I was going to tell you anyway. There'll be an opening coming up in my company in a few months." A lie, but meaningless compared to the other lies of the night. "It'll be perfect for you."

"I just said—"

"Look, we can argue over the details later. Right now, just tell me you'll agree to be my wife for a few months."

Her expression went blank. "That long?"

Why did the question annoy him? It wasn't as if he'd gone down on his knees and offered her his heart.

"I don't know," he said bluntly. "However long it takes, okay?"

She swallowed. He could see the movement in her throat and that made him remember the softness of her skin there, just there, at the hollow where he could see the swift beat of her pulse.

She shoved back her chair. "I need time to think."

"There is no time." Urgency crept into his voice. "The Harper woman will be watching us like a hawk. And I told her we'd be getting married right away, remember?"

Ana's eyes darkened. "Why is everything all about you? *You* came up with that ugly lie, and it was all because *you* forced yourself on me!"

"I what? Ana! Dammit, what the hell are you doing?"

A stupid question. What she was doing was bolting from her chair and racing out of the restaurant. Linc cursed, shot to his feet and dropped a handful of bills on the table.

The captain hurried over. "Mr. Aldridge, sir, is everything—?"

Linc didn't bother answering. He ran, oblivious to the stares, the whispers, flung the door open and stepped onto the street.

Clouds had been scudding high over the city's concrete canyons most of the day. Now those clouds had opened up. A warm, light rain was falling, drawing a green, woodsy scent from the sycamores that stood like sentinels along the curb.

Where the hell was Ana?

There! Half a block away, running barefoot, her spiked heels clutched in her hand. Linc took off after her, caught her and spun her toward him.

"Forced myself?" He jerked her to her toes. "You wanted what happened as much as I did, lady."

"That is not true!"

The rain was coming down harder. Drops of it glittered like diamonds on the tips of Ana's lashes.

"Stop lying to yourself."

"*You* are the liar, Lincoln Aldridge. Liar, liar, li—"

Linc kissed her. Ana tried to twist free but he thrust his hands into her hair and held her fast, angled his mouth over hers, kissed her and kissed her, without mercy, without pity...

Without stopping, until, at last, she sobbed his name. *Lin-cone,* the way he loved to hear her say it, and slid her arms around his neck.

He groaned, drew her closer. She was so soft. So delicate.

Somebody laughed, somebody else whistled. "Hey, man," a male voice said, "get a room."

Slowly, Linc raised his head. He looked at Ana's rain-bedraggled hair, her gently swollen mouth, her lashes damp with rain or maybe tears. He had hurt her tonight; he knew he would always despise himself for it, just as he knew what he had to do now.

"Ana." He took a deep breath, then slowly expelled it. "What I did tonight—it was inexcusable." He lowered his forehead to hers. "You're right. Asking this of you was wrong. I'll find a way to deal with—"

Ana laid her fingers lightly over his mouth.

She was watching him as if she were trying to see deep inside his soul. If she could, what she'd see wouldn't make him proud. What he'd just told her was the truth. All of this was his fault.

He'd built his life around discipline. Not just clawing his way into college or putting his life's blood into building Aldridge Security, but everything he'd done to survive his childhood, to ensure that Kath had a chance at a better life.

Now Kath was gone and he'd screwed up so badly that he was on the verge of losing all that remained of her. But to try and make Ana help him clean up the mess he'd made was dead wrong.

He took her hand in his and kissed it.

"I'll find a way, and it won't involve you. I should never have—"

"I'll do it, Lincoln." She took a deep breath. "I'll marry you and stay married for as long as you want me to."

THEY AGREED to tell no one the marriage would be a sham, and not to tell Ana's father about it at all.

Mrs. Hollowell's excitement made Ana feel guilty.

"Oh, that's wonderful," she said. She kissed Ana, hesitated, then blushed and kissed Lincoln, too. "I wish you all the happiness in the world! Jenny's a lucky little girl."

Only Linc's attorney knew the truth. He met with them the following morning, spoke pleasantly, explained the details of the agreement he'd drawn up and then said he'd like to see Linc alone for a couple of minutes.

"Do you know what you're doing?" he demanded, once the door shut after Ana.

"I know precisely what I'm doing, Charles. I'm gaining permanent custody of my niece."

"Lincoln. This woman—"

"Ana, you mean?"

"This woman, Lincoln... You know nothing about her."

"I know all I need to know."

"This innocent appearance of hers—"

"Charles. I know you mean well, but I haven't come here for your advice. I've already decided to marry Ana."

"And then what? Suppose, when the time comes, she refuses to file for divorce?"

"Suppose the sky falls? It's not going to happen, Charles. She's no more interested in making this thing permanent than I am."

"Indulge me, okay? What would happen, do you think, if this woman—"

"Ana," Linc said coldly. "She has a name."

"What if Ana changed her mind? Never mind. Let *me* tell *you*. You'd be up a creek without a paddle."

"Why would she do that? I just told you, she's not interested in staying married."

"She might be interested in money. Lots and lots of money." The lawyer folded his arms. "Who knows what she might demand to go ahead with the divorce?"

"She isn't interested in money."

"I'll let that bit of naiveté go by. What about sex?"

Linc narrowed his eyes. "You're my lawyer," he said coldly, "not my shrink."

"There are no rules about marriages like this, Lincoln. You can have sex or not. It won't change anything legally, but it could muddy the emotional waters."

"Just draw up the contract, Charles."

"Answer the question first."

Linc felt a muscle flex in his jaw. "There won't be any sex."

"Well, that's something."

"I'm happy you're happy," Linc said, his tone still icy.

"One last question. What if the time to dissolve the marriage comes and she refuses to grant you a divorce? Would you file instead?"

"Of course."

"On what grounds?"

"You're the lawyer. You tell me. Hell, this is twenty-first-century America. Divorce is easy to come by."

"But no less messy than fifty years ago. You are, in case you've forgotten, a very, very wealthy man."

"Charles—"

"And you're well-known. Your name is in the news about as often as my great-aunt Tillie pets her cat."

"You have a great-aunt Tillie?"

"This isn't funny, Lincoln. I want you to understand that when push comes to shove this contract, any contract, isn't worth the paper it's written on if one party or the other decides to ignore it."

Linc raised an eyebrow. "Are you telling me you're not the *wunderkind* you claim to be?" he said drily.

"She'd be in position to take a bushel of your money and, in the process, drag your name through the mud."

Linc's expression sobered. "If the truth about the marriage became public after I gained custody of Jenny, could the courts take her from me?"

"After you gain custody? No. You wouldn't lose her."

"In that case, draw up the contract. Let me know when you want us to come in and sign it."

Ana was in the waiting room. When she saw Linc, she rose to her feet. He took her arm and they walked to the elevator.

"He wanted to warn you," she said softly.

Linc thought of saying she was wrong, but how many lies could a man tell?

"He's a good lawyer," he said, just as softly. "I pay him for legal advice and he felt obligated to offer it."

"What did he say? That I was after your money? That I would not divorce you when the time came?"

Linc pushed the call button. "Pretty much."

"And what did you say, Lincoln?"

He swung toward her. "You still say my name that way. 'Lin-cone.'" His voice roughened. "As if there's only you and me left in the world."

"You know that isn't—"

He didn't let her finish the sentence. Instead, he lowered his head, touched his mouth to hers, lightly, gently, then with growing hunger. She leaned into him, let herself fall into the kiss before she gasped and pulled back. "It will be a marriage of convenience," she said breathlessly. "That means—"

The elevator doors swished open. It was crowded.

"—no sex."

Someone giggled. Ana felt her face heat. She stepped into the car, Lincoln by her side, and refused to make eye contact with him until long after they were home.

CHAPTER EIGHT

MRS. HOLLOWELL left early the next evening, which gave Linc the chance to tell Ana what he'd planned.

"There's this guy I play racquetball with. He's a judge. I've dropped by his chambers a couple of times. I thought I'd ask him to marry us. His chambers are handsome, plus he's a nice— Why are you shaking your head?"

"I don't want to be married by your friend, Lincoln."

Linc raised his eyebrows. "Because?"

"Because he will think he has to say something personal."

"And?"

"And I would rather not make this more of a lie than it already is."

"Really?" He could hear his tone hardening. This was no blissful occasion, but it wasn't exactly a funeral, either.

"Yes. Really."

"So, you want to do what? Act as if we're planning a visit to a dentist who doesn't believe in Novocain?"

To his surprise, she laughed. She had, he thought, a lovely laugh.

"I know it seems silly but I feel guilty. We're lying to everyone."

He felt guilty, too. Not so much about lying to the world but about… He wasn't sure, exactly. Maybe it had to do with what this day should be like for Ana, because no matter what she said, he was sure she would marry someday.

She was meant for the comfort and love of a man's arms, just not for his. No woman was meant for that. He was too removed. Too dedicated to his work. Relationships weren't his thing. A dozen women had told him that. So had Kath, only she'd been more blunt.

"You don't want to open up, Linc," she'd said. *"It makes you feel too vulnerable. I understand it's because of how we grew up, but you're going to regret it someday."*

Not true. It was the worst kind of dollar-store pop psychology—and, dammit, what did all this looking into his navel have to do with anything?

"Okay," he said briskly. "We'll get the license tomorrow, get married at City Hall as soon as the law says we can."

"Fine." Ana got to her feet. "What time shall I be ready?"

Linc rose, too. Oh, yeah. Definitely she looked as if she were getting ready for a trip to the dentist.

"It's only eight in the evening. Why are you going up?"

"I get up early."

"Me, too, but I go to bed later than this."

"So?"

"So," he said, watching her face, "we'll have to coordinate our hours. I'd lay odds newlyweds don't go to their bedroom a couple of hours apart."

Color swept into her cheeks; she looked as if he'd just

told her he had a predilection for wearing animal skins and dancing around campfires.

"What do you mean, *their* bedroom? Surely you do not think—?"

"Surely I do think," he said, walking around the table to her. "Mrs. Hollowell thinks we're getting married because we're crazy about each other." He smiled thinly. "Sleeping in separate rooms might put a dent in that."

"Lincoln." She took a step back. "No sex, remember? This is a marriage of—"

"I know what it is." Slowly, he hooked his hand behind her neck and drew her forward. "I also know we're going to have to make it look real." He put a finger under her chin, raised her face to his. Her mouth was trembling. The sight put a knot in his gut. "No sex doesn't mean we won't share a room. Or an occasional kiss." He lowered his mouth to hers. Kissed her gently. Waited for what he knew her response would be, that little sigh, the sweet moan…

What in hell was he doing? he asked himself, and stepped back.

"Good night," he said, as calmly if he hadn't just kissed her, as if he weren't aching to lift her in his arms and carry her to his bed.

Ana fled. He couldn't blame her. He'd run, too—except it was too late.

HE'D ASKED Mrs. Hollowell to take care of Jenny for the day.

Ana waited until the housekeeper left for the park.

Then she handed Lincoln a piece of paper. At first, he thought it was a shopping list.

Then he looked more closely.

1. No sex.
2. Do you have a chaise longue in your dressing room? If not, please order one. It is where I will sleep.
3. Signs of affection should be brief and occur only if someone is observing us.
4. No sex.

He looked up. She was standing with arms folded and lips compressed. He told himself not to laugh.

"You have one item listed twice."

"I thought it a very important item."

He nodded. His soon-to-be-wife was definitely an interesting woman.

"Well?"

Linc handed the paper to her. "No problem."

"Including the chaise longue?"

"Including the whatever-it's-called."

"Thank you. I thought you might be opposed to some of my requests. I am happy to see that you are not."

"They're fine."

Kissing her last night had been a momentary lapse in judgment. A man shared his home with a gorgeous female, he was bound to react. It wouldn't happen again. As for the *chaise* thing—he'd call Macy's and order one right after they went to City Hall to apply for a license. Or after they went to Charles's office and signed the prenup.

Somewhere in there he'd take care of it.

The prenup was as thick as a dictionary. Linc, who'd been dealing with his lawyer long enough to trust him, signed it after a cursory look.

Not Ana. "I would prefer to read it through," she said.

It took her an hour.

Charles tapped a pencil against a pad of yellow legal paper, watched the clock, watched a couple of pigeons on the ledge outside the window, watched the people in the office across the street.

Linc watched Ana.

She frowned, chewed on her lip, made notes. She was wearing one of her dress-for-success suits and she'd pulled her hair into a knot at the nape of her neck, but strands had escaped and fallen against her cheek.

She pushed them back impatiently.

Linc thought about doing it slowly. Very slowly, so he could bend down and breathe into her ear, touch the tip of his tongue to it.

He shot from his chair. Ana and Charles both looked up. "Just stretching my legs," he said brightly. "I'll be back in a minute."

He went out of the office, paced the corridor, counted to a hundred, then headed back.

Ana saw him and scowled.

"What?"

"This clause about payment…I told you, I want nothing for my part in this."

"Yeah, and I told *you* that you deserved something."

"This money is out of the question. I do not need it. I will not take it."

"Independence is expensive, Ana. You want to be on your own when this is over, you'll want that check."

"I will not accept money, Lincoln!"

"Fine. Scratch out the clause and initial it. That's the way. Here, I'll initial it, too. Okay. Now, just sign the damned contract."

She glared at him. Then she scrawled her name on the document and stood up. "I will wait outside," she said, and marched out without a backward glance at Lincoln or Charles.

Linc waited until she'd closed the door. Then he took an envelope from his pocket and put it on the desk.

"What's this?" Charles said.

"A check, made out to Ana."

"But she said—"

"I know what she said, but I'm not going to let her do all this for me without compensation. Put it away until this thing is over. I'll give it to her then."

His lawyer nodded. "An excellent idea."

"Yeah," Linc said—except the truth was, nothing about this idea felt the least bit excellent.

THEY MADE A QUICK STOP at Tiffany's for a plain gold band, then hurried to City Hall, where Linc produced his birth certificate and Ana produced her passport.

Linc took out his wallet. Ana took out hers.

"I will pay half the fee," she said.

He decided not to argue. Her accent had grown so thick that soon he'd need an interpreter to understand her.

The clerk issued their license. In twenty-four hours, he said, they could marry.

Back home, Jenny grinned and held out her arms. They played with her for a while. Ana said she would take over, but the housekeeper tut-tutted.

"Don't be silly, dear! Tomorrow's your wedding day. You go and relax with Mr. Aldridge and leave the baby to me."

But once they were alone Ana said she was exhausted. "It has been a very long day, Lincoln. I think—I think I will go to my room."

Linc tried to see past his fiancée's wooden smile. Was she angry at what he'd forced her into, or was she terrified?

Suddenly, he had to know.

"Ana. Listen to me. I promise, you'll be fine—"

Her eyes flashed. "What do you know of how I will be?"

He thought about pulling her into his arms. Showing her that he knew, that he would never hurt her...

His mouth thinned. Did she think this was any easier for him? Because it wasn't. Why would he want to get married, even if the marriage was a lie? Why would he want to marry a woman who didn't want to marry him?

"What I know," he said coldly, "is that you've agreed to perform a role in a charade and I expect you to do it well."

"Do not worry, Lincoln. I will be the best actress the world has ever seen."

"Just remember that," he said, and even though he hated the way her mouth trembled, he stood his ground in silence as she ran up the stairs.

LATE THE NEXT AFTERNOON, they stood before a clerk at Centre Street. Two minutes later they were husband and wife.

"You may kiss the bride," the clerk said, smothering a yawn.

Linc knew there was no need for what Ana had labeled a "sign of affection." Nobody was, to use her word, *observing* them, except the clerk and a stranger pressed into duty as a witness. Still, they were in a public place. The pretense might as well begin now.

He turned Ana to him.

Brides were supposed to glow, but her face was the color of milk. And when he tilted it to his, he saw the glitter of tears in her eyes.

His heart constricted.

"Ana," he said softly, "I'm sorry. For what I said last night, for today…"

She shook her head. "Never mind. We're doing this for Jenny. It's all right."

It wasn't all right at all, and he knew it. He kissed her. Kissed her tenderly. Until she melted against him and he tasted the salt of her tears on her soft mouth.

My wife, he thought. *My wife.*

And then the clerk said, politely, that there were others waiting and it was going on closing time. Linc put his hand in the small of Ana's back as they left the building and felt her trembling. He slid his arm around her waist. She stiffened, but then she leaned into him the way she would have done if the ceremony binding them together had been real.

HE HAD ARRANGED for Mrs. Hollowell to stay overnight to care for Jenny.

Ana had objected, until he'd pointed out that his housekeeper would be the one person who'd be in a position to comment on their marriage, if that became necessary.

Mrs. Hollowell had said of course she'd stay, but wouldn't it be better if she took the baby home for the night? She had grandchildren so she had all the things Jenny might need. He'd thanked her and said that wouldn't be necessary.

Now, watching Ana, he knew he'd made a big mistake.

Mrs. Hollowell had set out champagne and caviar. Ana didn't notice. She'd filled the sitting room with vases of white roses and freesia, which was more than he'd thought to do, but Ana didn't notice that, either.

The housekeeper was giving her worried looks. Ana was supposed to be a happy bride. Instead, she looked like a woman who'd lost her best friend. Who knew what she might say or do? What if she blurted out the truth about their marriage?

He had to do something, he thought, and gently gathered Ana into his arms.

"You must be exhausted, sweetheart," he said, smiling, hoping she'd get the message and smile in return. "Why don't you go upstairs? Take a long bath, even a nap. I'll be up after a while."

She not only got the message, she all but sighed with relief. "I will do that, Lincoln. Thank you for thinking of it."

He waited until she'd left the room, then he turned to Mrs. Hollowell.

"My wife's been under a lot of stress," he said. "She's worn out."

"Yessir," his housekeeper said evenly. "You haven't given her time to breathe."

A day of firsts. He'd never been married before and his polite housekeeper had never before commented on his personal life.

"That offer you made," he said, "to take Jenny for the night... Is it still good? Ana and I need some quiet time together."

That won him a smile. "Two minutes to get the baby ready, Mr. Aldridge, and we'll be on our way."

"I'll phone for my car. And Mrs. Hollowell?" Linc smiled. "Thank you."

HE GAVE ANA AN HOUR.

Then he knocked on his bedroom door. *Their* door, he reminded himself, and felt the tension in his gut.

Ana opened it. She'd worn one of those dress-for-success suits for the wedding and she was still wearing it now. She was also wearing an expression that could best be described as halfway between disbelief and anger.

"Someone moved all my things!"

"Well, yeah. Mrs. Hollowell. She suggested it and—"

"You should have asked me."

"We went through all this, remember? You're my wife. You sleep with me."

"I have no intention of sleeping with you."

"A figure of speech," he said, holding up his hand.

"And what," she hissed, "is this?"

Bewildered, he started to look around. Ana muttered something, grabbed his lapel, hauled him into the room and shut the door.

"Do you want Mrs. Hollowell to hear us, Lincoln?"

Maybe this wasn't the time to tell her Mrs. Hollowell was gone.

"What's the problem?"

Ana swept her hand around the room. "What do you see?"

"Uh—"

"Dresser. Chest. Tables. Chairs. Bench. Lamps," she said, answering her own question. "Now come into the dressing room. What do you see?"

Linc cleared his throat. "Clothes?"

Ana folded her arms and glared at him. "Do you see anything even resembling a chaise longue?"

"A chaise...?" *Damn!* "I forgot. In the rush, I just... I'll order it tomorrow."

"And where, pray tell, am I to sleep tonight?"

He looked at her, at the beautiful eyes flashing with anger, at the defiance, the courage, the spirit his Ana radiated...

"Here. It's a big bed. You take one side, I'll take the other."

She glared at him for what seemed a very long time. Then she narrowed her eyes.

"Touch me," she said through her teeth, "and you are a dead man."

He believed it.

CHAPTER NINE

ANA lay wrapped in her robe, all but clinging to the edge of the bed, as far from Lincoln as she could manage.

The clock read 2:22 a.m. She had not slept at all.

Lincoln, on the other hand, had gone into the bathroom, come out in a pair of sweats, climbed into the bed, put his head on the pillow and drifted off to happy dreamland.

This sham wedding was upsetting only to her. He'd gone through it without hesitation, saying "I do" and "Yes" and kissing her at the end of the ceremony as if their reasons for marrying were the same as everyone else's.

He wasn't supposed to have kissed her.

That was part of the deal. No touching. No kissing. A separate bed for her. He'd agreed to it all and now she knew just how much that meant. He'd touched. He'd kissed. Now they were sharing a bed.

Ana swallowed hard.

Maybe the real question was why she'd melted into that kiss? Leaned into his embrace? Why she'd wanted to weep when she saw the champagne, the caviar, the flowers that it had taken Lincoln's housekeeper to arrange?

She wasn't a bride. Not a real one. She was a woman playing a role opposite a man who thought marriage was an unnatural act. But so what? She thought the same thing.

There it was again, that ridiculous sting of unwanted tears. Ana blinked them back and looked across the endless expanse of bed. Lincoln still hadn't stirred. For all she knew, in a little while he might even start to snore.

Such a romantic wedding night.

She sat up, eased from the bed and the room. She thought about stopping at the nursery to check on Jenny, but Mrs. Hollowell was sleeping there and the last thing she wanted to do was rouse the housekeeper. Instead, she made her way downstairs and onto the terrace.

The late summer night was warm. Below, a lone taxi prowled south along Fifth Avenue. Across the street, the trees stood like silent sentinels in the darkness.

This time, when Ana's eyes filled with tears, she let them come.

What a fool she'd been to marry Lincoln. Hadn't she realized this would not work? That to live this kind of lie would be—?

"Ana?"

She spun around. Lincoln was standing in the doorway. Her heart did a stutter step. He was so beautiful. So masculine. He was her husband—and she could still remember the taste of his mouth, the scent of his skin…

"Lincoln. I didn't mean to wake you."

"You didn't." He stepped outside and leaned his elbows on the railing beside her. "I wasn't sleeping. I just figured it was simpler to let you think I was." He sighed. "And I know exactly what you were thinking just now."

She felt the rush of color in her cheeks. "You do?"

"You were thinking, what in hell did we do?"

"Oh." The breath whooshed from her lungs.

"Me, too. I thought it would be so simple. Get married, pretend everything's great. But it's turning out to be complicated." He turned around and leaned back against the railing. "Well, we'll just have to uncomplicate it."

"How?"

"I don't know," he said gruffly. "And frankly, I'm not up to figuring it out at this hour. The only thing I'm sure of right now is that we never had supper."

She looked at him. "Didn't we?"

He grinned. "No. Not even that caviar. You were too busy chewing me out for forgetting to order the bed."

"About that…" Ana hesitated. "I shouldn't have been so angry. With everything you had on your mind—"

"I should have remembered. I'll take care of it tomorrow, I promise." He touched the tip of his index finger to her nose. "Right now, it's the middle of the night."

"I know. I'm just not very sleepy, that's all."

"What you are is hungry."

She would have said he was wrong, but her belly gave an unladylike growl of affirmation.

"See?" he said, laughing. "So, let's have something to eat, okay?"

He held out his hand. Slowly, she took it.

"I suppose I could find something in the refrigerator and make sandwiches."

"Forget that. We'll do takeout."

"At three in the morning?"

"This is New York, sweetheart. The city that never sleeps." He turned on the kitchen lights, drew a stool from the counter and watched as she scooted onto it. "And bachelors know all about takeout. Mrs. Hollowell only started cooking for me after Jenny came along." He opened drawers, cupboards, poked through shelves and finally fanned a dozen menus on the counter in front of her. "Pick one."

"You decide. I'll be happy with whatever you choose, Lincoln."

Lin-cone. There it was again, that softness in her voice, that way she made something as simple as his name seem to shimmer. There was that smile, too. He'd wondered if he'd ever see it again after the fiasco about the unordered bed, the fiasco of the entire day. He'd moved too fast, hadn't taken the time to ease her fears or maybe even make her see how good this could be, being together for whatever time they had.

Hell.

Linc grabbed for a menu, then for the phone.

"Chang's Kitchen," a voice sang in his ear. "What would you like?"

Ana, Linc thought, and the realization stunned him.

HE BUILT A FIRE and they ate seated on oversized silk pillows before the hearth. He set out heavy white napery and Baccarat flutes that he filled with the chilled champagne.

Ana laughed when she saw how much food he'd ordered. Moo shu pork, orange chicken, shrimp in black bean sauce and half a dozen other things sent their fragrance wafting into the air as he opened the white take-out boxes and arranged them in a circle.

"No plates?"

"No plates. No forks. Just chopsticks. Trust me," he said solemnly. "It tastes better this way."

She smiled and dug in. He waited a while, watching as she transferred small bits of food to her mouth. Once or twice she licked the chopsticks. Damn if it didn't make his belly clench.

"What?" she said, laughing. "Are you going to criticize my chopstick technique? I'll have you know my very first nanny was born in China. Well, Taiwan. She had me using sticks before I was five."

"A nanny, huh?"

Ana lifted a shrimp to her mouth. "A long succession of them. Nice, mostly, but I think it must be nicer to be raised by your mother."

"Probably."

"Probably? Didn't your mother—?"

"She took care of herself," he said, shrugging as if it hadn't mattered when it damned well had. "I took care of me."

"And your sister," Ana said softly. "Kathryn was lucky to have you in her life."

"She was my sister," he said simply. "My responsibility."

"And you are a man who takes responsibility to heart."

How had this conversation grown so serious? This wasn't a night for that. It was a night for being alone with Ana. For realizing how important she had become to him. For wanting—for wanting—

"Ana."

What he was thinking must have been right there, in the way he spoke her name, the way he looked at her. Color rushed into her face. Carefully, she put down her chopsticks.

"It is late," she said, rushing the words together. "Mrs. Hollowell will probably be coming down in a little—"

"She's not here. She took Jenny home with her."

Ana stared at him. "Why?"

"Because this is our wedding night."

"No." Her voice was a whisper. "It isn't."

"It is, Ana. No matter the circumstances. I thought it would be easier this way, not having someone else here in the morning."

He was right. Lincoln, the ever-responsible man. She forced a smile.

"Thank you."

"What are you thanking me for, Ana?" His voice roughened. "That you won't have to pass an early-morning inspection? Or that you won't have to make love with me?"

Ana felt her heartbeat quicken. *Get up right now,* a voice inside her ordered. *Get up and walk out of this room!*

"Because what I want, more than anything in the world," he said, "is to make love with you."

"No. You should not say—"

"I should. I've told enough lies lately. Tonight, at least, I'm going to speak the truth."

She sat very still, feeling his gaze on her skin like a silken caress. She knew he wanted her. She knew it the way every woman knows when a man wants her.

And she wanted him.

"Ana? There's a drop of sweet-and-sour sauce on your mouth."

All she had to do was pick up her napkin and touch it to her lips. But she was an adult. Independent. Capable of making her own decisions.

"Where?" she whispered, and saw the heat flare in his eyes.

"I'll show you."

He leaned forward and covered her mouth with his. It was a long, sweet kiss; his lips were cool, the abrasion of his end-of-day beard against her skin sent a tingle of electricity down her spine.

"Did you get it all?" she said against his mouth.

"Not yet. There's more…"

So much more, Ana thought, and then, somehow, her lips were clinging to his. Parting beneath his. His tongue was in her mouth and she…

She was on fire.

"Lincoln. Please. Kiss me. Kiss me. Kiss—"

The bedroom was too far away. He knew he'd never make it that far. He, the man who prided himself on his self-control, could never seem to manage it when it came to this woman.

Instead, he drew her down against the soft pillows. Kissed her, drank in her sweet moans and whispers as he undid the sash of her robe. It fell open around her, an ivory chrysalis exposing his Ana to his eyes.

She was exquisite.

Small, rounded breasts tipped with deep rose. A slender waist that blossomed into a woman's hips. Long, elegant legs. And at the junction of her thighs a cluster of pale gold curls that seemed to beg for his caress.

Her skin was flushed with color; she was trembling, as if she'd never been with a man. Selfishly, even though he knew better, he wished it were true.

"You're beautiful," he whispered.

Gently, he cupped her breasts, watched her face as he swept his thumbs over her nipples. She moaned and he bent to her and kissed her throat, the slope of her breasts, the delicious crests. She made a little sound in her throat and he felt a wave of hot, raw need sweep through him. He wanted her now, wanted to bury himself inside her, but she deserved more from this night and he was determined to give it to her.

He kissed her breasts again. Drew the sweetness of her nipples into his mouth. Kissed her navel, her belly. Kissed the delicate whorl of gold. Parted the petals of that most beautiful of flowers...

And touched her.

Ana screamed and came apart in his arms.

He drew her close, held her, rocked her until she calmed. A fierce sense of fulfillment swept through him, knowing he had done this for her. For his wife.

"Lincoln?"

Her voice shook. He kissed her, pulled off his sweats and came back to her again, covering her with his body as she sighed his name. Slow down, he warned himself, but her cries were the aphrodisiac men had sought through all eternity.

"Ana," he said, "look at me."

Her lashes lifted. Her eyes met his.

"Yes," she said, and he let his swollen sex brush against hers. God, he thought, surely he was going to die from such pleasure…

Sweet heaven! He didn't have a condom.

He jerked back. Felt his erection starting to fade with the shock. But Ana reached between their bodies and closed her hand around him.

"Ana," he said, trying to hold on to sanity. "Ana, sweetheart…"

She tilted her hips. "Please, Lincoln," she whispered, and the world blurred as he surged forward and thrust deep into his bride's feminine heart…

And tore through the fragile barrier of her virginity.

THEY LAY ENTWINED, his arm around her, her head on his shoulder, her leg over his.

Linc's heartbeat slowed. The room came back into focus and so did his brain. God, what had he done? He had shredded his no-sex promise to Ana. He had taken her virginity. And as if that weren't enough, he had committed the ultimate sin.

He'd made love to her without a condom.

The room was cool, the air chill against his sweat-slick skin. Ana had to feel it, too. Carefully, never letting her go, he reached for her discarded robe and drew it over them.

"Sweetheart." He rose on his elbow, just enough so he could see her profile, half-hidden by strands of golden hair. Where to start? he thought, gently thumbing it aside.

She sighed. "You want to know why I didn't tell you I was a virgin."

"No. Yes. That, too. Dammit, why didn't you?"

"I don't know." She looked up at him and smiled. "Maybe because it was none of your business."

"Of course it was my business," he said, even though he knew she was right. They'd never intended to become lovers; why should she have told him anything so personal?

"Besides, even if I'd wanted to, when was the right time? Would you have had me say, 'Lincoln, this moo shu pork is delicious and, oh, by the way, I am a virgin'?"

A deep laugh rumbled in his chest. "Okay. Maybe not like that, exactly, but…" Gently, he brushed his mouth over hers. "How come you didn't slug me when I said maybe you'd come from your lover that night we met in Rio?"

"Mmm. I should have." She smiled. "But I took pity on you. I knew you were furious because I'd violated your security system."

"Mostly I was furious at myself for losing control and kissing you." His tone grew husky. "If you knew how many times I thought about that kiss after I got back to New York…"

"I'll bet you thought about your security system, too. 'How could that woman have defeated it?'" she said, in almost perfect imitation of his low growl.

Lincoln grinned and nipped lightly at her throat. "Are you going to tell me?"

"It's very complicated, Lincoln. I sat down at a computer, worked up some algorithms…" She grinned at the look on his face. "I memorized the code when Papa set it. You think I'd let a hotshot *Norte Americano* keep me from getting outside for a nightly run without bodyguards?"

"A run?" His voice rose. "Alone, in those hills? For God's sake, Ana! Anything could have happened to you."

"But nothing did." Her voice softened. "In fact, Lincoln, I don't think anything at all ever happened to me in my entire life until now. This was—it was wonderful."

"Yes," he said gruffly. "It was. But—" He tried to say it lightly. "But I broke rules one and four."

"No sex," she said softly.

He nodded. "Can you forgive me, sweetheart? I swear, I didn't plan—"

"It was my choice, too. That's why I came to New York, remember? To live my own life, not anyone else's."

But she was part of his life now, Linc thought. Except she wasn't. When this marriage ended, she would go her own way. It was what she wanted. What he wanted, too.

Wasn't it?

"Lincoln? What's the matter?"

"Nothing. I just—just—" He took a deep breath. "Ana. I didn't use a condom."

She nodded. "I know."

"I'm healthy, sweetheart, but I could have made you—"

"This is my safe time of the month, Lincoln."

"Yeah, but just so you know, should anything happen—"

"I'm an adult. I take responsibility for myself."

There it was again, another arrogant little statement about independence. He admired her for it, but would it be wrong if she leaned on him, just a little? If she needed him, just a little? If she—if she felt something for him besides desire?

"Ana." He drew her tightly against him. "Ana—"

She silenced him with a kiss, not wanting to hear how grateful he was that she'd married him for Jenny's sake, because, if he did, she knew she would not be able to let the lie pass. She would have to tell him the truth. That she loved Jenny, yes, but that what she'd done was for him.

She had fallen in love with her temporary husband, even though loving him would surely break her heart.

CHAPTER TEN

LIFE was wonderful.

Jenny was a delight. Surely a baby like no other. Bright. Sweet. Absolutely adorable.

And Lincoln...Lincoln was everything a woman could want. Generous. Attentive. Tender. Intelligent. Charming and gorgeous and sexy and passionate.

Sometimes, lying in his arms at night, Ana would imagine what life would be like if their marriage were real. She didn't want to think that way; it hurt too much to know it would not happen. But her thoughts drifted to how it would feel to be with her husband forever, and her throat would constrict.

Maybe she made some little sound, maybe Lincoln could sense something, because, inevitably, he'd turn her toward him.

"Sweetheart?" he would whisper. "What are you thinking?"

"Nothing," she would say, and thank God for the darkness of the bedroom that kept him from seeing how close she was to tears.

Sooner or later all this would end. Lincoln would

come home and tell her that their deception had worked, that Jenny was his, that their marriage had run its course.

That was how she'd thought it would go. In the end, it was not like that at all. He didn't come right out and tell her. Instead, he just began to change.

He came home late. Meetings, he said. Last-minute stuff.

He left early. Breakfast appointments, he told her. Unavoidable.

But the surest indication of what was happening came at night. He began letting her go to bed alone. The press of work. Reports to read, plans to make...

"You understand, don't you, Ana?"

Yes, she said, yes, of course.

When he finally came to bed, she pretended to be asleep. Sometimes, he'd climb in beside her so carefully she knew he was determined not to wake her, and she'd want to sit up and tell him not to worry, that she would not let him make love to her even if he tried.

A lie, because every once in a while he'd suddenly roll toward her, wake her with his kisses, take her in his arms and love her with a passion that bordered on frenzy. She'd seen a movie once about a soldier leaving for war. He'd made love to his wife that way. It was how he'd said goodbye.

Life was not a movie, but it wasn't a fairy tale, either. There would be no happy ending here.

Then came the morning—this morning—when she knew it was time to admit the marriage was over. She'd awakened to find Lincoln at the window, fully dressed, staring out at the park.

"Lincoln?" she'd said, sitting up, drawing the duvet

to her chin because, for the very first time, she hadn't wanted to face him naked.

Slowly, he'd turned toward her. What she'd seen in his face had made her breath catch. "We have to talk."

Not yet, she'd thought. Oh, please, not yet...

"Now, if you like. Or this evening, Ana. Whichever you prefer."

She'd known she needed to compose herself. Weeping in front of him would be too humiliating. So she'd lied. She'd said she'd gotten her period during the night. Her back ached. She had cramps. Talking tonight would be best.

Lincoln had breathed what could only have been a sigh of relief. Why wouldn't he? It was almost four weeks since they'd made love without a condom. Her responsible husband would have stood by her if she were pregnant...

But that wasn't what he wanted.

It wasn't what she'd wanted, either. Amazing how what you wanted could change.

He'd nodded. Asked if he could get her some tea. Responsible to the end, she'd thought, and stretched her lips into a smile.

"Don't worry about me," she'd said brightly, and she'd held the smile until he left the room without kissing her, without a backward glance, without anything to show that, for a little bit of time, they'd been lovers.

It was only then that she'd let herself weep.

Now, sitting on a bench in Central Park, sitting near the statue of Alice in Wonderland by the model boat pond with Jenny asleep in her stroller, a bright autumn sun beating down from a cerulean-blue sky, Ana wondered how she would get through tonight's conversation.

She would, though. Lincoln had married her for Jenny; she had married him for love. That wasn't his fault, it was hers, and she would never let him know that she—

"Miss Marques?"

Startled, she looked up and saw Lincoln's attorney standing beside the stroller.

"May I join you?" he said, even as he sat down beside her.

She knew, instinctively, this was no accidental meeting.

"What are you doing here, Mr. Hamilton?"

"I stopped by Lincoln's place. Lincoln's housekeeper said I might find you here."

Lincoln's place. Lincoln's housekeeper. And he'd addressed her as Miss Marques. Nothing like reminding the hired help who and what they were.

"I wanted to speak with you privately, Miss Marques. I hope you don't—"

"You've come to tell me Jenny's custody has been settled."

She spoke the words through wooden lips, knowing, as she'd known for days, they had to be true.

Hamilton raised his eyebrows. "Well, that's a relief. I thought there might be a problem."

Ana's throat tightened. "What do you mean?"

"The ruling came through more than a week ago. I suggested to Lincoln that the three of us meet right away, but—well, I gather he thought he'd have some difficulty sharing the news with you."

A week? Lincoln had known for all that time but he had not told her. Had he been silent out of pity? Or had

Lincoln, the ever-responsible man, been waiting to find out if she were pregnant?

"So, on his behalf, as his attorney and his friend…"

"Please. You do not have to say anything more." Ana rose to her feet. "Lincoln and I had an agreement and now there is no longer a need for it."

"I'm glad you're taking this so well, Miss Marques." Hamilton stood up, too. "We can set an appointment for our meeting. Or…" He held out an envelope. "Or we can deal with the remaining legality right now."

She took the envelope and stared at it. "What is this?"

"Your check."

"My what?"

"I know you insisted on crossing out that clause in the contract, but Lincoln feels you've earned yourself a generous— Miss Marques?"

Ana released the brake on Jenny's stroller and began pushing it toward the park exit, her pace quickening as she heard the traffic on Fifth Avenue.

"Miss Marques," Hamilton called, but she saw no reason to answer. She saw no reason to do anything but take Jenny home, kiss her goodbye and get out of Lincoln's life as swiftly as possible.

To think he'd imagined he had to buy his freedom from her…

Tears blurred her eyes. She blinked them back and kept going.

"WHAT DO YOU MEAN, she's gone?"

Mrs. Hollowell stared at her employer. His voice was low and dangerous, his face white, his eyes bright and hard as emeralds.

"Just that, sir. Ana is—"

"You did nothing to stop her?"

"Me? How could I have stopped her, Mr. Aldridge?"

"How in hell do I know? You were here, not—" Linc stopped and drew a deep breath. He had to get control of himself, fast.

"I'm sorry," he said. "Let's start over. Ana's gone. She packed her things and left?"

"Yes."

"No note?"

"No, sir."

"No forwarding address?"

"No, sir. I told you. She told me to take care of Jenny. Then she called a taxi and—"

"Nobody just calls a taxi and disappears." So much for control. Linc ran his hand through his hair, then started over. "What brought it on? Did she say?"

"Only that she should have left a long time ago." Mrs. Hollowell bit her lip. "She was crying, sir. And when she kissed Jenny goodbye… Oh, it was awful."

Awful, and his fault. If he hadn't been afraid she'd turn him down, if he'd taken his wife in his arms anytime during the whole miserable week and said, *Ana, the court has given Jenny to me, but I don't give a damn how badly you want your independence, I love you and I'm not going to let you leave me,* at least he'd have had a chance.

His last hope had been that maybe she'd conceived his child and he could use that to make her stay married to him. Then, this morning, she'd launched into that little speech about getting her period.

And she'd been smiling, as if she was glad he understood there'd be nothing binding her to him once the terms of the contract were met.

So he'd walked away rather than say something he'd regret, spent the day trying to figure out a way to approach her that would change her mind.

In midafternoon he'd thought, Screw this. Forget about work. Forget about a plan. He'd just go home, take Ana in his arms, tell her he adored her and that she had to feel the same way about him, she had to…

Except she was gone.

"Mrs. Hollowell. Exactly what happened here today?"

"Nothing out of the ordinary. Well, except maybe Ana seemed a little, I don't know, sad. So when Mr. Hamilton stopped by after lunch, looking for her—"

"My lawyer was here?"

"Yes. Looking for your wife. And since she'd seemed a bit down, I thought perhaps a little visit with someone would cheer her up. I told him she'd gone to the park and that I knew she almost always sat near the Alice statue."

"Charles Hamilton went to see Ana?" Linc said in a low voice.

"As far as I know, he did. And, oh, I almost forgot. There was one other thing. When your wife returned home…" The housekeeper dug in her apron pocket. "She left this on the kitchen counter, Mr. Aldridge. I didn't know whether to throw it out or—"

Linc stared at the bits of paper in Mrs. Hollowell's outstretched palm. He took them, spread them on the counter, shuffled the pieces…

And groaned.

He was looking at the check he'd made out to Ana and

given to his lawyer for safekeeping, right after they'd signed that goddamned contract.

At the time it had seemed the responsible thing to do.

"Charles," he said through his teeth, crushing the pieces of paper in his fist, but he knew better than to give in to his fury. There'd be time to deal with it later.

Now, finding Ana was all that mattered.

WHERE WOULD SHE have gone? Home to Brazil? He didn't think so, but anything was possible.

He took his Porsche. It was a fast car and every minute counted. When he'd started doing business in Brazil, he'd stored the phone numbers of all the airlines that flew to Rio from Kennedy in his cell phone.

Now he punched them up. Only one had a flight leaving, and it was leaving soon. Was an Ana Maria Marques on the passenger list? Nobody would tell him. Security was his business so he understood why they wouldn't, but if his Ana was on that flight…

He drove like a madman, ignored blaring horns and raised middle fingers, but by the time he reached the airport the plane was gone. Five hundred bucks slipped to a counter agent got him the information he needed.

Ana had not been on the plane.

Where next? There were eight million people in the city. How was he going to find one woman, one incredible woman whom he loved with all his heart?

Think, he told himself furiously, *think.*

The hotel where she'd originally been registered? Where she'd stashed all those suitcases filled with her dress-for-success suits? It was as good a guess as any.

He got there fast, skidded the Porsche into the no-parking zone in front of the door and ran into the lobby.

"Ana Maria Marques," he said to the desk clerk. "Is she registered here?"

She was, but the guy wouldn't tell him her room number. More security, and Linc, the security expert, wanted to reach across the desk and grab the man who was only doing his job and shake the information out of him.

Yeah, but that would only get him arrested. So would banging on the doors on every floor, yelling Ana's name.

He took another look at the front desk. The hotel was old. The clerk had a computer, but a wall of numbered mail slots stretched behind him. Did they use those or were they for show?

Only one way to find out.

Linc got the hotel's number from a stack of brochures on the desk and punched it into his cell phone. The clerk answered; Linc said he wanted to leave a message for Ana Maria Marques. He made something up, held his breath, watched as the clerk wrote it down—and stuffed it into slot 916.

He ran to the elevator. Halfway to the ninth floor it hit him that maybe Ana had been crying because she was angry he hadn't told her they didn't have to stay married anymore. She'd torn up the check, but that didn't prove anything. She was hot tempered and impossibly independent.

And she'd left him.

What kind of woman did that to a man who loved her? Okay, so he'd never said the words, but she should have known. When a woman loved a man, she knew what he felt for her. Women were supposed to sense those things, dammit.

The elevator doors opened. Linc stepped onto the ninth floor and started walking.

Ana had to love him—or what was he going to do with the rest of his life?

ANA PEERED at the thermostat in her room and edged it up another notch. It was set on high; she had not yet taken off her jacket and still, she was shaking. Maybe she was coming down with something? Or maybe it was what she'd seen on that little stick in the bathroom a few minutes ago?

No. She would not think about that now. Though why she hadn't thought to check until after she'd lied about her period this morning…

Tea. Hot tea. That was what she needed. She phoned Room Service, placed the order, then sat down on the edge of the bed.

What now? She had to make plans. Go home to her father? Not an option, especially now. She would remain in New York. Find a job. A place to live. One step at a time, and not one of those steps would involve weeping over Lincoln.

He had needed her to care for Jenny and warm his bed. Then he hadn't had the courage to tell her that was all finished, so he'd let his lawyer do it for him, with money.

Tears welled in her eyes. She was a fool to cry over such a man.

The knock on the door surprised her. Room Service. She'd almost forgotten. She wiped her eyes with the back of her hand, went to the door, released the security chain…

And gasped.

"Ana—"

She slammed the door in Lincoln's face.

He knocked again. Pounded the door until it shook. Ana reset the chain and cracked the door an inch.

"Go away!"

"Open this door, Ana."

"Are you deaf? I said—"

"This is an old hotel. That chain might as well be made of paper clips. Open the door or, so help me, I'll kick it down."

She stared at him. The grim look on his face said he would do exactly that. Her mouth narrowed; she shut the door, undid the chain and turned the knob. Lincoln stepped inside and began to shut the door.

She stopped him. "Leave it open."

"You should know better than to open a hotel door without looking through the peephole."

Ana folded her arms. "Thank you for your professional advice. I will remember it for next time."

"Well, the odds are you won't need it next time."

Her eyebrows rose. "And why is that?"

"Because the next time you're in a hotel room, you'll be with me."

"I do not work for you anymore, Mr. Aldridge. I quit my job."

"You can't quit your job."

"I most assuredly can."

"Actually, *job* is the wrong word."

"It is the correct word to describe a nanny's duties."

"But not the duties of a wife."

She looked so cold, sounded it, too. And that rigid posture, the voice saying "Mr. Aldridge" in tones that would have given a penguin chilblains... He'd known his Ana was upset, but the truth was he didn't know if it was because she didn't want to see him or because she was surprised to see him. Now, as color flowed into her cheeks, he felt the first stirrings of hope.

"I am not your wife. At least, I will not be for very long. I phoned your attorney's office and left him a message. I told him to start divorce proceedings as per our contract."

"My attorney is an ass."

"Because he did what you were too much the coward to do?"

"Because," Linc said, starting slowly toward her, "he knows all about the law and not a damned thing about the human heart."

"For that you would need a physician." Ana took a half step back. "Stay where you are, please, Mr. Aldridge, or—"

"Or what, Mrs. Aldridge? Are you going to call Security and ask them to throw your husband out of your room?"

"You are not my husband. You are—you are—"

"I love you, Ana."

Ana's heart seemed to bump against her ribs. "You are an excellent liar."

"I adore you."

"Is that the reason you told your lawyer to give me that check?"

"I wrote that the day we signed that damned contract. I wasn't going to let you put your life on hold without giving you something for it. How in hell was I to know

Charles would take it into his head to deliver it? Ana. Listen to me. I love you!"

She wanted to believe him. Oh, she wanted to! But there was just so much pain her heart could take before it shattered.

"Why are you doing this?" she said, hating the way her voice broke. "Lincoln, I'm not going to play these games anymore. What are you doing?" she said, which was a foolish question, because what he was doing was reaching for her and gathering her to him. "I just told you—"

"No games," he said softly. "Not anymore. Come back to me, Ana."

Tears rose in her eyes. "None of this is necessary. I know that Jenny is legally yours now."

"Jenny is ours, sweetheart. If you're willing, I'd like us to start adoption proceedings."

"Lincoln." Ana began to weep. "Do you really love me?"

Linc drew her into his arms and kissed her. His kiss said everything she'd ever longed to hear, and as she wound her arms around his neck she realized he had been kissing her that same way since the first time they'd made love.

"Last night," she whispered against his mouth, "you were so removed…"

"I'd been trying to find a way to tell you about Jenny, but I was afraid you'd say you were happy for me and now it was time you went on to live your own life."

"For shame, Lincoln," Ana said, laughing and crying at the same time. "Didn't you know how much I loved you?"

"I let myself hope, but when you said you'd gotten your period…" He leaned his forehead against hers. "It wasn't the news I'd hoped for, Ana. You're probably going to hate me for this but, see, I figured you couldn't possibly leave me if you were carrying my child."

"Our child," she said, smiling.

"That's what I meant. Our child. And—"

"I lied to you, Lincoln. I didn't get my period during the night."

He lifted his head and looked into her eyes. "No?"

"I didn't get it today, either." She moistened her lips. "A little while ago I took one of those home tests."

Could a man really survive without breathing? "Ana. Are you? Are we—?"

She nodded. "Jenny's going to have a little brother or sister for company."

He didn't move. Didn't speak. Just as her heart started to plummet, Lincoln lifted her off her feet and whirled her in a circle.

"Sweetheart. Ana. I love you so much…"

He kissed her. She kissed him back. And gradually they heard the sound of applause.

The Room Service waiter stood, smiling, in the open doorway. Half a dozen people were clustered behind him. They, too, were smiling. And clapping. Someone even whistled.

Ana laughed and buried her face against her husband's throat. Linc grinned at the little crowd.

"I," he said proudly, "am the world's luckiest man."

He gave his wife another long, tender kiss. When he finally lifted his mouth from hers, Ana sighed and looked deep into his eyes.

"Lincoln, my love," she said softly, "let's go home."

BACK TO YOU

Sarah Mayberry

A big thanks to Marsha for thinking of me for this anthology, and to Margaret for helping make the manuscript as good as it could be. None of my writing would get anywhere without the advice, support and inspiration provided by Chris, who really is my hero.

CHAPTER ONE

HE'S NOT supposed to be here.

Becky Taylor froze on the threshold of the restaurant. Across the room, Cal MacKenzie leaned against the far wall, tall and dark and gorgeous. After ten years, the unexpected sight of him stole her breath away and sent her heart hammering into overdrive.

He was supposed to be in London. He'd moved there five years ago with his new wife, and Becky hadn't had any word through the grapevine that he was back.

He had every right to attend the staff reunion—they were both ex-employees of Hannigan's Discount Emporium, a family-owned store that had paid many a student's way through college. The thing was, she wouldn't have come if she'd known he was going to be there.

Becky quickly corrected herself. Of course she would have come; staying away would have meant she still cared.

"Hey, look—Cal's here," her old friend Carolyn said behind her.

Becky forced a smile.

"How about that."

"Now it really is the old Hannigan's gang," Carolyn said.

"Yeah." Becky hoped she didn't sound as off balance as she felt.

She shot another glance across the room. This time Cal was staring back at her. He raised the beer in his hand in silent greeting, his blue eyes smiling at her.

It was a warm Sydney night in the middle of a hot Australian summer, but all the little hairs on Becky's arms stood on end. It had been a full decade since she'd last seen Cal, but he still had the same effect on her. Damn him.

Carolyn was already exchanging hugs and exclamations with the group of people nearest the door. Becky wiped her sweaty hands down the thighs of her jeans. She spotted a discreet sign for the ladies' room on the door to her left. Three steps, and she was closing the bathroom door behind her and sighing with relief.

A moment. That was all she needed. A short moment to get over the surprise.

She stared at her reflection in the mirror, unhappy with the dazed expression on her face.

He's here, get over it. It doesn't matter, it doesn't mean anything. It definitely doesn't mean anything to you.

She and Cal had gone their separate ways a long time ago. The memory of how shattered she'd felt when he called an end to their brief relationship might still make her squirm with self-consciousness, but the days of her mooning over him were long gone. She was thirty-one now, not twenty-one. She owned her own home, she drove a sleek and sexy sports car, and until recently she'd been in a live-in relationship with a successful, attractive man. She was worlds away from the girl she'd been when Cal MacKenzie had ruled her world. The only reason she'd felt that illicit surge of excitement when she'd seen his tall body standing there was because she'd been taken by surprise. He'd once meant something to her, now he didn't. End of story.

She squared her shoulders and dug out her lipstick, smoothing on a fresh coat then topping it with lip gloss. Her lips looked shiny and full when she'd finished. She fluffed her long, dark, curly hair and adjusted the hem on her red T-shirt. Determined to prove something to herself, she exited the bathroom and made a beeline for the far wall where Cal still lounged, laughing with a handful of men.

He straightened as he saw her approach. She found herself looking up into his tanned, handsome face, a hundred old memories washing through her as she noted the way his black hair still flopped over his left eye, and how his mouth still quirked up more on one side than the other when he smiled.

"Becky Taylor," he said. "Good to see you."

Before she could respond, he ducked his head and leaned close to plant a kiss on her cheek. For a few seconds she was swamped with his heat and scent. She had to blink to clear her head as he straightened again.

"Cal MacKenzie. Aren't you in the wrong hemisphere?" she asked, amazed at how casual and light and assured her voice sounded.

"Moved home last year," he said. He placed his empty beer bottle on a nearby table and angled his body so that he cut her off from the rest of the group he'd been standing with. Almost as though he wanted her all to himself.

She pushed the stupid thought away. She didn't care if he wanted her all to himself—she didn't want him. That was the important thing.

Sliding a hand into the back pocket of her jeans, Becky cocked her head to one side.

"Still in IT?"

"Yep. Started my own consultancy with a mate, actually."

"Brave of you. It's a pretty competitive field."

"We're doing okay," he said.

She'd already noted his Hugo Boss jeans, Gucci boots and the expensive Longines watch on his wrist. She guessed he must be doing very well—but then, Cal had always been modest. Even as a young man, he'd possessed a quiet confidence and charm that had drawn people to him. Herself included.

"I hear you're with David Jones now," he said, naming Australia's most prestigious department store. "Ladies' fashion buyer, is that right?"

Had he asked after her, or had someone told him what she did for a living?

"That's right."

"I suppose that means you've been jetting around, checking out the latest fashion shows?" he asked.

"As much as I can," she said. She could brag about Paris, New York and London, but she had no need to impress Cal. He was just an old work colleague. No big deal.

"I was admiring your boots when you came in," he said, and they both glanced down at her dark red, hand-tooled Western boots. "They look like the real deal."

"They are. Straight out of Texas."

She was very aware of the way his gaze travelled back up her jeans-clad legs and over her breasts before it returned to her face. She felt a flare of excitement when she saw the desire in his eyes.

Unbidden, a handful of sense memories raced across her mind: the feel of his long, strong fingers stroking her body, the way he used to whisper in her ear as he drove her to her climax, the aching, needful fullness of his body moving inside hers.

She licked her lips and tucked her other hand into her back pocket to stop herself from reaching for him.

Then she realized what she was doing and she snapped to attention.

Pathetic. Ten years, and he cocks his little finger and you're ready to go on the spot. Too sad for words, Taylor.

"So, is your wife here?" she asked pointedly. Time to nip this flirtation—if that was what this was—in the bud.

Cal held up his left hand, displaying his ringless fingers.

"Divorced," he said. "Papers just came through. How about you?"

Divorced. He was divorced. Which meant he was free. Available.

"I'm not married," she said evasively.

"But you're living with someone, aren't you?" Cal asked.

Becky blinked. He *had* done his homework.

"Not anymore."

He looked pleased. She glanced away to break the spell he was weaving around her. She'd always found him fatally attractive. Right from the very first day when she'd looked up from reading a book in the staff room at Hannigan's and Cal had been standing in the doorway, a dark-haired god with blue eyes and a roguish smile. She'd been nineteen years old, and his innate charm had hit her like a freight train.

Even though she knew it smacked of retreat, she cast a look over her shoulder, scanning the party for an escape route.

"Look, there's Cheryl. I haven't seen her in ages," she said with relief. "I'd better go say hi or she'll kill me."

She had a smile fixed firmly in place when she turned back to him.

"Great to see you, Cal," she said.

Before he could say anything else, she turned and walked away.

CAL WATCHED her walk all the way across the room. More specifically, he watched her ass. Becky had always had a great ass—full, high, firm—and time had not altered it one iota.

God, she looked good. And she was single. He couldn't believe his luck. If he was completely honest with himself, she'd been the main reason behind his appearance at the reunion tonight. Sure, he'd wanted to catch up with a few old buddies, but it was Becky who had really drawn him. For ten years, the memory of their time together had burned bright as the hottest, most sexually satisfying time of his life. They hadn't been able to get enough of each other. He could still remember how desperate he used to be to get his hands on her smooth, creamy skin after a full shift working alongside her. More than once they'd wound up in the backseat of his car in the parking lot or in the dark corner behind the box crusher in the stock room, tearing at each other's clothes until he was inside her, giving her what they both wanted.

Was it any wonder that his thoughts had gravitated toward her now that he was a free man again?

He kept his gaze on her as she joined the group of ex-Hannigan's employees near the bar. Her hair was longer than when he'd known her. Back then, she'd kept her curls short and well-tamed, but he liked the way they cascaded around her shoulders tonight, the overhead lighting picking out rich highlights in the tumbled, dark mass. She'd put on a little weight, just enough to make her hips rounder and her breasts fuller, but her face was exactly the way he remembered it—the small, upturned nose, the full lips, the big brown eyes. She had the smoothest, clearest skin of any woman he'd ever known, and he could still recall the way he used to chase the blushes across her body when he had her naked in his bed.

Cal registered the tightness in his jeans. If he didn't stop staring, he was going to embarrass himself in a very public way. He hadn't expected to be so struck by her. When he'd hoped that she'd be here, when he'd speculated as to whether the old fire would still be there between them, he hadn't imagined anything like the heat that had ripped through him the moment he saw her. It had honestly been as though the years had fallen away and they were two kids again—two kids who desperately wanted to jump each other's bones.

Across the room, Becky laughed and brushed a stray curl away from her cheek, tucking it behind her ear. Even though he'd been staring at her shamelessly for the past few minutes, she hadn't glanced his way once.

He was forced to a reluctant conclusion—that the heat he was feeling was one-sided and only one of them was interested in bone-jumping.

It had been a long time between drinks; it had been crazy to think that there might be something left between them. Just because his thoughts had constantly drifted to her over the years, wondering what she was doing, who she was with, who was to say that hers had done the same?

Which left him standing alone at a reunion with no beer in his hand and a hard-on in his jeans. Not exactly a recipe for social success.

Forcing himself to look away, Cal shoved a hand into his pocket and rejoined the group of men he'd been hanging with before Becky entered and rocked his world off its axis.

He had the answer to the question that his body had asked when he received the invitation to the reunion—yes, Becky was still the hottest woman he'd ever known. And no, he would not be getting a chance to relive history.

A damn shame, but he would survive.

BECKY WAS so tense and wired after she got home from the reunion that her T-shirt was damp with perspiration. Nervous energy, caused by pretending that she didn't care a hoot about Cal all night. What a joke.

The truth was, she'd been painfully aware of his every move. His laugh, who he was talking to, what he ate or drank. Seeing him so unexpectedly had really thrown her for a loop.

If there was one saving grace to the whole evening, it was that she was a better actress than she'd ever given herself credit for. Despite how she'd been feeling privately, she was pretty damned sure that no one had guessed how she really felt—least of all Cal himself. She'd been cool with him every step of the way, even when he'd approached her again after dinner and spent half an hour lounging in a chair talking to her and Carolyn about old times. She'd been supremely conscious of every pass his blue-eyed gaze made over her body and her face—but not once had she allowed him to see how much his slow, lazy appraisals affected her.

Being with the Hannigan's crowd had been the perfect incentive to keep her guard up. Carolyn had been well aware of her crush on Cal all those years ago, and she'd been thrilled when Becky and Cal had finally gotten together. When it had all fallen in a heap after just a month, Carolyn had been a sympathetic and supportive friend, but Becky's pride had demanded that she keep the extent of her hurt to herself. To Carolyn and the rest of her Hannigan's colleagues, she and Cal had had a fling for a few weeks that hadn't worked out. They'd both moved on, and only Becky knew how big the hole was that Cal had left in her heart—and that was the way she wanted it to stay.

As Becky shed her sweaty clothes and stepped beneath the shower, she forced thoughts of Cal to one side. He was the past, history. She wanted to wash him off the way she was washing away the stress and tension of her evening. Down the plughole with him, and may he never blight her life again. He'd wreaked enough damage already, thank you very much.

After towelling herself dry, she slid into bed and switched the light off. Closing her eyes, she acknowledged to herself that she was pleased to have survived the evening with her dignity in tact. Willing sleep to come, she slowly relaxed her body into the mattress.

She should have known better. In the months following their breakup, dreams of Cal had tortured her endlessly. Tonight, she was revisited by them with a vengeance.

There was no narrative to her dreams, just flashes of memory twisted into new shapes by her subconscious. Images of Cal's tall, strong body naked and ready for her, the too-familiar need to be close to him pulling at her, the tearing hurt of knowing that having had her, he didn't want her anymore.

She woke panting, the sheets twisted around her legs. She growled low in her throat as she rolled from her bed and grabbed the low-dose sleeping tablets she kept in her travel kit to help conquer jet lag. Downing one with a mouthful of water, she returned to bed, smoothed out the sheets and pummelled her pillow into a new shape.

"Get out of my head," she told Cal, even though she felt a little crazy doing it.

Rolling onto her side, she stared at the darkened square of her bedroom window until the tablets kicked in and she drifted into dreamless sleep.

Tomorrow was another day—a beautiful, fresh, Cal-free day. Bring it on.

You're thirty-one, Cal. Too old for this kind of crap.

It was three in the morning, and he was standing naked in the living room of his penthouse apartment, staring out at the darkened waters of Sydney Harbour. To his left, the bridge hung like a fairy-lit coat hanger in the sky, and all around the harbor, lights twinkled in the predawn blackness.

Everyone was asleep—except for him. He was too horny to sleep. Too restless and unsettled. He should have asked Becky out tonight. He'd been waiting to get her alone before he tried his luck in case she shot him down in flames, but it had never happened. Possibly because she hadn't wanted it to happen. The jury was still out on that one. Now he wished he'd thrown caution to the winds and just asked her, witnesses or no witnesses.

He walked into the kitchen, fumbling in the dark for a brandy balloon before pouring himself an inch of the golden liquid. Back in the living room, he hit the play button on his stereo and sank into the comforting soft leather of his couch. The mellow sounds of Coldplay filled the room as he sipped at the brandy and let his mind wander.

In the twelve months that he'd been back in Australia, a lot had changed in his life. Generally he had a sense that they'd changed for the better. His marriage hadn't survived the changes, but he was becoming more and more philosophical about that. In the end, he and Natalie had wanted different things. When she'd pushed him too hard, he'd pushed back.

He liked being back in Sydney. It was such a dynamic

city, full of brash confidence and energy. And the weather—it was unfair even to think of comparing the gray heaviness of a London winter with the clear blue skies of home. Then there was his company. He and his partner, Daniel Strong, had attracted an exclusive set of clients, all of them high-end, and business was booming. Hence his penthouse apartment and very nice lifestyle.

He was quietly satisfied with all that he'd achieved in his thirty-one years, give or take one divorce and a few foolish decisions here and there along the way. So why was he sitting buck-naked on his sofa, swilling brandy in the vain hope that it would send him to sleep?

Becky Taylor. She of the perfect ass and the creamy breasts and the fiery passion of yesteryear. Closing his eyes, he relived the moment when she'd walked in the door tonight and stood there in all her red-cowboy-booted glory.

To hell with it. He was going to ask her out. As soon as it was remotely close to business hours, he'd look up her number at David Jones and call her. That was the only way he was going to get any closure on this; he felt it in his bones.

As though he'd finally given his tired body what it needed to sleep, he suddenly felt gritty-eyed with weariness.

"About time," he muttered to himself as he downed the last mouthful of brandy.

First thing tomorrow, he was making his play.

"BECKY, how are you?" the deep voice asked.

Becky's fingers clenched the phone receiver and she shifted to the edge of her seat.

"Cal? How did you get my number?" she queried stupidly.

"I looked it up. I wanted to ask you something, something I should have asked you last night at the reunion."

Becky swiveled in her chair and stared out at the spectacular view she had of Sydney's Hyde Park, a swathe of oak-and-plane-tree-dotted open space that created an oasis in the middle of the city.

"Yes?" she asked cautiously.

A surge of excitement raced up her spine. She squeezed her thighs together, sending a silent signal to her body—*Not on your life, pal. Not in a million years is* that *going to happen.*

"Will you have dinner with me?"

She was holding her breath, and she let it ease out slowly. Cal was asking her out. She hadn't imagined the spark of interest in his eyes last night. He still found her attractive. He wanted to explore that attraction.

All very good reasons to say no. But she hesitated, the word on the tip of her tongue. The silence stretched between them as her mind raced. If she said no, what would he think? That she wasn't up to the temptation? Worse, that she still had feelings for him? Pride demanded that she protect herself, as it had demanded all those years ago that she walk away from their brief relationship with her head high when he told her he wasn't ready for a big commitment, that things were moving too fast for him.

"Sure. When were you thinking?" she said.

It was her turn to be on the receiving end of surprised silence. He hadn't expected her to say yes. Interesting.

"How about tomorrow night?" he suggested. "Café Sydney?"

"I love it there. Sure. Shall we say eight?"

"I'll be there."

"You'd better be, since you called me," she said.

He laughed, the sound low and deep and compelling.

"See you, Beck," he said. Then she was listening to the dial tone.

Regret kicked in immediately. Was she *insane?* She had no business going to a cosy dinner with the man who had snapped her heart in two so efficiently all those years ago. Talk about being a glutton for punishment. Why on earth would she put herself in such a precarious position, especially when it was clear that Cal wanted to sleep with her again?

She was reaching for the phone before she realized she had no way of contacting him. She didn't know the name of his business, and she was almost certain he wouldn't have a publicly listed home number. A quick check on the Internet confirmed it. She slumped back in her seat and slapped her forehead with the palm of her hand.

"Stupid," she said, just as a familiar face appeared in her office doorway.

"Oooh, self abuse. Please don't stop on my account," Gareth said, swaying his way toward her guest chair.

Gareth was her opposite number in male fashion, and so gay that one of the secretaries had jokingly dubbed him "super gay" at the office Christmas party one year. It was a badge Gareth wore with pride—literally. In the annual Gay Pride parade last March, he'd worn a cape and a skin-tight Lycra bodysuit with a specially designed

SG insignia on his chest. Now, he folded his long, slender legs and rested his beautifully manicured hands on them as he waited for her to continue.

"It's not the same with someone watching," Becky told him.

"Tell me about it," he said, rolling his eyes dramatically. "This is why I always advocate video cameras—if you must share, technology makes it so much less intrusive."

Becky laughed. "Sometimes I think you have a Ph.D. in innuendo."

Gareth looked pleased. "I do try, darling. Now, tell Uncle Gareth what's wrong. You know I always offer the best advice."

It was true—for an outwardly frivolous person, he was very perceptive. Or, as he liked to put it, his "emotional IQ topped out at freakin' genius."

"Just wrestling with a ghost from the past," she said, shrugging. "An old flame asked me out to dinner, and I stupidly said yes."

Gareth's eyebrows wiggled.

"How old is the flame? And is there a spark still?"

"Ten years. And it's dead and gone. Just my pride left to rake over the coals, really."

"But he wants to reignite it?" Gareth asked, really getting into the whole fire metaphor thing.

"I guess so. I need to track down his phone number and cancel."

Gareth looked down his nose at her, and somehow she found herself telling him everything: how she'd fallen for Cal the moment she met him, how she'd found out almost straightaway that he had a girlfriend, how she'd worked alongside him for two years, the tension between them building every day. And how she and Cal had gotten together the moment he broke up with his girlfriend and fireworks had exploded between them.

"We saw each other almost every single day for a month. I utterly adored him. And then he told me that he wasn't ready for another serious relationship after coming out of three years with another woman."

"Ouch. How old were you both?"

"Twenty-one when we broke up. Intellectually, I understood where he was coming from. He was a good-looking guy, he was studying, he'd been tied down for three years. He wanted to party. But I felt like I'd been given the keys to the kingdom then had them snatched back again. I'd been in love with him for a year, and I only got to have him for a month. Not nearly long enough."

"Poor Becky," Gareth said.

"Yeah, well." She sat up a little straighter. "Anyway, it's all ancient history."

"Uh-uh. No way. You have unfinished business with this man. He cut you off before you were ready. You need to readdress the balance. You definitely can't cancel. What you have to do, Becky, my girl, is knock that man off his feet, dazzle him utterly, then walk away and leave him with his tongue hanging out and his zipper bulging. Revenge," Gareth said, eyes wide for dramatic effect.

It was a compelling argument. She loved the idea of letting Cal think he was charming her all night, only to pull the rug out from beneath him at the last minute. It would give him a small taste of his own medicine.

"You're tempted, I can tell," Gareth said. "I should warn you I have a Ph.D. in temptation, too."

"It seems a little petty," Becky said.

It was a token objection, and they both knew it. She was already imagining the look on Cal's face when she sashayed away from him. Not that she'd be able to see his reaction, not having eyes in the back of her head. But she could imagine it. Oh, yeah, she could imagine it.

"Petty, schmetty. Life hands us very few moments to be true divas, Becky. We have to grab them with both hands and hang on tight." Gareth clutched at two fistfuls of air, hauling them flamboyantly toward his thin chest.

"Okay. I'll do it," Becky said impulsively.

Gareth smiled and clapped his hands. "Girlfriend, you will *so* not regret this," he crowed.

Becky grinned back at him, feeling empowered all of a sudden. If she were a man, she'd beat her chest and give a Tarzan yell. Instead, she sat back and crossed her legs, feeling very feline and satisfied.

Yes, indulging in a little revenge fantasy was petty. But it wasn't as though anyone was going to get hurt, was it? Just Cal's ego a little, perhaps. She was certain he had plenty to spare.

"I'll need a new dress," she said.

"Oh, yes. And killer shoes. And underwear—something really slutty."

Becky raised an eyebrow.

"It's a psychological thing," Gareth said. "Trust me. He will never know it's there, but you will. You'll feel like a warrior queen."

A warrior queen. After years of feeling not good enough and discarded.

It sounded like a damned good exchange to her.

CHAPTER TWO

HER CONFIDENCE lasted until she was standing in front of her bathroom mirror the next evening, mascara wand in hand. Her whole body was shaking so much she was in serious danger of taking out an eye. She had to steady her wrist with her other hand before she could get a decent coat on.

Not a great sign.

She glanced down at her Slutty Avenger underwear. Her breasts were pushed up by a black satin-and-lace balconette bra. She wore matching panties and black garters and sheer black stockings. She was dressed to tempt and seduce. She should be feeling in control.

She *so* wasn't.

Becky reached for the deep red silk dress she and Gareth had chosen for tonight's dinner. It was part of the latest shipment of couture they'd received from Paris—a sleek, fitted, cocktail-length dress with a startlingly low back and neckline and a slit up one side. If she sat right, Cal would get an eyeful of stocking and garter. She'd practiced for ten minutes earlier in front of the mirror and was confident she had the move nailed.

She slid her feet into a pair of suede stilettos in the

same deep red. They made her feet ache after about five minutes, but like the underwear, they made her feel sexier, stronger, braver than she really was.

She sprayed on perfume, hitting all her pulse points. Then she picked up her elegant clutch purse. She was ready.

She was also trembling with anticipation and nerves.

So much for being the Slutty Avenger.

She took a cab to Café Sydney. Traffic was light and she arrived early. Taking the elevator to the top floor of the heritage-listed Customs House, she veered away from the restaurant's reception desk and made her way to the ladies' room. Sitting on the closed lid of a toilet, she waited a full fifteen minutes before reemerging.

Childish, but her knees were knocking together and she needed every bid of edge she could get.

Cal rose to his feet as the waitress led her to him. He'd scored a coveted balcony table that offered them privacy and a spectacular view of the Opera House and the Harbour Bridge.

"I was beginning to think you'd stood me up."

He had no idea how close she'd come to doing just that.

She went to flick her hair over her shoulder, then remembered she'd worn her curls in a sophisticated updo. She dropped her hand lamely to her side.

Smooth, Becky. Real smooth.

"Traffic was bad," she fibbed.

He smiled, the left side of his mouth quirking up just a little bit more than the right.

"I ordered champagne. I hope you still like it."

He looked deep into her eyes as he said it, and a fierce, hot memory rose up inside her—Cal pouring champagne over her breasts, Cal dipping his tongue into her belly button to suck out precious drops, the cold fizz of champagne bubbles tingling between her thighs.

She opened her mouth to say something sassy and clever and tantalizing.

"Yes."

His smile widened. He was wearing a charcoal shirt with French cuffs and a pair of black wool trousers. Discreet cufflinks glinted at his wrists. His hair gleamed darkly in the candlelight. His skin was tanned, and his eyes looked incredibly blue by contrast.

He was so damn sexy. She wasn't sure what it was about him that had always got to her so badly. Sure, he was good-looking, but she'd slept with other good-looking men. And yes, he was charming, but so were a lot of other guys. There was just something about the knowing, slightly naughty look in his eyes, and the ready curve of his lips, and the way he seemed so comfortable in his own skin....

He signaled the waiter and a glass of pale-yellow champagne appeared in front of her. Cal raised his.

"To old friends," he said.

She slid her fingers around the cool glass of the champagne flute.

"Friends? Hmmm."

That was what the Slutty Avenger would say, right?

He tilted his head to one side. "Okay. To old lovers."

She couldn't exactly argue with that.

She hoped like hell that her hand wouldn't shake when she lifted her glass.

"Much more accurate," she said. "I think we were too busy having sex to ever really be friends."

He laughed. "True. Maybe I should have said to great sex, in the interests of being really accurate."

She raised her glass to her mouth. Her hand was blessedly steady. The champagne tickled her tongue and tasted pleasingly dry in her throat.

"Nice."

He sat back in his chair. "So, tell me about the last ten years," he said.

She crossed her legs, but the table blocked his view of her stockings. She frowned. She hadn't thought about that minor detail when she'd practiced earlier that evening. She *so* wasn't cut out for this femme fatale business. Definitely an amateur.

"What do you want to know?"

"How did you get into fashion buying?" he asked. "You were studying economics when we were working together."

She explained that she'd dropped out of her degree in the third year and worked her way up from the shop floor, and he told her about his start-up IT company. By the time they'd given their orders and worked their way through their starters, some of the tension banding her chest had eased.

Probably the champagne had a bit to do with that. By her count, she was on her third glass by the time their mains were slid in front of them. She felt as buoyant and full of potential as the bubbles beading her glass.

"I like your hair long," he said as the waiter moved away from their table. "It suits you."

It was the first personal comment he'd made since their toast.

"I keep toying with cutting it short again, but it takes so long to grow. And the in-between stage was a bitch. I felt like a human fuzz ball for months."

"Don't cut it," he said. His gaze slid over her face before delving into the deep shadow between her breasts.

That quickly, the tension was back between them. She squeezed her thighs together under the table, aware of the heat building between them.

She eyed his body and wondered if he still had the strong tan lines he'd had as a younger man. He'd surfed and spent a lot of time in the outdoors, and she could still recall the way the rich nut-brown of his flat, muscled belly had given way to paler skin low on his hips. She could also remember how quickly she could get him hard, and the way he always stared intently into her eyes as he slid inside her, hard and hot and ready…

"I've thought about you a lot over the years," Cal said, his words an uncanny echo of her own thoughts.

He cut a slice off his porterhouse steak. "Wondered what you were doing. Who you were doing it with."

Her heart kicked against her ribs and she swallowed a huge lump of lust. All she could think about was what it would be like to be with him again. To feel his skin against hers, his breath in her ear, his body moving against hers.

Their eyes locked across the table, and she knew he was thinking the same thing.

If she was really the Slutty Avenger, she would be doing a victory dance right about now. She had him exactly where she wanted him—hot for her, putting himself on the line. All she had to do was string him along for another hour or so, then sashay away, leaving him with a hard-on and the bill.

But she wasn't the Slutty Avenger. Not by a long shot. She was practically panting, and a throbbing ache echoed her heartbeat between her thighs. She wanted him. Bad. Just as bad as when they'd both been twenty-one years old and full of raging hormones.

She stared at him, her mind working like a hamster in a wheel, trying to get a grip on the situation. He was too sexy, too tempting. She wasn't going to be able to walk away from the invitation in his eyes.

As soon as she admitted as much to herself, a strange relief flooded through her. She was going to sleep with him. She was going to run her hands over his body and let him run his hands over hers. She was going to taste his skin and welcome him inside her. They were going to revisit the past in the most physical, real way possible.

But it will just be sex. That's all. I'll take what I want from him, and I'll walk away, she promised herself. A variation on her original plan, and nothing more.

It would be even more effective this way. She'd get to have a good time, and finally put the ghosts of the past to bed. And she'd get to walk away leaving *him* wanting more.

She closed her eyes for a second, savoring the knowledge of what was to come. Then she opened them and locked eyes with him again. His blue gaze was dark and smoky with intent. They stared at each other, neither of them eating.

She smiled a slow, anticipatory smile. She felt light, as though the champagne she'd been drinking had carbonated her blood. He smiled back at her. Her breathing was shallow, her belly muscles tight. Her breasts tingled, and she didn't need to look down to know they were already hardening with desire.

"Are you hungry?" he asked, his voice a low rumble.

"Not for food," she said.

He stood in one smooth, powerful move. "Then let's get out of here."

She stood. He stepped close and took her hand, looking deeply into her eyes.

"I thought I'd exaggerated how sexy you were in my mind," he said. "I thought there was no way you could live up to my memories."

His gaze swept over her, and she felt a surge of feminine power. He wanted her as badly as she wanted him.

He turned, tugging on her hand as he pulled her toward the reception desk so he could take care of the bill. She eyed his broad shoulders as they walked, his words echoing in her mind.

He'd thought about her. And he thought she was sexy. Sexier even than his memories of her.

Triumph and relief and need coursed through her. He shot a glance across to her as he handed over his credit card. The animal need in his eyes made her forget everything sane and sensible.

No man had ever affected her quite like Cal. No man had ever gotten her as hot or made her feel as decadent and wanton and wild.

Trepidation twisted in her stomach as she remembered how she'd felt in the weeks and months after they'd parted ways all those years ago. Empty and dissatisfied and terrified that she'd never find another man who would make her feel as good.

Was she about to make a very stupid mistake? Was she willfully deluding herself that she could handle this situation, that she could handle him?

"Come on," Cal murmured near her ear as he found her hand with his again and pulled her toward the elevator.

She followed him because she wanted to and because she had to. But she wasn't completely gone. No matter what, she would not stay the night with him. She made the commitment to herself as the elevator doors closed and Cal put his arms around her from behind and pulled her back against him.

Her breath got caught somewhere between her lungs and her throat as he splayed one big hand over her belly and the other just under her breasts.

"This is a great dress," he said, the warmth of his chest pressing against her bare back. "I've been wanting to get you out of it all night."

"That was pretty much the idea," she said.

She felt the warm, gentle press of his lips on the side of her neck, followed by the wet lick of his tongue. Desire shot through her like lightning as she arched her neck to allow him greater access.

"Becky, if you had any idea what you do to me…" he murmured against her skin.

Her whole body was trembling with need and anticipation. His hands clenched the fabric of her dress as he pulled her closer. She could feel the hardness of his erection against the curve of her bottom.

This felt so good. *He* felt so good.

She twisted in his arms so that she was facing him. She rose up on the balls of her feet and kissed him, her lips opening over his, her tongue sliding inside the hot, slick darkness of his mouth to caress his tongue, to suck on it, to bite it gently, suggestively.

Cal groaned low in his chest and grabbed her butt, dragging her closer to him and grinding his hips into hers.

"I don't think I can wait," she confessed as they broke from their kiss.

His cheekbones were dark with desire, his lips glistened from their kiss. He slapped a hand toward the buttons on the elevator wall, and the elevator stopped at the next floor.

Without a word they both stepped into the muted darkness of a four-sided balconied walkway that ran around the open space at the centre of the building. While Café Sydney occupied the top floor of Customs House, several prestigious businesses had their headquarters there. Becky figured they must have exited onto one of the commercial floors.

They walked the length of one side of the walkway until Cal found a waiting area tucked into the corner of the building. Two floor-to-ceiling walls of glass came together to offer yet another amazing view of the harbor.

Neither of them gave it so much as a glance.

Cal moved in on her with intent, his fingers sliding up her neck and into her hair as his mouth angled down on hers. His tongue was hard and demanding in her mouth as his body pressed against hers. The pins and combs holding her hair in place fell to the ground and her hair was suddenly loose about her shoulders.

"I've been wanting to do that all night, too," Cal murmured as he kissed his way across to her ear.

She gasped as his tongue traced the inner curve before plunging inside. She was so ready for him it physically hurt. She reached for the buttons of his shirt, sliding them open by feel alone as Cal continued to plunder her ear.

Then she had her hands on his chest. His skin felt hot and smooth and she pressed her palms flat against him and curled her fingers possessively into the resilient strength of his pectoral muscles. He was bigger, broader than when they'd been younger. She mapped his width with her hands, then found his nipples and began to tease them.

His hands found the zipper at the back of her dress. The hiss of it descending was a seductive whisper. Cal lifted his head from her ear to gaze at her as he pushed her dress off her shoulders. Red silk pooled at her waist and he mouthed a four-letter word as he took in the creaminess of her breasts pouring over the black satin cups of her bra.

His hands slid up her ribcage and onto her breasts, cupping them, molding them. Then he pushed the satin down beneath her breasts and his fingers found her nipples.

He pressed kisses into her neck as he teased her with his hands, squeezing gently, flicking his thumbs back and forth, shaping her with his palms.

"Everything is better than I remembered," he said against her skin, his voice rough with desire.

She was so overwhelmed by sensation and lust that she could barely think. She knew she should probably be more worried about the fact that Cal was pressing her against a thick glass window, and that anyone glancing across from one of the neighboring buildings could see them. She simply didn't care. There was only one thing on her mind—satisfaction. She wanted Cal inside her, pounding into her, giving her what she'd fantasized about in the unacknowledged, dark corners of her mind for ten years.

Her hands shook as she reached for his belt buckle. His erection strained against the zipper of his trousers, thick and powerful, a promise she was about to collect on. He sprang into her hands as she released him. So hard. So silky and yet so strong at the same time. She wrapped her fingers around him as he lowered his head to her breasts and sucked a nipple into his mouth.

She clenched her hand around him as need pierced her, arrowing through her body to where she throbbed for him. He bit her nipple, then sucked it, hard.

She was panting, and so was he. He smoothed his hands down her hips, found the hem of her dress. She moaned as he slid his hands up her stockings. Then he was caressing naked skin, and his fingers were gliding between her legs to where she needed him the most.

The firm press of his fingers against the damp satin of her panties made her moan again. He gave an appreciative sound in the back of his throat as he stroked her once, twice. Then he slid his hand inside her panties and into her slick readiness.

A shudder racked his body as he felt how wet and hot she was. She pushed his trousers and boxers down his hips, then stroked her hand up and down his shaft. Her thumb found a single bead of moisture on the plump head of his penis and she knew he was just as turned on as she was.

"Becky," he groaned against her breast.

"Yes," she said.

His thumbs hooked into the waistband of her panties and pushed down. She took over when they reached her knees, stepping out of them. Cal immediately pushed her back against the window and hooked one of her legs up over his hip. She felt the delicious pressure of his hard-on sliding between her folds. Then he slid inside her, big and hard and thick.

"Oh, boy," she panted as she stretched around him. Her memory had been holding out on her, big-time. He felt so right, so perfect inside her.

He huffed out a laugh.

"Oh, boy? Is that the best you can do?" he asked. His hands gripped her bare backside as they both savored the moment.

She stared into his eyes. "I can do a lot better than that."

She tilted her hips and started to tell him what he was doing to her, her words a whisper against his skin as she kissed his neck and his mouth and his ear and his chest. Cal's grip intensified on her butt as he began to thrust into her—long, slow, powerful strokes that pushed her closer to the edge with each penetration.

She lifted her other leg so that he had her entire weight.

She hooked her ankles together behind his back, gripped his shoulders and held on for dear life as he pressed her against the glass and pounded into her with increasing urgency.

"Yes," she sobbed as her climax began to sweep her away.

Cal's mouth found hers. Her desire peaked. She opened her eyes and gazed into Cal's blue eyes as she came and came and came, her body tightening around his, her breath harsh and desperate. His lips pulled back into an animal snarl as he found his own climax, but his eyes never left hers. He stared at her the whole time that his body lost itself in hers, his fingers clutched into her backside, his thighs trembling.

For a few precious seconds afterward, he rested his forehead against hers and they simply breathed together. Then he released his grip on her butt and she slid down his body and stood on her own two feet.

Her body vibrated with satisfaction and the echo of passion. Her breasts were still wet from his kisses. Her dress was rucked up around her hips, the silk crushed.

She pushed her hair back off her forehead. Cal was busy tucking himself back into his clothes. She tugged her bra up over her breasts and slid her arms through the sleeves of her dress.

"Could you zip me?" she asked, turning her back to him.

His fingers were warm against the skin of her back as he eased the zipper along its tracks.

She wasn't about to climb into her underwear in front of him. Instead, she bent to collect her panties and stuffed them into her evening bag. Very elegant. She was sure there was a paragraph covering just this situation in an etiquette manual somewhere, but she'd never read it.

Cal was buttoning his shirt, and she watched him slide the last button home.

Time to walk away. Time to regain the dignity she'd lost ten years ago when he'd broken her heart.

"Well, Cal, dinner was lovely," she said with what she hoped was a casual smile.

"What we ate of it, you mean," he said drily.

She shrugged a shoulder.

"Dessert was worth it." She took a step forward and pressed a kiss to the angle of his jaw. "Thanks. It was great to catch up."

He frowned as she turned away.

"Where are you going?" he asked. He sounded surprised.

"Home. Where else?"

"I thought we could go back to my place," he said.

Despite what they'd just done together, a hot rush of desire washed through her as she thought about what that would mean. More Cal. Much more.

What could it hurt? You still won't stay the night. And you'll get him out of your system once and for all.

Becky frowned. She'd been chipping away at her own resolve ever since she'd said yes to Cal's dinner invitation. She had to draw the line somewhere, or there'd be precious little of Operation Dignity left to salvage. And then she'd be back where she'd been all those years ago—left gasping and needy when Cal had had his fill of her.

"I've got an early start tomorrow," she said. "But thanks for the offer."

"Right."

She forced a smile. She had to get out of there before the word *yes* escaped her lips.

"See you round, Cal," she said.

Then she turned on her heel and walked away.

CAL STARED as Becky walked away from him once again, her high heels clicking on the tiled floor.

They'd just had stupendous, gut-wrenching sex, and she'd calmly put herself back together and said goodbye as though it was nothing special.

Not what he'd expected. Not by a long shot. But then, none of it had been. He'd known he was still attracted to her. The reunion had illustrated that in no uncertain terms. But he hadn't expected to be so hot for her that he'd abandon dinner and find the nearest dark corner to bury himself in her. He was a seasoned, experienced businessman, for Pete's sake. Not a randy kid anymore.

And he hadn't expected it to feel so good to be with her again, to touch her, taste her. She'd felt familiar, but also excitingly different, and she'd been so turned-on that he'd almost embarrassed himself before he could give her what they both wanted.

He frowned. He still couldn't believe she'd just asked him to zip her up and then left him standing there. In the old days, Becky had been affectionate, warm. She'd never been able to get enough of him. And he'd never been able to get enough of her. All that intensity had scared the shit out of him hard on the heels of his breakup with Virginia, his long-term girlfriend. As blown away as he'd been by the sex, as much as he'd always enjoyed Becky's wit and sense of humor and sharp take on the world, he'd felt as though he was jumping feetfirst into another serious commitment. He'd been twenty years old. It had freaked him out. All his mates had been partying, seeing the world, having one-night stands. And he'd been in danger of turning into Mr. Monogamy.

He'd told Becky how he was feeling, that he wanted to pull things back, lighten up. She'd been upset. She'd cried. But then she'd pulled herself together. She'd said she understood where he was coming from. They'd worked alongside each other for a whole year after their short, tumultuous relationship had ended, work buddies who knew each other's bodies really, really well.

He'd still been hot for her. He wasn't a saint. They'd been so good together, he'd been unable to look at her without remembering. He'd even tried to score with her again on a casual basis when he'd had too much to drink at one of the Hannigan's Christmas parties. She'd turned him down. Then the next thing he knew, she'd quit, and the only contact he'd had with her was through the staff grapevine.

Cal ran a hand through his hair, then checked to make sure his fly was closed and his shirt buttoned properly. Crossing to the elevator, he punched the button and checked his watch. It was only ten. If she'd come home with him, they could have had all night.

Get over it, Cal. She didn't want anything more than what she got. Suck it up and move on.

He told himself the same thing when the urge to call

her gripped him the next day. Badgering Becky with phone calls was not going to change anything.

Still, his hand hovered over the phone. He laughed at himself. He felt as though he'd regressed ten years. Time to take his own advice and get over it. They'd had a great night, a one-off. End of story.

A MONTH LATER, Cal found himself sitting in a church in the richy-rich Melbourne suburb of Toorak on a sizzling summer day, watching another former Hannigan's friend, Carolyn, walk down the aisle to marry her high-school sweetheart, Phil.

Even as he marveled at the fact that their relationship had survived the transition into adulthood and beyond, he found his gaze constantly drawn to the pew near the front of the church where Becky sat. She looked gorgeous in a dark green dress with tiny black flowers on it. Her hair was loose around her shoulders, and he spent almost as much time watching her as he did the bride and groom.

Afterward, at the reception, he arrived early in the ballroom and saw they were sitting at neighboring tables. He hesitated only a second before switching placecards with the man sitting next to her. If someone had put him on the rack and shone a light on him and demanded he tell them why he wanted to sit next to her, he would have said it was because he liked Becky. He always had. But it was also because he felt as though there was unfinished business between them. And yeah, he wanted to have her again. So sue him—sex that great didn't come along too often, in his experience.

She raised an eyebrow when she entered the ballroom a few minutes later and found him seated at her table.

"I could have sworn Carolyn said she was putting me next to Roger Lee," she said.

He gave her his best faux-innocent look, and she shook her head and laughed.

"You always were used to getting your own way," she said.

"To the victor the spoils."

He stood and held her chair out for her.

"Wow. Next thing I know, you'll be throwing your tux jacket over the nearest puddle for me," she said.

He inhaled her spicy-fresh perfume as she sank into the chair. She smelled as good as she looked. And he already knew she tasted twice as good.

"What can I say? I've picked up a little polish over the years."

She eyed his suit knowingly. "More than a little."

She reached out and rubbed the fabric of his lapel between thumb and forefinger.

"Armani, yes?"

He shrugged, quelling an adolescent surge of pride that she'd noticed his expensive threads.

"If you say so."

Her eyes brightened with amusement. "Don't tell me—you have so many designer tuxes in your wardrobe, you can't remember which one you brought down to Melbourne with you?"

He smiled back at her. "Something like that."

"Oooh. Big guy. I bet you own your own company and everything."

She laughed then, and the low huskiness of it hit him in the gut. He shifted in his chair, aware that he was rock-hard for her all over again. His gaze dipped to the swell of her breasts, outlined by the silky fabric of her dress.

"You look great," he said.

The smile was gone from her face when he looked up and their eyes locked. Something dark and hot flickered in the depths of her big brown eyes, and she swallowed visibly.

A slow smile curved his lips. He might be hard, but she was just as aware of him. He knew it the way he knew the earth wasn't flat, the way he knew cats hated dogs and dogs hated postmen.

"Where are you staying?" he asked.

"The Hyatt. You?"

"The Adelphi," he said, naming one of Melbourne's smaller, boutique hotels.

She licked her lips. He flicked his eyes toward the bridal table where Carolyn and Phil were talking and laughing with family and friends. It was going to be a long few hours while they waited out the meal and the speeches and the dancing. Until he could get Becky alone again.

He made it to the end of the main course before sitting next to her and not touching her the way he wanted to became too much for him. He felt like a kid again, out of control. He wanted what he wanted—and he wanted it *now*.

She was talking to the person sitting on her other side, and he waited impatiently for her to turn to him.

"Want to go for a walk?" he asked.

"A walk?" She arched an eyebrow at him, a smile quirking the corner of her mouth.

"Yeah. A walk."

He found her knee under the table.

She sucked in a surprised breath.

He slowly pleated the soft fabric of her skirt beneath his fingers as he gathered it up, inch by inch. She stiffened in her chair as his hand found her silky stockinged leg.

"Tell me you're wearing garters again," he said, fascinated by the way her pupils had dilated with desire.

"Stay-ups. Garters ruin the line of this dress," she said.

He glided his hand up her thigh until he hit bare flesh. She shivered. He slid his hand higher and encountered the smoothness of her satin underwear.

"What color?" he asked quietly.

Her eyelids masked her eyes for a beat before she answered.

"Red."

"One of my favorites."

He stroked her through the satin, and she bit her lip.

"Cal," she said.

He wasn't sure if it was a plea or a warning. He knew what he wanted it to be. Leaning back in his chair, he glanced toward the entrance to the ballroom, then back toward the bridal party.

"I figure we've got about fifteen minutes before they even think about cutting the cake," he said.

She took a deep breath.

"Yes."

WHAT AM I doing? One look, one touch and I'm trailing after Cal again, looking for someplace to get hot with him. This is insane. I'm insane.

Becky knew she should pull her hand free and go back to the table and ignore Cal for the rest of the evening. She also knew she wasn't going to. She'd been dreaming about him for four weeks, ever since their dinner. She might have walked away from him, but he'd gotten under her skin.

Not like when they were kids. Definitely not like that. She'd assured herself of that fact over and over. This was purely a sex thing. But it had still driven her crazy for the past month.

As Gareth had said when she'd given him a shame-faced, bare-bones report of her evening at Café Sydney, she sucked at being the Slutty Avenger.

Right now, however, revenge was the last thing on her mind. As always with Cal, lust had short-circuited her higher brain functions. She wanted to get off. Nothing else. She was even prepared to miss dessert for the privilege.

"In here," Cal said, and he opened a door in the hallway they were traversing and pulled her into a linen cupboard.

She laughed. "You've got to be kidding," she said, looking around at the cramped space lined with shelves piled with tablecloths and napkins.

"I'd never joke about something this serious," he said.

Then he kissed her, pressing her back against the door, one hand finding her breast through her dress, his thumb teasing her nipple into hard, demanding arousal.

"You get me so hot," he said.

She couldn't speak. She was too busy gasping as his other hand slid up under her dress and inside her panties.

"Ohhh."

He grinned at her, a wicked, knowing grin.

"Spread your legs for me, baby," he said.

She did so mindlessly, watching as Cal shrugged out of his suit jacket and threw it onto a shelf behind them. Then he was on his knees, lifting her dress, tugging at her underwear.

Her knees went weak as she understood what he wanted to do. He'd always been so good with his mouth and hands. He was one of the few men she'd been with who genuinely got off on the act of pleasing a woman.

She flattened her hands against the cool wood of the door as she felt the warmth of his breath between her thighs. And then he was tasting her, his tongue by turns delicate and rough, his hands cupping her backside as he held her close.

She shuddered and bit her lip and closed her eyes. Within minutes, her orgasm washed over her with the force of a tsunami. Then Cal was unzipping his trousers, and she was gripping his big, hard erection and guiding him once more between her thighs.

"One day, we should really consider doing this in a bedroom," he said as he took her full weight and pressed her back against the doorway.

"Shut up and kiss me," she panted.

Afterward, they put themselves back together in silence. Becky slipped out of the cupboard first and made a beeline for the ladies' room. She closed her eyes briefly when she caught sight of her reflection. She looked like a woman who'd just had two orgasms in a linen cupboard—cheeks flushed, hair mussed, lipstick smeared halfway up her cheek.

"You are such an idiot."

The woman staring back at her knew it, down to her bones. She was playing with fire. And there was only one inevitable result—she was going to get burnt.

No more. No matter what it took, this had to stop now. Before she did something even more stupid than sleep with Cal.

She took a deep breath. Then she started to erase the telltale signs of their encounter.

CHAPTER THREE

THREE WEEKS LATER, Becky stepped out of the shower and reached for the towel folded neatly on the corner of the vanity. She blotted her face dry, then briskly toweled off her body. Naked, she crossed into the bedroom to find her clothes.

"Stay the night," Cal said the moment she entered the room.

He was sprawled across his bed the way she'd left him after they'd made love for the second time that evening, deliciously naked against chocolate-brown sheets.

His blue gaze followed her every move as she reached for her underwear and began to dress.

"I can't. I've got—"

"An early start at work tomorrow," Cal said drily.

It was the same excuse she'd used every time she'd seen him over the past few weeks.

"Tomorrow's Saturday, Becky," he said, propping himself up on his elbows. "That one's not going to cut it."

"I was going to say it's my nephew's birthday, and I promised my sister that I'd go over early and help her set things up."

"What, at six in the morning?"

She pulled her linen trousers over her hips.

"No, but I've got some running around to do before I get there," she said.

Cal dropped flat onto his back and crossed his arms behind his head. For a few minutes there was nothing but the sound of her clothes rustling as she finished dressing.

"Is there some kind of unspoken rule against you staying the night that I don't know about?" he asked quietly.

Yes. It's the only way I can retain control of the situation. This way, we get what we need from each other, but I can't fool myself that it's anything more than what it is.

"It's easier this way," she said.

"How? It's two in the morning. Wouldn't it be easier just to go to sleep? I promise I won't snore or steal the sheets."

He kept his tone light, but she could hear the edge beneath it. She grabbed a scrunchie from her handbag and pulled her hair into a haphazard ponytail. This conversation had been coming for a while. Perhaps they should have had it up front when he'd called her after Carolyn and Phil's wedding. That way they would have clarified the ground rules going in. She'd thought they'd been pretty obvious, but apparently they were about to get even more so.

"Are you saying you want to turn this into a relationship, Cal?" she asked bluntly.

He blinked. The surprise in his face was like a slap. Clearly, having a relationship with her had not even crossed his mind.

"I've only been divorced three months, Becky. I'm still finding my feet again, remembering what it's like to be single."

She reached for her handbag, keeping her head down as she blinked rapidly. What had she expected him to say? Yes? That he saw her as more than just a warm body? That he'd asked her to stay because he wanted to wake up and find her lying beside him, not because he wanted to have more sex with her?

Maybe. Even though she'd convinced herself that she'd gone into this with her eyes wide open.

History repeating itself.

The thought lent steel to her spine. She eyed Cal coolly.

"You're not interested in anything else," she stated for him. "And neither am I. This arrangement suits me fine, and I would have thought you'd be happy with it, too."

Cal's gaze narrowed. There was a long silence as he studied her, apparently trying to work something out.

"So this is just about sex?" he said.

"Hasn't it always been?"

She busied herself with digging her car keys from her handbag, aware she was walking a dangerous emotional line. The truth was, she was close to sitting on the edge of the bed and crying like a baby. Or like the rejected young woman she'd been all those years ago when he'd first cut her loose. Because this was what had always been at the heart of the problem of her and Cal—she loved him, while he only loved having sex with her.

Cal sat up and reached for his boxers.

"I like you, Becky," he said.

She forced a smile. "I know that. I like you, too. But let's not pretend it's anything other than what it is. We're not kids anymore, we don't need to dress it up."

"Is that why you said no to dinner tonight? Because you didn't want to dress it up?"

"Yes."

He stared at her. He was pissed, she could see it in the firm line of his mouth.

"So you're happy to screw me in fifty different ways, but you don't want to break bread with me?"

If she thought his reaction was anything more than piqued pride, she'd be jumping with joy.

"If I wanted dinner and movies and whatever else, I'd be in a relationship. And that's the last place I want to be," she lied. "I've got a lot going on at work right now. This suits me. If it doesn't suit you, then I understand. It's been fun."

Where was this calm, cool voice coming from? She felt as though someone else had taken over her body while the real Becky quivered in the corner feeling nauseous and shaky and weak.

Cal rubbed the stubble on his chin.

"So we're what? Bed buddies?"

"Yeah," she said.

"And anytime I want some action, I just call you?"

"Yep. And ditto for me. No need to ask each other to the movies or out for dinner or whatever."

"For your information, I really wanted to see that new George Clooney movie last week."

She simply raised an eyebrow at him. They'd wound up skipping the movie and going straight to bed.

"Yeah, all right, point taken," he said grudgingly.

"I'll call you in a few days," she said.

"Hang on."

Cal stood and moved close. He slid a hand behind her neck. He kissed her, his tongue slow and silky in her mouth. His face was full of promise when he raised his head.

"You could stay a little longer, couldn't you?"

She searched his eyes, trying to find something more in them than sexual hunger. She already knew he was hard again, his erection straining against the soft fabric of his underwear. It would be so easy to let things start up again, to fall back into bed with him. She gripped the cold, hard metal of her car keys, hanging on to her self-control.

"I really have to go," she said.

"Okay."

He leaned in again for one last kiss, but she turned away, pretending she hadn't noticed. She suddenly knew she couldn't handle having him touch her right now. Her skin felt as fragile as gossamer. If he touched her, she was afraid it would rupture and all her feelings would tumble onto the floor between them and he'd see the truth.

She made it to her car before hot tears spilled down her cheeks.

She loved him so much. Seeing him again, sleeping with him, had resurrected all her old feelings and then magnified them tenfold. She'd thought she could handle the situation, that she could sleep with him and prove something to herself and to him.

She'd thought she could show him that she didn't

care. That he hadn't hurt her. That she hadn't felt rejected and humiliated and somehow lacking all those years ago.

But Cal had grown into a dynamic, sexy, fascinating man, so much more compelling than the young man she'd fallen in love with on the shop floor all those years ago. In bed, he was instinctive, passionate, daring. Just looking into his eyes was enough to turn her on. And he had a great sense of humor and a knowing wit that never failed to make her laugh.

He was the man of her dreams. Again.

And once again he didn't want her.

She forced herself to remember what he'd said: *I've only been divorced three months. I'm still finding my feet again, remembering what it's like to be single.*

Just like last time, only then he'd been young and full of juice and feeling trapped after three years with one girlfriend.

They were both excuses. He didn't feel the same way about her. Never had, never would. She had to face that fact now and stop kidding herself.

She hunched in on herself as her shoulders shook. Her chest ached, and she rubbed her sternum with the heel of her hand, over and over. It hurt. She loved him so much, and it physically hurt that he didn't love her back.

Even though she was an experienced, grown woman now, for a few weak moments she allowed herself to ask the old, old questions.

What's wrong with me that he doesn't love me? What don't I have that he's looking for? Aren't I beautiful enough? Clever enough? Funny enough? Am I too needy? What's wrong with me?

"God!" she moaned, disgusted with her own wallowing.

Talk about a pity party. If she was listening to a friend vomit up all this tragedy, she'd give her a swift kick in the butt and tell her that the problem wasn't with her but with Cal, or fate, or pheromones or some crazy mix of all those things that decreed that people did or didn't fall in love with each other.

She was smart, attractive, a good person. She didn't need Cal's approval or love anymore to prove that to herself. It might hurt that she'd been foolish enough to fall for him again, but just as he'd become a more compelling, nuanced, multifaceted version of the young man he'd once been, so had she become a more sophisticated, confident woman. She didn't need Cal or his love. She *wanted* it, but it was not essential to life as she knew it.

She scrubbed at her wet cheeks with her hands. No doubt she looked like a mad-ass raccoon, sitting here in her car on a darkened city street outside Cal's apartment block with mascara smearing her face.

She started her car and pulled away from the curb. A curious calm settled over her as she drove. She felt both lighter and heavier. At last she'd acknowledged the truth of her and Cal: it was never going to happen between them.

No more pretending she was just having a fling with him for old times' sake or proving something to herself or him. It was over between them, for good this time.

It wasn't until she was pulling into the driveway of her small Victorian terrace house in Woollahara that she wondered what she was going to do when Cal called her again. She'd just spelled out the rules of their involvement in no uncertain terms—sex, no strings, no commitment. How was she supposed to back out of their deal when she'd gone to so much trouble to assure him she wasn't even remotely emotionally invested in their relationship? She couldn't very well tell him the truth—that she'd finally admitted to herself that she still loved him, which made having sex with him a really bad idea since he didn't feel even remotely the same way.

Switching off her car, she rolled her eyes at her own pride. That was what had gotten her into this stupid mess in the first place, after all. Pride had made her accept that first dinner offer. And pride had made her put on that dog-and-pony show tonight in his bedroom. And now pride was squirming in her belly at the thought of turning Cal down when he next suggested they hook up, just in case he guessed how she felt.

Okay, pride *and* lust. It would be hard to say no to more of his beautiful body and clever hands. To know that she would never again hear him sigh her name against her skin as he made love to her. That she would never again be filled with the sweaty, needy, greedy desire for him that gripped her every time they saw each other.

Tough cookies.

Her jaw hardened as she let herself into her house. She could go cold turkey on the sex. And she could definitely suck up a bit of damaged pride since the only alternative was to keep sleeping with Cal in order to maintain her facade of not caring. There was no way she was doing that to herself—making love to a man she loved but who only *liked* her was not something she was signing on for, thanks. She'd never been into sadomasochism. Self-delusion, yes. But not willful self-hurt.

She'd avoid him for a week or two, then tell him that she had a big work project coming up and she wanted to concentrate on it. Or better yet, that she'd met someone. He was in no position to challenge her. They'd made no commitments to each other. And if he suspected something deeper was going on…well, she could live with that. Whatever it took to get him out of her life once and for all.

And next time there was a Hannigan's reunion, she'd ask if he was going to be there before she blithely walked in the door and was blindsided by him all over again.

Later that morning she woke to churning nausea and just made it to the bathroom in time to lose what was left of last night's dinner. She put it down to the situation with Cal, and possibly the shrimp cocktail she'd grabbed after work with Gareth before joining Cal at his place.

When she threw up Sunday morning, and then Monday morning, an impossible suspicion began to form in the back of her mind. Tuesday morning, she rinsed her mouth out after what was becoming her traditional prebreakfast barf and reached for her packet of contraceptive pills. No stray pills remained in the blister pack, which meant she hadn't forgotten to take one. Not this month, anyway. She pulled open the cabinet behind her mirror, scrabbling around to see if she'd left last month's blister pack lying around, so she could check that, too. She hadn't. She sighed. The odds of her being pregnant were incredibly slim. She'd been on the pill for over five years. Even if she *had* slipped up, her body would have to have been poised on the starting block, ready to explode into fertility at the first hint of an opportunity. What were the odds of that happening?

Then her gaze fell on the bottle of antibiotics she'd been prescribed last month for a nagging ear infection. She'd wanted to take care of it before she had to fly to Melbourne for Carolyn and Phil's wedding, she remembered.

She'd glanced at the bottle dozens of times over the last few weeks as she brushed her teeth and did her makeup and her hair, and not once had the familiar warning printed along the bottom of the label registered. But today it did. Big-time.

Warning—Antibiotics may decrease the effectiveness of birth control pills.

Her mind went blank. A rushing sound filled her head. She sat down on the closed toilet lid and stared at the towel rack.

She'd thrown up four mornings in a row. She'd also taken antibiotics, then had wild monkey sex with Cal in the linen closet at her friend's wedding.

She pressed her hands to her breasts and squeezed them gingerly. Were her boobs bigger? Unusually tender? Different in any way?

She didn't think so. She stared down at her belly. It looked the same as it always had—as though she needed to really commit to doing two-hundred sit-ups a day if she wanted killer abs like Cameron Diaz.

Was it possible that right now there was a tiny new life growing behind her belly button?

She stood. She hadn't showered or had breakfast, but she didn't care. There was a convenience store on the corner, and she knew for a fact that it had pregnancy tests because she'd often noted them when she picked up milk and pitied the poor woman who was so desperate to find out whether she was pregnant that she bought her test from the quickie mart.

Hah.

She dragged on a skirt and T-shirt, not bothering with a bra, and slid her feet into flip-flops. She slung her purse over her shoulder and slammed out her front door. Once she was in the street, she became acutely aware of the fact that at thirty-one, her breasts were not as up to going out in the world sans support as they used to be. She kept her arms crossed over her chest the whole way to the convenience store.

She couldn't be pregnant. She'd have to be the unluckiest woman in the world. She'd been taking antibiotics for five days, and she'd had sex with Cal once in that time frame. Unless he possessed some kind of supersperm, there had to be another explanation for her nausea.

There was one test left on the shelf, and she lunged at it as though a horde of other desperate women might appear at any moment. She handed over cash and was out the door again in the space of a few seconds.

She tore the pack open as she walked back home, uncaring now that her breasts bounced with every step. She rapidly scanned the instructions. All she had to do was pee on a stick. She eyed the plastic indicator window. It had better say what she wanted it to say. Otherwise…she wasn't quite sure what she would do.

Ten minutes later, she sat on the edge of her bathtub and stared at the blue cross in the indicator window.

She was pregnant.

Her head spun. She didn't want to be a single parent. She wasn't really sure if she wanted to have children at all. It was something she'd discussed on and off with Jack before they'd split up, but they'd never gotten beyond the talking stage. When they'd gone their separate ways, she'd been profoundly grateful that the only people they'd had to consider were themselves.

But now the decision to have children had been taken out of her hands. She was going to have Cal MacKenzie's baby.

She gasped as the top threatened to float off her head. She bent over, gripping her knees as she shoved her head between them. Slowly the world stopped rocking and rolling.

A thought slid into her mind. She could take care of it. She didn't even have to tell him. She didn't have to tell anyone. One trip to the clinic, and this moment, this feeling would be history.

She stood and crossed to the telephone. Punching in a number, she counted one ring, then two, then three rings before her sister answered at the other end.

"I need to talk to you. Do you have work today?"

Amy worked part-time, but Becky could never remember which days.

"No. I was actually going to come into the city and raid your shoe department. Can't beat that staff discount."

"Amy, I think I'm pregnant." Becky closed her eyes.

God, she couldn't even say it properly. "I mean, I know I am. I just did a test."

There was a moment of profound silence.

"Oh my God. This is fantastic. You know I've always wanted the kids to have cousins."

Despite how desperate she felt, Becky smiled. Amy had been hassling Becky to hurry up and pop out kids for years now. Her sister was such a natural mother, she probably couldn't comprehend that news like this might be unwelcome, not to mention downright scary to Becky.

"Well, I'm glad someone's pleased," Becky said.

There was a short pause. "I'm sorry. I'm such a doofus. I just assumed you and Jack must have gotten back together…." Her sister trailed off, waiting for Becky to fill in the gaps.

"No. I've been, um, seeing Cal MacKenzie. You know, from back in college."

"Cal MacKenzie who broke your heart? That Cal MacKenzie?"

"That's the one."

"Isn't he married?" her sister asked.

"Not anymore."

"Thank God. Sorry, but I know how you always had such a thing for him and I thought for a moment there that maybe you'd let yourself get sucked into something ugly because you couldn't say no to him."

Becky rested her forehead on her hand and closed her eyes.

"Does that mean I can come over?" she asked. She didn't like how small and sad her voice sounded, but there was precious little she could do about it.

"Of course you can! Don't be an idiot. You could come over even if you'd humped a football team's worth of married men. You know that. What time should I expect you?"

"I need to phone in sick to work. Maybe an hour?"

She didn't feel even a moment's compunction about taking a sick day. She figured finding out she was unexpectedly pregnant by her teen crush gave her the world's biggest get-out-of-jail-free card.

"How many weeks are you?" her sister asked when she opened her front door an hour later.

"Four weeks. I think. I guess I'll need to have a scan or whatever to confirm that. Is that what happens next?" Becky asked.

Her sister pulled her into a bone-crushing hug.

"You're going to keep it," Amy said. "I'm so pleased. When you said it was Cal's and you sounded so miserable about it, I wondered."

"Of course I'm keeping it. Maybe when I was a kid I wouldn't have. But there's no reason why I can't look after a baby and be a good mum now. I've got my own place, a good job. You and Mum will help out. I'll get by."

Becky hadn't realized how much had fallen together in her mind during her shower and the drive over. The first rush of panic had subsided. She was pregnant, and it was unplanned, but she could handle it. She *would* handle it.

Amy frowned. "What about Cal? Where does he fit into all of this?"

"He doesn't," Becky said firmly.

"Why not? He made half a baby, same as you. Why shouldn't he handle half the consequences?" Her sister had her hands on her hips and a martial light in her eye.

Suddenly Becky remembered that her sister had never been Cal's biggest fan.

"Because I love him desperately, and he thinks I'm just a great lay," Becky said bluntly.

Her sister opened her mouth then shut it again without saying anything.

"Exactly," Becky said. "I am not going to spend my life eating my heart out over a man who will never feel the same way toward me that I feel toward him. Been there, done that, didn't keep the T-shirt. Having this baby tie us together forever is bad enough."

Instantly she realized what she'd said. She pressed a hand to her stomach and ducked her head to address her navel. "Sorry, little guy. I didn't mean that the way it sounded."

Her sister's eyes filled with tears as she noted the small gesture. Becky shook her head adamantly.

"No. We are not going to cry, Amy. I can't afford to. I have to sort this out. I need to come up with a way to tell Cal. And I need to set everything up so that he can see that I don't need anything from him."

"You could just not tell him, if you're so worried about it," her sister said. "Thousands of women don't."

Becky instantly shook her head. It was an easy way out, but she couldn't take it.

"No. I want my baby to know who his father is. What I don't want is Cal feeling obligated or trying to take control. He can be a part of the baby's life, but not mine."

She still wasn't sure how she was going to keep the two things separate, but she would find a way. She had to.

"Good luck with that one," Amy muttered.

"What's that supposed to mean?"

"Men come over all me-Tarzan, you-Jane when they find out they've planted a seed. Trust me on this. Craig was practically pounding his chest when I found out I was pregnant with Kyle."

"That's because he loves you and you guys had been trying for ages. This is different. Cal is different. He's a newly single guy, fresh from a divorce. He's got a new company, he's making money. He just wants to have a good time. He doesn't want the commitment of a baby. He definitely doesn't want it with me."

Her sister blinked rapidly again and Becky pointed at her.

"If you make me cry, you're going to have to go inflate a dinghy or something because it's going to be a while before I stop."

Her sister hugged her close.

"I'm so sorry. I've always wanted you to have kids so you could experience how amazing it is. I just never imagined it would be like this."

Becky closed her eyes and hugged her sister back.

"I know. Me either."

CAL SLID two champagne flutes onto his kitchen counter, then stole a black olive from the bowl he'd placed nearby. Sultry music played on the stereo, and a tray of antipasto sat alongside the bowl of olives and the champagne bucket. The lighting was low, he was fresh from the shower, and the harbor was putting on its usual spectacular nightly show.

For the fifth time in the last fifteen minutes, he checked his watch. Becky was late. He'd called her earlier in the week to tee up a time to see her, but he'd had to wait until Friday for her to be free. A whole week since he'd had her naked in his arms. Was it any wonder he was feeling distinctly edgy?

He ran an eye over his arrangements again, sliding the olive bowl a little more to the left to stop it crowding out the antipasto platter. He was just about to replace the plain glass champagne flutes with the cut-crystal ones he'd brought back from London when he realized what he was doing.

Fussing. Primping like an old lady expecting the vicar for tea. Or like a nervous man determined to woo a woman into bed.

Except he didn't need to do that, did he? Becky had made that more than clear last Friday. This thing they had together was about sex and nothing else. Whenever he felt the need to get off, he didn't have to come up with the pretext of dinner or a movie or a theater show before he could get her naked. He just had to pick up the phone and she'd arrive, ready to head straight into the bedroom and get busy.

He frowned. He wasn't sure why their deal left him feeling uneasy. On the surface, it was every man's wet dream. He craved Becky's body. Several times a day he was visited with memories from their sessions together. The clench of her hands on his butt as she urged him to go harder, faster. The taste of her on his lips. The way her body shuddered and then turned soft and languid after she came. Today, he'd been sitting in a quarterly update meeting with his business partner when he'd had a flash of Becky's face as she savored him riding high inside her.

It was crazy to question the gift he'd been given—great sex with no obligations. After the way things had ended with Natalie, it was just what he needed. She'd become so clingy toward the end, so jealous and possessive. He'd lost count of the number of times she'd accused him of having an affair. He'd been working like a dog to pay for the lifestyle they'd become accustomed to—there was no way he'd had time to squeeze in a little extra on the side, even if he'd been so inclined. Perhaps if she hadn't had trouble finding a job she enjoyed in the U.K., things might have turned out differently. But she'd been restless, dissatisfied, and she'd funneled all her anxiety into their relationship. Ironically, she was the one who'd wound up having the affair. Out of boredom, she'd said. And because she'd wanted to make Cal jealous and test his love for her.

He guessed that the fact that he'd been able to walk away from his marriage with relatively few scars was evidence that perhaps he hadn't loved her as much as he'd thought he had. He'd misjudged her. He could admit that to himself now. He'd assumed Natalie's confidence was a part of her and not just a mask that she put on like the makeup she insisted on wearing every day, no matter what.

His thoughts shifted to Becky. She was the polar

opposite of Natalie. Dark to Natalie's blond, and genuinely confident, a woman with a career and life of her own. She'd always had backbone. Always known what she wanted and gone for it. It was one of the things he admired about her the most.

The doorbell chimed. On his way to answer it, he adjusted the dimmer switch, brightening the room to normal levels. He picked up the remote for the stereo and killed the smoochy music, too. For some reason, he felt stupid for trying to turn their evening into anything other than what it was.

"Hey. I was getting ready to call out the search choppers," he said as he let her in.

She gave him a tight smile and slipped past him into the apartment.

He frowned. Something was wrong.

She hadn't changed out of her work clothes, for starters. She always went home to change before meeting him. She hadn't quite met his eye when he'd opened the door, either.

"Are you okay?" he asked as he joined her in the living room.

"I'm fine," she said, but he caught a flash of distress in her big brown eyes. He stepped closer and placed a hand between her shoulder blades, rubbing her back soothingly.

"You're as stiff as a board."

She shrugged a shoulder, almost as though she was trying to shake his touch off. Then she stepped forward, out of his reach. She turned to face him, her hands clenched together in front of her.

"There's no easy way to do this. I had this big speech planned, but I'm just going to say it. I was taking some antibiotics before Carolyn and Phil's wedding, and I didn't think about what that might mean. And then I started throwing up this week."

He stared at her, confused. What was she saying? That she was sick? That something was wrong with her? A wave of protectiveness and fear raced through him. He didn't want Becky to be sick. Not when he'd just found her again.

"Cal, I'm pregnant," she said.

Two very simple words, but they changed his world forever.

CHAPTER FOUR

"Pregnant." Cal stared at her, his brain not quite putting two and two together and getting parenthood.

"As in having a baby. Our baby, to be specific."

Stupidly his first thought was for the champagne. "You won't be able to drink, then," he said.

She stared at him, and he shook his head.

"God. Sorry. I'm just...I don't know."

"It's a lot to take in." Her voice was flat, distant.

"You're on the pill, right?" he said, confused.

In the back of his mind, he was aware that there were other things he probably should be saying. Reassuring, supportive things. But he'd just been hit with the biggest surprise of his life and he didn't have a manual of political correctness on hand to guide his every move.

"Like I said, I was on antibiotics for an ear infection before Carolyn and Phil's wedding, and apparently they can affect the body's absorption of the pill in some people."

"Right."

Becky dropped her handbag onto the kitchen counter.

"I want to keep the baby, Cal," she said in a rush. "I know having a termination is maybe the smarter thing, but I think I could be a decent mother and saying no to this baby because it's not convenient doesn't sit well with me."

Cal scrubbed his face with his hands. He felt as though his brain was filled with marshmallow. Why couldn't he think straight? He was painfully aware of Becky watching him, waiting for him to say something.

"I know this is a big shock," she said after a short silence. "The last thing you want in your life."

Cal found himself staring at Becky's stomach. In a few months time, she was going to get big and round. She'd start walking with one hand on the small of her back and the other on her belly. People would want to touch her in the street.

She was having his baby. Their baby. A baby that was half him, half her.

"When are you due?" he asked.

"Carolyn and Phil's wedding was early January, so I guess that means it will be sometime in September."

"Right." Plenty of time to get things organized. To get his head around this.

"I want you to know that I've got things covered," she said. "I've spoken to my sister and my boss at work and my mum, and I can take six months maternity leave and my sister and my mum have offered to look after the baby between them when I go back to work so he won't have to go into childcare. I own my own home, I earn a good salary, I'm looking into getting a nice safe hatchback instead of my Audi."

He frowned. "Why do I feel like we're in a job interview?"

"I'm trying to explain that you don't need to worry about anything. I'd like for the baby to know who you are, to spend time with you when he or she is older, I guess, but until then there's really no reason why this should mess with your life too much."

Cal stared at her. "You're having a baby, Becky. My baby."

"Our baby. And I know this is the last thing you need or want in your life. There's no need for you to feel trapped or anything like that."

"That's the second time you've said that," he said, his frown deepening.

"What?"

"That this is the last thing I want in my life."

"It's true, isn't it? You just got divorced three months ago. You're still finding your feet, remembering what it's like to be single again."

Why did he feel as though he'd heard those words somewhere before?

"That doesn't mean I'm not going to step up and meet my obligations. I'm thirty-one, Becky, not some kid who's going to bail at the first sign of trouble."

"I told you, you don't need to feel obligated. The baby and I are all taken care of—there's nothing for you to do."

"What if I *want* to do something? You'll need help financially, for starters."

Her full lips pressed together and her chin came up.

"I don't need your money. I told you that."

"There is no way I'm standing by and letting you shoulder the burden of bringing up our child on your own," he said.

Her lips got even thinner.

"Fine. I'll keep a record of what I spend on the baby and you can pay half. Anything else?"

"What about doctor's visits, that kind of thing? That's going to be expensive."

"I have insurance, it's covered."

"You'll need a specialist. I'll ask my brother for a recommendation." Andrew's speciality was orthopedics, but he'd know who was the best.

"I've already booked an appointment with my sister's doctor."

"Maybe we should hold off on that. My brother might know someone better."

"My sister has had four children with Dr. Martin. She trusts him, and so do I."

Her jaw was set, and her hands were crossed over her breasts. She looked the very picture of stubbornness.

"Would you like me to come to the doctor's appointment?" he asked.

"Why?"

"Why the hell do you think? To support you."

She threw her hands in the air.

"I don't need your support, Cal, and I don't want it. We're two people who happen to have good sex together, but that's it. Under any other circumstances, we'd sleep with each other until one or both of us got bored, then we'd go our separate ways. Just because this has happened shouldn't change that."

"We're a little more than two people who sleep with each other," he said. "We've known each other for more than ten years, Becky."

"No. We haven't spoken to each other for ten years. We knew each other a little when we were at university. That's it. I wouldn't even call us friends."

He'd never thought her big brown eyes could look so cold.

"Well, I consider you a friend," he said stiffly. "We worked together. We've slept with each other, I enjoy your company."

"Yeah, and when I left Hannigan's we never said another word to each other until the reunion. That's not how friends behave, Cal. Friends call each other up and drop each other e-mails every now and then. Friends are there in good times and bad. We only ever did the good times."

He shifted his feet, shoved a hand into the front pocket of his jeans.

"I thought about you. But it would have felt wrong to make contact. I was married."

She stared at him, color rising in her pale cheeks.

"Doesn't that just prove my point? It's like I said the other night. We were only ever about the sex. And just because this has happened doesn't change anything."

She slid her handbag up onto her shoulder. "I'll call you once a month to keep you up to speed on everything during the pregnancy, and I'll send you copies of the scans or anything else that comes along. We can work out child support things closer to when the baby is due, if that's what you want to do."

She headed for the door, leaving him staring at the space where she'd been standing.

"Wait a minute," he said.

She turned on the threshold of his apartment, her face perfectly calm and composed. How could she be so together when he was reeling, trying to come to terms with the fact that his whole life had changed?

"Be honest with yourself, Cal. You're a party guy—always have been. You've got this place and a sporty car and a business that's making lots of money. I know you probably feel like you have to say and do the right thing, but I don't need anything that you have to offer. I certainly don't need you coming along for the ride out of guilt. Let's just take it as read that you're off the hook and move on, okay?"

She walked away, her stride long and sure. He stared at her back until she stepped into the elevator car.

At about the same time, he started to get angry.

Phrases from their conversation circled his mind.

This is the last thing you need or want in your life.

You're a party guy—always have been.

And his personal favorite: *Let's just take it as read that you're off the hook and move on, okay?*

Becky had walked in the door, broadsided him with the news of her pregnancy, then bulldozed him into a corner with about a million assumptions about who he was and what he wanted. She'd subdivided her pregnancy into neatly apportioned lots, and generously agreed to allow him access to one or two of them. He could see scans. She'd give him updates. She'd like the baby to know he was its father, and for him to have contact with the child once it was old enough.

She didn't want his money or his friendship, and she certainly didn't want him holding her hand through any of it. All she'd ever wanted from him, it seemed, was what was between his legs.

We were always only about the sex.
I wouldn't even call us friends.

Out of all the things she'd said, those two last comments burned him up the most. Yeah, it pissed him off that she thought he was some feckless playboy asshole tooling around in his Porsche, more than happy to turn a blind eye to the fact that he'd gotten someone pregnant because it might cramp his style. What the hell did that say about her opinion of him, for freak's sake?

But the thing that really got his blood boiling was the way she kept rewriting history. They *had* been friends, no matter what she said. Before they'd slept with each other, they'd spent hundreds of lunch breaks and tea breaks talking in the staff room. Every staff function, they'd wound up in a corner somewhere, making each other laugh. Yes, there had been plenty of suppressed flirtation in all of those encounters, but they'd liked each other, as well as lusted after each other.

He ran his hand through his hair, then glanced around his apartment. The champagne, the food, the stereo and lighting he'd set up and then chickened out on at the last minute—it all seemed to mock him.

He'd always wanted kids someday. He and Natalie had tried for a short while when they'd first arrived in London, but his work had become so hectic that they'd both agreed the timing wasn't right. Then their relationship had started to dissolve and the idea of kids had been well and truly off the agenda.

Now he was going to be a father. And he was damned

if he was going to let Becky draw a neat little box on the ground and tell him he couldn't step outside its bounds. He had rights. He wanted to be a part of his son or daughter's life.

And despite the cool look in Becky's eyes, despite the fact that she was clearly, utterly unthrilled to find herself linked with him for life, he wanted to help her. She might not be prepared to acknowledge it, but there had always been more to them than sexual attraction. There was a reason why he'd backed off all those years ago. The same reason that she'd been the first person he'd thought of when he was single again.

Grabbing his car keys, he headed for the door.

BECKY WAS still shaking by the time she let herself in her front door. Telling Cal she was pregnant had been one of the hardest things she'd ever done.

She dressed in her favorite pair of threadbare flannel pyjamas despite the heat. She needed the comfort of the familiar. If she was the kind of woman who went in for soft toys, she'd be clutching one to her chest right about now, too. Instead, she sat on the couch with her knees pulled tight to her chest.

If she could go back in time to the night of the reunion and change things, she would. She'd turn around the moment she saw Cal, and simply walk out the door. So what if her old friends and work colleagues guessed that she still had feelings for him? A bit of self-exposure was better than this.

She rested her chin on her knees and tried not to remember the things he'd said when she'd given him the news. He'd talked about meeting his obligations. He'd used the word *burden*. She scrunched her eyes tightly shut and grit her teeth.

A burden. The last thing she wanted was to be considered a burden in Cal MacKenzie's life. Not when she loved him. Not when she craved his touch and longed for the sound of his voice.

Tears burned at the back of her eyes. She swallowed them down. She hadn't cried since that night outside Cal's apartment, and she wasn't going to now. She was going to have a baby, and that child needed her to be strong and sure. From now on, every decision she made affected both of them. The days of thinking and behaving selfishly and impulsively were over.

She uncurled from her position on the couch. She felt vaguely nauseous, and she groaned. Her sister had explained that just because it was called morning sickness didn't mean it only happened in the mornings. She'd added that she'd thrown up day and night for twelve weeks with her first child, and had warned Becky that the same might happen to her. It seemed her prediction was spot-on.

"Great. All I need," Becky muttered.

The sound of someone pounding loudly on her front door made her jump on the spot. She stared down the hallway at the glossy black door, knowing who was on the other side and dreading yet another conversation with Cal.

"Becky, I know you're in there and I'm not going anywhere so you might as well let me in," he yelled.

It was past ten, and she was sure that her neighbors

wouldn't appreciate her having a yelling match through her front door.

Cal glared at her as the door swung open between them.

"I didn't even have your address," he said tightly.

His hair stood up in unruly spikes as though he'd been running his fingers through it, and his cheekbones were dark with emotion. He brushed past her, inviting himself into her home.

"I had to ring Carolyn up and ask her for your address, because I don't know where the woman who is pregnant with my child lives," Cal repeated as he swung around to face her in her living room.

Becky stood in the doorway, feeling at an acute disadvantage in her baggy pyjamas when he was fully dressed.

"It's never come up before," she said.

"Because you didn't want it to come up," he said. He stabbed a finger at the air between them. "Ever since we hooked up again you've been calling the shots. You decide when we'll meet, where we'll meet, if you'll stay the night or not."

"I didn't hear you complaining." She crossed her arms over her chest. She could feel her heart hammering against her ribs, and nausea swirled in her belly.

"I have over twenty employees," he said. "People who rely on me to pay their mortgages and keep food in their kids' mouths. I ring my parents once a week and try to see them at least once a month, and I donate to a bunch of charities."

Becky shook her head. What the hell was he going on about?

"Cal—"

"I'm not an asshole, Becky. I don't spend my spare time partying with morons and driving around in my car showing the world how great I am. I was married for five years, and I was faithful for every one of them."

She stared at him. "I wasn't aware that I said you were an asshole who did any of those things."

"Yeah, you did. You said I was a party guy. That I always have been. That's not me. Maybe for a few years when I was in my early twenties, but not anymore."

"Okay. Well, I'm sorry if I offended you. I was simply trying to make a point. This is unexpected news, not something you planned for or even remotely want. And I'm prepared to take care of everything. So it doesn't need to make too much difference in your life."

Despite her reassurances, Cal's frown only deepened.

"You're doing it again, making assumptions about who I am and what I want and how I feel."

Becky opened her mouth, then closed it without saying a word. She didn't know how to respond to him.

"What do you want, Cal?" she finally asked.

"I want to help you. I want to do this with you. I want us to start acting as if we actually like each other."

She stared at him. He had no idea what he was asking for.

She'd worked for a year with him after their breakup, and it had been hell. Every time she'd had to go to work she'd felt half-hopeful that something may have miraculously changed since she last saw him and he'd have realized what he'd thrown away. And every time she'd had to listen to him laughing and joking about what he'd done on the weekend with his buddies, the other girls he'd met, the good times he'd had. Every work shift she'd had to face the fact that having fun with his friends was more important, more valuable to Cal than what they'd shared together.

She wasn't going through all that again.

"I've told you what I want to do. I've told you I'll take care of everything. You don't have to feel that this is a burden you have to take up or a responsibility or an obligation."

"Jesus, Becky." Cal looked to the ceiling as though seeking patience. His blue eyes burned with intensity when he returned his gaze to her. "This is not a burden to me, and if you say it one more time I'm going to get really pissed. I'm thirty-one years old, and I've always wanted to have children. I want to be a part of this."

Becky shook her head, instinctively rejecting what he was saying. She couldn't handle knowing these things about Cal. She didn't want to know that he was responsible and mature, that he'd been faithful to his wife. She definitely didn't want to know that he wanted a family.

She wanted him to be a playboy, an attractive, sexy guy she'd stupidly fallen in love with, but who would never make her happy, even if he did love her in the same way that she loved him. She wanted him to be unsuitable, impossible, out of the question. Because if he wasn't, it made the fact that he didn't love her too hard to deal with. He went from being a guy who would never settle down to a guy who wanted to settle down. A guy who wanted a family. A guy who wanted all the things she wanted—but who simply didn't want them with her.

"I don't think I can do this right now," she said.

"Tough. I'm not letting you push me into a corner and tell me what's what again," Cal said. "I'm sick of hearing you tell me what you think I am, how this is the last thing I want and how I'm thrilled to be single again. You don't know me at all, Becky."

He was standing too close, and he was too big and tall for her little living room. She felt cornered, overwhelmed. He had no idea what he was doing to her, what this meant to her.

"Don't put all this on me," she said. Suddenly she felt incredibly, incandescently angry. Not just at Cal, but at life, at the unfairness of loving a man who would never love her back. And angry at herself for putting herself in this situation in the first place.

"You said those things, Cal. *You* said you'd only been divorced three months, that you were just getting used to being single again. *You* called the baby a burden, not me. So don't you dare tell me I'm putting words in your mouth."

He frowned. "You're taking it out of context."

"Really? I asked you if you wanted a relationship with me, and you told me you'd only been single for three months. What was I supposed to take from that, Cal?"

He stared at her. "Are you saying that you want to have a relationship with me?" He sounded incredulous, mystified.

Becky stared at him, at his gorgeous face and strong, lean body. Why did she have to fall in love with him all those years ago? And why couldn't she get over him now?

Suddenly she felt bone weary, utterly exhausted. There was no way she could protect herself from Cal now that she was pregnant with his baby. There was no way she could allow him access to their child and hope to quarantine him from the rest of her life. He was going to be a part of her life forever. Unattainable, but always there.

"Don't worry. I'm not going to make this any more awkward than it already is," she said. She blinked furiously and turned away. "Do you want a coffee?"

Maybe they could both calm down, sit down and hammer out some kind of arrangement.

Cal caught her arm before she'd taken two steps.

"What do you mean by awkward? What's awkward about you wanting a relationship with me?"

She tried to shrug him off. "It doesn't matter."

"Yes, it does, Becky. There's been enough unsaid bullshit between us. Say what you mean for once."

She glared at him. "Why should I? Why should I lay everything at your feet so you can pick it over and see if any of it interests you? I'm done with being rejected by you, in case you hadn't noticed."

He dropped her arm at last. "If you're talking about when we were kids, we both know the timing was wrong," he said.

Years of anger and hurt swelled inside Becky.

"You have no idea, do you? You think that just because you walked away from what we had easily, it was the same for me. I loved you, Cal MacKenzie. I worshipped the ground you walked on. I used to look forward to going to work just so I could see you. I thought you were the funniest, the smartest, the sexiest guy I'd ever met. I was so jealous of your girlfriend. And then you broke up with her, and suddenly you were mine. For four whole weeks."

She took a deep breath, distantly aware that Cal was staring at her, his face pale.

"And once you'd screwed me every which way, you dumped me like yesterday's garbage. And I realized exactly what I meant to you."

"That's not how it was," Cal said tightly. "You meant something to me."

He took a step forward, but she held up a hand, warding him off.

"I know exactly what I meant to you—hanging out with your buddies and chugging beers and having sex with nameless girls was more important to you than what we had together."

"That's not true," he said, frowning. "I thought you were fantastic, Becky. God, I was obsessed with you. I used to feel so guilty when I was with Virginia because you were all I could think about. You were the reason we broke up. When we first got together, it was so good, so intense, you blew my mind."

Nausea rolled up the back of her throat. She didn't want to hear this. Didn't want to hear Cal try to justify or explain. She shouldn't have said anything. Laying out her hurts before him was worse than pathetic. She didn't want his sympathy. She definitely didn't want his guilt.

"Stop," she said. "Don't say another word. Let's just agree that I was an idiot and you had a nice time and that history has just repeated itself."

Cal stepped forward and grabbed her shoulders. She

could feel the heat from his body, smell his aftershave. Helpless tears filled her eyes. Why did he have so much power over her?

"Will you let me finish? You were never just a good time to me, Becky. Being with you was the most intense, amazing time of my life. The way I used to feel when you were lying in my arms... Like my chest wasn't big enough for my heart. When we were together, all I wanted to do was get as close to you as possible. And when we weren't together, I couldn't stop thinking about you. I picked up the phone ten times for every one time I called you."

He stared down at her, his blue eyes compelling, his face tight with intensity.

"I didn't break up with you because I didn't care, Becky. I broke up with you because I cared too much, and it scared the shit out of me. When I was with you, I thought about houses and babies and being together forever. I was twenty years old. I had no idea what to do with any of that. It freaked me out. I loved you with everything I had. That's why we broke up."

Becky blinked. Cal had loved her? All those years ago, he'd broken up with her because he'd loved her too much and he couldn't handle it?

It was such a huge twist on what she'd accepted as the truth, she could barely comprehend what he was saying.

Even as her emotions overwhelmed her, bile rose in her throat and the nausea that had been threatening all evening took control of her body.

Becky clapped a hand to her mouth, spun on her heel and raced for the bathroom. The door hit the wall with a bang as she shoved it open. Then she was on her knees, her body convulsing as she lost her dinner to the toilet bowl.

Her hair hung around her face as she retched. She was vaguely aware of Cal entering the bathroom behind her. She desperately wanted to tell him to leave her alone, but was in no state to do so. Then she felt him gently gathering her hair, holding it at the nape of her neck as her stomach rebelled yet again.

The warm weight of his hand landed in the middle of her back as the nausea retreated.

"Are you okay?" he asked quietly.

"Water would be good," she said, keeping her back to him.

Her hair fell free again as he stood and moved to the vanity. She heard the rush of water filling a glass as she reached up and pressed the flush button.

"Here."

He passed her the water and a wet towel. She rinsed out her mouth until the acid taste was gone, then wiped her face.

Finally she turned around to look at him, shifting on the cool tile until her back was to the wall. He was crouched down beside her, a concerned look on his face. They stared at each other for a long silent moment.

"I'm guessing that was morning sickness?" he finally asked.

"Yep. According to my sister, I've got another eight weeks of it to look forward to."

She drew her knees into her chest. Cal sat down, leaning his back against the bathtub so that they were facing one another. Cal's gaze searched her face for a few long beats before he started talking.

"That night when we went out to dinner, I told you that I'd thought about you over the years. Not just about the sex, Becky. I thought about that great dirty laugh you have. And the way you always get so fired up for the underdog. And the fact that you're so strong and independent that sometimes it would drive me crazy when you wouldn't let me buy you dinner."

She smiled faintly as she remembered the running argument they'd had over her paying her own way.

"You were the only reason I went to the reunion, you know. I wanted to see you again. I wanted to know if I still felt the same kick in my gut every time I looked at you."

She eyed him across the space that separated them.

"Do you?"

"Oh, yeah. Might even be worse now. Maybe I understand what I threw away all those years ago when I chickened out."

Becky held her breath. What was Cal actually saying? She'd been uncertain of him for too long to take anything he said at face value.

"When I told you I was just getting over my divorce, I wasn't saying that I wasn't interested in a relationship with you," he said. "I don't want to be one of those tragic guys who gets divorced and then marries again in a few months time because he can't stand being on his own. And you told me you weren't interested in a relationship. You told me your career was important to you. That we were about sex and nothing else."

Becky squirmed a little as she considered their conversation from his point of view. She'd been so busy protecting herself that she hadn't considered what signals she'd been sending Cal. She'd been so sure she knew the score where he was concerned.

"I thought that was how you felt," she said.

"You didn't give me a chance to say anything else. You were pretty clear that being with me was just about what happened in the bedroom."

Her gaze slid over his shoulder as heat rose into her cheeks. She felt ridiculously exposed and foolish.

"I thought you knew," she said. "I thought it was obvious how I felt and I was simply trying to hold on to a little dignity."

"Like I said, there's been a lot of unspoken bullshit between us. Me trying to find out if I threw away the best thing in my life all those years ago, and you throwing how not interested you were in my face at every turn."

Was that what she'd done? She'd thought her reaction to him, her longing, was evident in every glance she sent his way, in every gesture, in every word out of her mouth. She'd felt as though her love was written in the sky, huge and obvious.

"I've never been not interested in you, Cal," she said quietly.

"I realize that now. And I'm sorry I hurt you so much all those years ago, Becky. I wasn't ready for us. I think I knew on some level that I'd hurt you badly, but I never really admitted it to myself. That would have made it impossible for me to try to start things up with you again. And that was something that has been in the back of my mind ever since I knew my marriage was over."

Becky felt something hot and wet splash onto her hand, and she realized she was crying.

"Don't cry," he said. His face was twisted with regret. "I can't stand seeing you upset."

The gentleness in his voice fed the hope in her heart, and the tears fell faster. She was too scared to believe in what was happening between them, what they were both admitting to each other. She'd wanted this all her adult life.

"Becky," he said, and then he was in front of her, drawing her into his lap and holding her close as he pressed kisses onto the top of her head, her forehead, her wet cheeks.

"Please don't cry. I'm sorry I hurt you. And I'm sorry I didn't push harder when you started talking about us just being bed buddies. I should have told you how I felt, what I wanted straight up."

Becky clutched at the soft fabric of his shirt, feeling the warmth and the heat and the realness of him.

Cal. After all these years. Holding her so tightly, so closely that his voice vibrated through her body when he spoke.

"Tell me now," she whispered brokenly. "Tell me now what you want."

He took a deep breath, then she felt the nudge of his finger beneath her chin as he encouraged her to lift her face up. Tears sheened her eyes as she swallowed and met his gaze.

"I love you, Becky. I want to build a life with you.

When you told me you were pregnant tonight, all I could think about was that of all the women in the world, you were the one I wanted this to happen with."

Becky absorbed his words into her soul, the certainty in his voice and the sincerity shining from his face filling the empty spaces that doubt had made inside her.

"Say it again," she said, lifting her hands to cup his face.

"Which bit?" he asked, the shadow of a smile on his lips.

"All of it."

He cupped her face in turn, his thumbs brushing the tears from her cheeks.

"I love you, I love you, I love you," he said.

He opened his mouth to say more, but she closed the space between them and pressed her lips to his. She could taste the salt of her own tears, and she could taste him, and her heart ached in her chest as she understood that she finally had the dream. After all these years, Cal loved her. They were going to be together the way she'd always wanted. And they'd made a baby together. A baby they'd watch grow together. Maybe there would be other babies, too.

She felt desperate to be as close to Cal as possible, and she began tearing at his clothes as their kiss deepened. He seemed to understand and share her need, and they peeled each other's clothes off between clinging, wet, soul-searing kisses, their hands caressing bare skin as it was uncovered, fingers clutching greedily.

Then her back was flat on the cool tile of the bathroom floor, and Cal's warm weight was on her. She felt the hardness of his erection between her thighs. She tilted her hips to invite him inside, and he filled her with his body.

"I love you," she said. "I love you so much, Cal."

"I love you, Becky," he said. "And this time, I'm going to make sure I get it right."

He began to move, and they locked eyes as the magic that had always existed between them began to heat their blood. She didn't look away once as he stroked into her, one hand cradling the nape of her neck as though she was the most precious thing in the world to him. Quickly her climax built, and still she held his gaze. She could see the love in him and his own passion rising. She could feel the tension in his body, and she loved him with her hands, mapping his strength, molding him to her, wanting to get as close as it was possible for two people to get.

"Becky," he breathed.

"Cal," she answered.

They came together, offering their vulnerability to each other along with their bodies.

Afterward, Cal rolled onto his side and pulled her against him as they both gasped for breath. Becky's heartbeat was still pounding in her ears when Cal turned his head to one side to look into her eyes.

"Marry me," he said, his face suddenly very serious and determined.

She stiffened, the old caution rising inside her. She opened her mouth to speak, but Cal pressed a finger to her lips.

"Before you answer, all I want to hear is what you want. Not what you're worried about or what you think is right or what you think I want. What do *you* want?

What's your heart telling you right now, Becky?" he asked, his voice vibrating with intensity.

She blinked, and the last, unacknowledged puzzle-piece of her dream slid into place. It was crazy, the two of them making so many decisions so quickly. So many things could go wrong….

"Yes. My heart's saying yes."

Cal closed his eyes, and when he opened them again she saw a world of relief and satisfaction and happiness in them.

"Like I said, this time I'm going to get it right," Cal said. Gently, he tugged her closer still and Becky rested her head on his chest, savoring the heavy thud of his heart beneath her ear.

For the first time in more than ten years, she allowed herself to experience her love for him as a blessing and not a curse. Emotion filled her, expanding her chest, her belly, warming her arms and legs. Cal loved her. He wanted to marry her. She was going to have his baby. Their baby.

Cal kissed her again, and she felt the glide of his hand as he found her belly. The palm of his hand cupped her gently, reverentially. Becky smiled against his mouth, and she felt him smile in return.

"It's going to be all right, isn't it?" she whispered.

"It's going to be more than all right," he said. "It's going to be amazing."

Looking into his eyes, Becky knew it was the truth.

EIGHT MONTHS later, Mrs. Becky MacKenzie gave birth to a five-pound, seven-ounce baby girl. She and Cal had argued over names the entire course of the pregnancy, but they both took one look at her and decided she looked exactly like a Poppy Kathleen. After an overnight stay in hospital, all three went home to the three-bedroom Californian-style bungalow that Becky and Cal had bought together near the sun and surf of Bondi Beach in Sydney's east. Poppy was mostly oblivious to proceedings, but Cal and Becky were both acutely aware of the occasion—and blissfully, achingly happy that life had handed them a second chance to get things right.

FORGOTTEN LOVER
Emilie Rose

To the very special friends who stick—even through the hard stuff. You know who you are.

CHAPTER ONE

"TALIA RIVERA. Where is she?" Jake asked the woman stationed at the emergency-room registration desk.

"And you are?"

If she had to ask she wasn't a fan of his show.

"Jake Larson. Someone from Grady Memorial called me and said Talia had been brought in by ambulance."

Jake tried to stifle his impatience with protocol while the hospital employee checked his ID and then her computer to verify he was the one the hospital had contacted.

"Have a seat in the waiting room, Mr. Larson. Someone will be right with you," she drawled in a thick Georgia accent.

Jake didn't have time to sit. Friday afternoons were always hectic. He had a customized Viper back in the shop awaiting the finishing touches. The owner had paid half a million for Jake's expertise and wouldn't appreciate a delay in delivery. He also had to prepare for next week's taping of *Larsonize This!* But curiosity demanded he find out why Talia had given his name as a contact when he hadn't seen her in four years.

He turned away from the desk, went through security and entered the crowded waiting area. Not in the mood to talk shop or sign autographs, he avoided making eye contact, ignored the few empty vinyl seats and found a place to stand outside the main traffic pattern.

Unwelcome but familiar smells and sounds inundated him, reminding him of a time he'd rather forget. Nothing smelled like a hospital. And then there were the moans and whimpers, almost drowned out by the blare of a TV tuned in to a soap opera. Before social services had removed him and his siblings from their parents' home when Jake was eleven, the E.R. had been the Larson family's only health-care provider.

His gaze roamed the room. There were kids everywhere. Crying ones. Dirty ones. Pale, silent ones. Shouldn't they be in a separate pediatric waiting room? Did they really need to be exposed to the drugged-out junkie muttering in the corner or the drunk heaving in the trash can?

Jake wasn't crazy about children. His years in the foster-care system had taken care of that.

But he wasn't that poor kid anymore. He made a good living customizing cars for his cash-laden clients, and his weekly TV show specializing in taking the average Joe's clunker and turning it into a one-of-a-kind collector car had made him famous and increased his business tenfold.

"Jake Larson?" a woman in a white scrub suit, her salt-and-pepper hair scraped back from her face, called from a doorway.

Bodies perked up around him as recognition dawned. These people represented his show's target demographic, the ones who wrote the hundreds of letters that arrived each week, begging to have their ragged rides Larsonized. Any other day he'd stay and yak. Not today.

Jake moved swiftly toward the woman. "Yes."

"I'm Sue. Ms. Rivera's nurse. This way." She briskly led him down a corridor crowded with curtained-off beds and past a sign that read Red Zone. His gut turned to lead. That didn't sound good. *Red* implied urgent.

"Ms. Rivera is in the Red Zone because of her head injury," she explained, as if she'd followed his gaze. "Her CAT scan and MRI are clear, but there are gaps in her memory that concern us."

"What do you mean gaps?"

"She doesn't know where she is or what brought her to Atlanta," Sue said over her shoulder. "She has partial amnesia."

"Amnesia? Get real."

Sue stopped in her tracks, turned and nailed him with a hard stare. "Her condition is very real, Mr. Larson."

She pivoted on her squeaky rubber-soled shoes and resumed walking. The deeper they penetrated into the E.R. the more the sounds and smells of misery bombarded him with memories. Bad ones. Of broken bones and bloody gashes, of being dragged away from his crying, pleading mother.

Sue rounded a corner and abruptly pulled back a curtain. "Talia, Jake's here."

Talia. Jake jerked to a halt. She'd changed, and yet she hadn't, but his reaction to her was the same as the first time they'd met. His heart rammed against the wall of his chest like a crash-test car and his mouth dried.

Her brown eyes looked huge in her ashen face. A purple knot marred her forehead. Another swollen bruise surrounded a small cut high on her left cheekbone that had been sealed with strips of tape—the kind he kept in the garage for when he didn't have time to drop everything and dash to the doctor's for a quick stitch or two. Dark, wavy hair, longer than the short, chic style he remembered, had been tucked behind her ears and fell to her shoulders.

He found no welcome in her expression, no enmity either. No anything. "Hello, Talia."

"Hi?" Her voice was little more than a tentative whisper.

Sue stepped forward. "Talia, do you remember Jake? His name and address were on the emergency card in your wallet. We called him when you couldn't give us any other family members' names."

Talia's bottom lip wobbled almost imperceptibly before her straight white teeth pinched it still. Fear invaded her features as she searched Jake's face. She shook her head and winced. The hand not connected to an IV lifted and touched her temple beside the bruise. "I'm sorry. I don't."

The sucker punch of her words winded him. She'd *forgotten* him? *Forgotten* the nights she'd spent in his bed, in his arms, the countless times he'd lost himself in her body? *Bull—*

"You are the correct Jake Larson, aren't you?" Sue asked. "You know Talia?"

Jake inspected Talia through narrowed eyes. What game was she playing? He didn't believe the amnesia garbage for one second. That was the stuff of the soap operas playing on the waiting-room TV, not real life. "We know each other. Very well."

Or so he'd thought before she'd packed up and moved out of his condo without even the courtesy of a goodbye. He'd returned from an out-of-town business trip and found her and her belongings gone and only a brief Sorry-this-isn't-working note as an explanation. He'd tried to track her down at work, but she'd quit her job and left town. He hadn't followed.

Sue's gaze found his. "There are gaps in her memory. For example, she knows the date, her name, her home address, her son's name, and—"

"Whoa." Jake recoiled. "Her son?"

Sue nodded to a pair of chairs pushed against the white tiled wall, their plastic backs facing Talia's bed. Jake had taken the lump on them for a pile of dirty laundry. Closer inspection revealed a small child curled beneath white blankets in a makeshift bed. Jake took a cautious step closer for a better look, but all he could make out was the top of a head covered in wavy hair the same glossy dark shade as Talia's, and a fan of lashes across sleep-flushed cheeks.

Talia had a child.

"Adam is the first thing Talia asked about, but I assured her he's been thoroughly checked over by our pediatric resident and he's fine. His car seat protected him."

Jake barely registered the nurse's words. His polo shirt with the Larson Ltd. embroidered logo suddenly felt tight and scratchy. He shrugged to ease the discomfort, but couldn't shake it. Thoughts clicked like a ratchet in his head.

His?

No. They'd had rules. An agreement. And she'd left

him. She wouldn't have skipped town if the boy was his, would she?

"How old is he?" he forced himself to ask through tight, numb lips.

Talia turned panicked eyes to Sue, who lifted a shoulder and said, "He's potty-trained, and judging by his teeth we're guessing he's no more than two-and-a-half. Talia's drawing a blank on Adam's age and his birthday, and he's either too young or too upset by the accident to tell us."

Two-and-a-half. Jake did the math. Too young to be his by six months. Thank God. He released the breath scalding his lungs.

Nonetheless, the uneasiness he'd experienced earlier didn't vanish. He shifted in his work boots. Wealth, success and the notoriety he'd gained since his series launched had taught him that almost everybody wanted a piece of him.

Talia had hinted about marriage before she'd left, but she'd backed off easily enough when he'd restated his intention never to get married or have kids. He'd told her then that his career would always be number one. If she'd wanted more than the no-strings affair he'd offered, she'd never let on.

But she'd left before he'd inked the TV series deal. Had she seen his face in the news, a magazine or on a calendar and decided to try again? Limelight was one hell of an aphrodisiac for some women. Or so he'd learned. But why come back now?

And if the boy wasn't his, whose was he? Had she turned to someone else soon after leaving Jake? Or had she left him for another man? Had she been two-timing him when they were together? A bitter taste filled his mouth.

"Talia was knocked unconscious," Sue interrupted his dark thoughts. "The standard protocol is to keep her overnight and repeat the MRI tomorrow morning to make sure she doesn't have a slow bleeder. You'll have to take Adam home with you."

Jake whipped his head back to the nurse. "Me? No way. What about the kid's father or Talia's?"

"Do you have a name and number for either?"

"No."

The nurse turned to Talia. "Have you remembered the names or numbers, hon?"

Talia's worry-widened eyes gave the answer before she shook her head and winced. "I—I don't. I just can't…"

"It's okay. It'll come." The nurse patted Talia's hand and turned back to Jake. "If you don't take Adam I'll have to temporarily place him with the Department of Social Services."

Jake flinched. He wouldn't wish DSS on any kid. Sure, there were success stories, but he and his siblings had been separated and hadn't reconnected in the years since entering the system. But that had been twenty-five years ago, and he wasn't still hung up on what-could-have-beens. He'd moved on and made a success of himself and his business. Larson Ltd. was practically a household name in certain circles, thanks to syndication.

He shook his head. "There has to be somebody else."

"Please, not social services. I'll think of someone else.

Just give me a minute." There was a desperate edge to Talia's voice that Jake hadn't heard before, and she gripped the bedrail so tightly her knuckles gleamed white in the fluorescent lights.

So she did remember what Jake had told her years ago. He scrutinized her pale face again, searching for another crack in her act, but her expression revealed the perfect blend of fear and bewilderment.

"We're running out of time, hon. Adam's going to wake up and get rambunctious like boys do. I'm afraid he'll get hurt." Sue looked at Jake.

He backed away mentally and physically. "I live alone and I work too many hours to look after a kid. Find one of her friends or a coworker who can take him."

"Don't you hear her? She can't remember anyone else and calls to her home phone are picked up by an answering machine. She thinks she and Adam live alone."

"If she remembers that, why can't she remember somebody who can keep the boy?"

The lines on Sue's face deepened into a scowl, revealing her irritation with him. "Talia, we'll be right back."

The nurse indicated that Jake follow her with an imperiously pointed finger. She led him around the corner. "Look, she's from out of state, and we don't know the full scope of her injuries yet. We can't turn her loose to collapse and possibly die from a bleed in a hotel room somewhere."

Alarm traveled like ice through Jake's veins, chilling him. He didn't want Talia back in his life, but he didn't want her dead, either.

Sue continued, "Her head injury looks mild, but the

partial amnesia is worrisome. It can be a sign there's more going on that we don't see yet. We can take care of her, but somebody needs to take care of Adam. He can't stay here. We're short-staffed and can't watch him. In another few hours this place will get Friday-night, payday crazy. He could get hurt or worse, some nut job could drag him out of here and we wouldn't even see it happen. We don't get to choose the quality of our patients, you know."

Jake recalled Friday nights in the E.R. all too well. Scary place for a kid.

"We're still waiting on the word from the North Carolina police. Sometimes out-of-state connections aren't as quick as we'd like."

"I'm not equipped to care for the boy." As lies went, this one was an act of desperation. As the eldest he'd been the only babysitter his younger siblings had had most days and nights while his parents worked two jobs each. But that had been decades ago. And he hadn't done such a great job. "Doesn't the hospital have a nursery for the employees?"

"We have a day care, but it's also short-staffed, has a waiting list and slew of regulations about immunizations. We can't just shove an extra child in there. Adam can tell you what he needs. He's quiet, but he talks."

Jake gritted his teeth and scoured his brain for a solution. He had to find a way out of this. "I'm not the man for the job."

"Yeah, well, until we hear differently you're the only one we got."

His gut burned as though he'd swallowed hot charcoal. "I want to talk to her doctor."

"I'll get him. But you need to think about that little boy in there, Mr. Larson. Adam's frightened and he needs someone."

Jake couldn't think about anything else. "That someone isn't me."

You'll have to take Adam home with you.

A shiver shook Talia. She hugged herself.

"Need another blanket, hon?" Sue bustled off without waiting for an answer, leaving Talia alone with the stony-faced Jake Larson, whose black polo shirt seemed to match his mood.

Talia didn't need a blanket. She needed her memory back. All of it. Not the spotty canvas she currently possessed.

Who was this man and why did the thought of him taking Adam send waves of fear rippling through her? She had a snapshot of Jake in her wallet along with a card bearing his name and phone number, written in her own neat handwriting. Although his hair was shorter now and the devastating smile and sexy glint in his eyes were missing, that face, with a chiseled jaw and tanned skin stretched tightly over high cheekbones, was unmistakable.

If she knew him well enough to carry his picture, why couldn't she remember him? But when they'd given her the wallet to go through, she'd looked at that photo and come up with nothing.

She bit her lip and studied Jake from his deliberately disheveled short, dark hair to his wide shoulders, muscled biceps, flat belly and lean khaki-encased hips.

He was the kind of guy to turn heads and quicken pulses. Hers included. But there were no memories attached to the physical attraction.

She dampened her dry lips. How well did she know him? He'd said *very well.* But what did that mean? Had she worked for him before she moved to North Carolina? Judging by the small car embroidered on his shirt beneath the words *Larson Ltd.,* she didn't think he was a doctor, and she had a strong feeling she worked in a medical setting. Not only had she understood all the jargon being thrown at her by the hospital staff, she'd been able to read her chart when the guy who'd brought her back from MRI had left it on the bed.

But she couldn't remember her son's birthdate or if he had any allergies—two questions the staff kept asking over and over. What kind of mother was she to forget such basic, critical information?

Her gaze returned to Jake's. Something in the way his bittersweet-chocolate-colored eyes traveled over her hinted at more than just friendship. Was she dating him? Sleeping with him? Warmth rushed her skin, chasing away the goose bumps.

Was he Adam's father?

My God, you don't even know who fathered your child.

And she couldn't exactly ask Jake. She'd be humiliated and he'd be insulted.

"Thank you for coming." She didn't know what else to say. Jake's dark stare unnerved her, and she needed to fill the silence and ward off her increasing panic.

If she had her cell phone she'd have other people to

call. Wouldn't she? People who might have answers to fill the Swiss cheese of her memory. People who wouldn't inspect her like bacteria on a petri dish. But neither the paramedics nor the police had found her phone at the scene of the accident. She knew she owned one, a pink one, and that she hated it and planned to replace it as soon as her contract ended.

But she couldn't recall her little boy's age. Trying had given her an excruciating headache. The doctors had offered to give her an injection to kill the pain, but they'd warned it would knock her out. She couldn't sleep. She had to watch her son and be there for him if he needed her. Gulping down the terror clawing at her throat, she glanced at the chairs where he slept in a small ball.

Adam. Her heart. Her world. Her everything.

How could she know that and not recall when or where he'd been born?

The police officer who'd come to the hospital to take her statement had told her she was lucky to be alive—a driver had turned the wrong way down an exit ramp and hit Talia's sedan head-on. He'd also said that if Adam hadn't been in the backseat he probably wouldn't have survived since the passenger side had taken most of the impact.

Talia didn't remember anything about the wreck. The last thing she recalled was searching for an exit off Interstate 85—but not which exit—and then she'd awoken in an ambulance screaming for Adam. There was nothing in between. And she had no idea why she and Adam were in Atlanta when they lived two states away.

"Why me, Talia? Why call me after almost four years

of silence?" Jake asked in a deep, gravelly voice that resurrected her goose bumps.

Four years? Not lovers then. At least not currently. And not Adam's father if the doctors were right about her son's age.

So who was Jake Larson? He wasn't the kind of man a woman would ever forget. Why couldn't she remember him? "I don't know."

Disbelief twisted his lips. "I'm not buying that."

He thought she was lying, and for once, she wished she was. "It's all I have at the moment."

And it wasn't nearly enough. How could she protect her son if she couldn't identify friend from foe?

She needed to go home. And as soon as the doctor returned she'd tell him so.

CHAPTER TWO

"WE THINK WE'RE DEALING with some kind of dissociative amnesia," the disgustingly young resident told Jake an hour later. "That's when the patient blocks out a traumatic event. Murderers often use this as a defense, claiming they can't remember the crime. Sometimes molestation or rape victims repress memories in the same way because they can't handle what was done to them."

Talia gasped and the doctor held up his hand—a hand that bore no calluses, Jake noticed. "None of those possibilities fits your profile, Talia. There are no APBs or warrants out for your arrest and no missing-person reports. Our state police checked.

"A second choice is hysterical amnesia. It's pretty rare, but it's another version of blocking out unwanted memories or something too painful to recall."

"Which do you think she has?" Jake asked, trying to pinpoint the intern and wondering why the guy didn't realize Talia had to be faking it. C'mon. Amnesia?

"We're not sure. The first isn't usually a result of trauma. The second is. So is the trauma linked or totally separate? We don't know." He shrugged his narrow shoulders and stroked his peach-skinned jaw. "Whichever she has, it is extremely important to her recovery and her mental health to let her memories return on their own. We think they will, given time, but if they don't and the lack of memories impedes her daily functioning, then we have options."

"Like?" Jake prompted, hoping the guy would come up with something to get Jake off the babysitting hook.

"Hypnosis."

More psychobabble. Didn't these people practice real medicine? Jake believed in facts. And so far he'd been told Talia's "illness" was one that couldn't be proved or disproved by tests or X-rays, which in Jake's mind meant it didn't exist.

"Mommy!" the lump under the blankets shrieked, and Jake nearly jumped out of his steel-toed boots.

"I'm here, Adam."

The child sprang up, shoved off the blankets and scrambled to the floor, riveting Jake's attention. Talia's son climbed into bed and snuggled in his mother's arms. She hugged him, closed her eyes and buried her nose in his hair. The hand she stroked over the shiny locks trembled.

The boy looked like her. Same mouth, wavy hair and honey-toned skin. His chin was more square than round like Talia's. Jake's gut twisted with something that felt a lot like regret, but was more likely hunger pains. He'd missed lunch to come here.

The kid tolerated Talia's tight hold for a few seconds and then squirmed. "Need to go potty."

Talia's eyes widened and then she bit her lip and looked at the doctor, who pointed to Jake.

Jake jerked as if zapped by a hot wire.

"C-could you take him?" Talia asked.

He frowned at the doctor, who shook his head, and then Jake scanned the E.R. for an available nurse, orderly, anybody. Everyone was knee-deep in something else. Damn. "Where is it?"

The intern/resident/whatever pointed toward the end of the hall.

"Adam, go with Jake," Talia said in a wobbly voice.

"Stranger?" the boy warbled.

Talia hesitated. Her worried eyes flicked to Jake and then back to her son. "No. Friend."

"'Kay." The boy slid from the bed and shoved his tiny warm hand into Jake's. Jake startled at the trusting gesture, and then he started walking. Fast. But he couldn't outrun the kid skipping beside him or the memories riding his back of having others depend on him.

And letting them down.

TALIA'S GAZE fixed on the tall man and small child heading down the hall. A suffocating panic rose within her. She clutched the bedrails and fought the urge to run after them. Gulping air failed to ease the choking sensation in her throat.

She forced her attention back to her doctor. "I don't understand. Why can I remember so much, but forget the important facts?"

"The brain is powerful. It can block out things that are too painful for you to recall. My guess is there's something you don't want to remember."

Aghast, she blurted, "But I do want to remember. I *have* to remember."

"Systemized amnesia is a subcategory of dissociative amnesia. It targets one specific event or person."

Talia's gaze returned to the hallway, searching for the man she couldn't remember and the child she adored. Both had disappeared.

Did she have a reason to want to forget Jake Larson? If so, why was his name the only one in her wallet, and why was she in Atlanta where, according to the nurse, Jake lived?

Filled with a sense of desperation and frustrated by the blank screen in her mind, she said, "You mentioned hypnosis. Let's do that now."

The doctor shook his head. "First we need to give your memories time to return on their own."

"But I must have a job to return to…or family or something. I just want to replace my car and go home. Please. Sign me out."

"For your own safety I can't do that. And I wouldn't suggest making any major decisions, like purchasing a car, until we have a handle on the amnesia. I'd definitely advise you against driving home. Flying's probably not a good idea, either, because of the cabin-pressure changes."

"But I can't be trapped in Atlanta. I don't know anyone here."

"You know Mr. Larson."

Did she? The hammer in her head pounded harder.

"I need to go home," she repeated. She knew it deep inside even if she didn't know why. "We can take the train or a bus."

"And who would watch your son if something happened to you on the trip? With an injury like yours it pays to be cautious. Stay with us twenty-four hours. Take a few days to ease back into the normal activities of caring for yourself and your son, and see how it goes. If you don't have any problems by the end of the week then you can plan your trip home. Who knows? Maybe by then your memory will have returned and all of your questions might be answered."

But what if they weren't? What if a week or a month or a year from now she still had blank pages in her memory?

How could she care for her son? If she couldn't even remember his birthday, what else had she forgotten?

Trapped.

Jake watched the social worker walk down the hall, taking Jake's last chance of escape with her. He didn't want a houseguest. But what choice did he have unless he let Adam go to a group home? Not the place for a little kid who'd just had his cage rattled. Sure, the social worker claimed it would only be a temporary measure, but that's what they'd told Jake when they'd separated him from his brothers and sisters. Temporary had stretched into forever.

He turned his attention to the pale woman in the bed. Talia didn't look any more thrilled by the circumstances than he was. The pain and worry lines etched across her forehead and around her mouth had deepened in the past hour, but she'd repeatedly refused the medication the doctor had offered because she said she wanted to keep an eye on her kid.

The only way she'd get any relief was if Jake took the boy and left. Hell of a dilemma. Both choices sucked.

Frustrated, he stabbed a hand through his hair. "I'll take Adam tonight. And if the Raleigh police can't find anybody else by the time they release you tomorrow, I'll put you up for a couple of days."

Her expression told him she hadn't missed his reluctance. "We could go to a hotel."

"You heard what the doc said about that. Too risky."

She bit her lip and finger-combed the boy's hair. "I guess so."

Adam smiled up at her from the inflated-latex-glove balloon Jake had made him to keep him from getting antsy. The trust in the kid's eyes brought back memories Jake would just as soon forget. Memories of his younger brothers and sisters, who'd once looked at him with hero worship. "We'll come back midmorning. I have a couple of errands to run, but he can tag along."

"I—thank you." She hugged the child tightly. "Adam, you get to have a sleepover at Jake's tonight. Be good for him, okay?"

"'Kay."

And even though she forced a smile, Jake could see letting the kid go was tearing her apart.

Sympathy dampened his resentment. "He'll be fine."

She nodded carefully and her eyes filled.

He'd never seen Talia cry. He had to get out of here before the waterworks started. For the kid's sake. And his. He held out his hand. "Come on, squirt. Let's go for a ride."

"Not so fast," said the nurse. "You'll have to have a

car seat before you can take him. There's a baby store one block down. We'll wait."

He had a reprieve, but only a short one.

THE KID stuck like flypaper.

From the moment Jake had jerked awake Saturday morning to find a warm little body curled against his spine instead of in the guest room where he'd left Adam, through checking Talia out of the hospital after lunch, the kid had stayed glued to Jake's side. Adam didn't say much. Jake had no idea whether that was normal for the kid or the result of the wreck, but he'd bet the boy didn't miss much, either. Those big brown eyes, so like Talia's, had followed Jake's every move.

Could Adam be only two and a half? Had to be. If anybody would know, the hospital pediatrician would. Adam wasn't telling. Jake had asked. Five times.

As soon as Jake extricated the kid from the new car seat, Adam squirmed free, bounced from the SUV and clamped one tiny hand in a vice grip around two of Jake's fingers, forcing Jake to use his free hand to open Talia's door and help her out.

She placed her hand in Jake's, and the warm contact sent shockwaves of awareness through him. He throttled back his response. No sense in repeating history. Especially a scenario that had ended badly.

"I'm sorry you had to buy a new car seat. I'll reimburse you." Talia alighted carefully, never lifting her coffee-colored gaze above his chin.

He released her the second she looked steady on her

feet. "The hospital insisted. Said yours wasn't safe after the impact."

"No. I guess not." He almost hadn't returned after he left the hospital yesterday to get the car seat. Talia wasn't his responsibility anymore, and he didn't have the time or energy to deal with her or her son.

But for the sake of their past friendship, Jake had bought the seat and then taken Adam back to the shop. His office manager had watched the boy while Jake completed the delivery of the Viper.

Because he'd wanted to find some other sucker to assume responsibility for Talia and her kid, this morning he and Adam had swung by the impound lot to search Talia's wrecked car for a name, a telephone number, anything that would get him off the hook. But his plan had backfired. He hadn't found anything useful, not even her missing cell phone. And seeing the crumpled heap of metal had made him sick to his stomach. He might not want Talia back in his life, but seeing how close she and her kid had come to dying had rattled him.

He returned his attention to his unwanted guest. Talia's eyes looked huge in her pale face as she scanned his six-car garage and then his large brick house in the same wide-eyed way her son had yesterday.

So sue him. He had money and he flaunted it. His impressive house was about as far as he could get from the tiny Alabama shack he'd shared with his parents and four siblings. He'd hired a professional to turn the house into a showplace. And it looked good…even if it did feel like a pricey hotel.

Talia dampened her lips. "This doesn't look familiar."

"You've never been here."

Her shoulders sagged and her lids fluttered. With relief?

"I asked my housekeeper to swing by and leave dinner in the fridge."

Adam tugged Jake's fingers. "Kin I hab a peanut butter sammich?"

No surprise there. The boy was an eating machine. He'd asked for a sandwich for dinner last night and another for breakfast and lunch today. Cut in squares. Not triangles. Jake had forgotten how picky kids could be. And how cute. But he still didn't want one depending on him. "Sure."

"Jake."

He turned. Talia hadn't moved from beside his Escalade. She braced a hand on the door.

"I'm sorry we're being so much trouble. Thank you for taking us in and for dealing with my insurance company."

He had an ulterior motive. Dealing with the insurance company would shorten her stay as his guest. "No problem. Your car's a total loss. Nothing worth salvaging. I retrieved your luggage and personal effects. Everything's inside. The cop cleared that with you, right?"

"Yes. Thank you," she said in a quiet voice.

He nodded and headed up the herringbone-patterned brick walk. He didn't want her gratitude. He wanted her out of his life and back wherever she'd come from. But first he wanted to know why she'd had his name listed as the only emergency contact.

And why she'd left him.

After unlocking the front door, he shoved it open. The kid bolted for the kitchen.

"Adam— I'm sorry. He's not usually so forward."

"Quit apologizing."

"I'm sor—" She bit off the words when he scowled. "Look, it's obvious you don't want us here. I promise we'll get out of your way as soon as we can."

Damn. He was being an ass. But making nice was difficult when he *didn't* want her here and was almost certain she was lying about the amnesia thing. He expelled a breath. "Come in."

She stopped in his foyer and indicated the faded green scrubs the hospital had given her. "Would you mind if I showered and changed before we eat?"

Traces of blood still matted the hair by her temple. The hospital had cleaned her up only as much as necessary to tend her wounds. They'd missed a few spots. He shut down the images of her hurt, bleeding and unconscious as quickly as they formed.

"Your stuff's in the room at the top of the stairs. First door on the right. Can you manage by yourself?"

If she needed help, he'd have to call his housekeeper to make another unscheduled Saturday visit.

"I think so."

"There's an intercom in the bathroom. Use it if you have to. I'd better check on the kid." He pivoted on his heel and left her in the foyer, but walking away couldn't prevent the memories of Talia with water beading on her long lashes and streaming over her smooth skin from forcing themselves forward.

They'd been good together. Damned good.

So why in the hell had she left him? And for whom? He intended to find out.

JAKE LARSON clearly did not want her around.

Talia might have lost her memory, but she hadn't lost the ability to sense when she was unwelcome. And while Jake had been patient and kind with Adam, he'd been cool to her.

What had she done to earn that frosty attitude? She wanted to know and she planned to find out.

Holding tightly to the elaborately carved banister, she descended to the foyer. Jake's house was a testament to his success, an exquisitely decorated showplace done in neutral shades, from the richest cream to the darkest chocolate. But it was soulless. There wasn't a sign of his personality anywhere. Too bad. Clues to this man she used to know might have helped fill in some of the missing bits of her memory.

She couldn't delay facing her reluctant rescuer any longer. Adam had been bathed and tucked into bed. Getting him settled had taken her a little longer than usual because he had been excited about his morning with Jake and spending a second night in Jake's house.

Following the shaft of light through the darkened house, she located Jake's study. He sat behind a wide polished desk with a diagram of some sort spread in front of him. His concentration was so deep he hadn't noticed her.

She knocked on the open door and he jerked up his head. "Did you need something?"

"I wanted to reimburse you for the car seat." Waggling

her checkbook, she entered the room filled with tobacco-colored leather and dark wooden furniture.

"Forget it."

"Jake, car seats are expensive and—"

"Do I look like I'm short on cash?"

"I wasn't implying you were. But you don't need to bite my head off." She didn't want to argue. Her headache had subsided somewhat, but it was still nagging in the background. She'd simply leave the check where he'd find it when she went home. She sat down on the sofa facing his desk. "I was also hoping you'd tell me more about…us."

He sat back and folded his arms across his chest. His closed expression had her bracing herself. "You walked out without the courtesy of a goodbye. What more do you want to know?"

She flinched.

Jake's gaze dropped to her chest and desire darkened his eyes. His nostrils flared. The contrast between the barely veiled hostility of his words and a look that said he'd seen her naked and would like to again confused her.

She felt her nipples contract and glanced down at the checkbook clenched in her fingers. Only then did she realize her pale-yellow cotton shirt clung damply to her breasts, revealing their areolas and the lace pattern of her thin bra. Adam was quite a splasher, and he must have gotten her wet during his bath.

She folded her arms. But embarrassment wasn't the cause of the heat circulating through her veins. Desire flickered to life deep within her. She tried to ignore it. How could she get turned on by a look from a man she couldn't even remember? Until she recalled everything and everyone she'd forgotten there was no room for passion in her life. No matter how tempting.

"I, um…meant what was my job? And what kinds of things did we do when we were…together?"

The leather chair creaked as he sat back. "You heard the doctor. You need to remember on your own."

"Yes, but—"

"Talia, I'm not playing this game. You managed to fool the doctors, but you haven't fooled me."

Her stomach bottomed out. "Do you think I don't want to remember? Do you think I like not being able to take care of Adam? Or that I like forcing my company on someone who wishes I were anywhere else?"

His lips compressed. "Go to bed. I need to get these plans done."

Stymied, she slowly rose. If she wanted to remember their past, it looked like she was on her own.

"Adam!"

The cry jolted Jake awake. He blinked in the near darkness and tried to get his bearings. His room. His bed. Talia's voice.

And then he noticed the warmth against his back and turned his head. The boy lay curled in a ball atop Jake's comforter for the second night in a row.

"Adam, where are you?"

"He's in here," he called out. Adam didn't stir.

Talia appeared in his open doorway. The pale moonlight streaming through his window illuminated her nightgown-clad form. Jake never bothered to close the bedroom curtains. No point. An acre of thick pines separated him from his nearest neighbor.

"Thank heavens. I panicked when I couldn't find him." The hand she pressed to her chest accentuated the shape of her breasts as she jerked to a halt just inside his room. He'd once worshipped those breasts. Not anymore. But like a damned teenager, he couldn't keep his eyes off them.

He sat up and the sheet fell to his waist. Talia's gasp rent the air. Even in the near darkness he couldn't miss her gaze raking from his shoulders to the puddle of Egyptian cotton at his hips, and then she knotted her fingers at her waist and averted her face, revealing the bruise and the surgical tape.

You are one sick puppy to be lusting after the walking wounded, Larson.

"I'm sorry. Adam likes to nap with my father. I guess he thought you were a good substitute." Her eyes widened and sought his as if she'd just realized what she said.

She'd certainly snagged Jake's attention with her slip. "You remember your father?"

"Yes." She frowned. "I don't know why I couldn't before."

Yeah, right. "Remember anything else?"

Her teeth worried her bottom lip. "I think I remember his phone number."

He reached for the cordless phone. "Call him."

She looked at his digital alarm clock and then him. "It's three in the morning."

Was he being inconsiderate to wake the man in the

middle of the night? "The hospital said they sent the local police to your house to look for next of kin. If your father heard about that he needs to know where you are and that you're safe."

"But the police said my neighbors weren't home. So who would tell my father?"

"Just call him...unless you have a good reason not to."

Jake had to get them out of his house. Sharing dinner with Talia and Adam had brought back too many memories. Listening to the kid's giggles and squeals echoing through the house this evening had been distracting. He had designs to work on and a final episode to refine, damn it. And seeing Talia's damp, clinging T-shirt after Adam's bath had been agonizing for a guy who hadn't gotten laid in months.

He scratched his bristly jaw with his free hand. When had he become too busy for sex? God knows he'd had offers.

Talia approached slowly, stiffly, and he noticed a bruise on her shoulder that he hadn't seen before. She had to be in pain, but she hadn't said anything. "Are you taking the pain pills the doctor prescribed?"

"No. They make me feel foggy and hung over." She took the phone from him. Seconds ticked past. Seconds filled with memories of Talia sharing his bed. Back then when she'd stopped a foot shy of his mattress it had been to do a slow, alluring striptease for him. Her scent filled his nostrils. His body heated at the memories of how she'd driven him insane with her hands and mouth.

Finally, she dialed a number. Even from a yard away he could hear the loud tones bleating through the phone, followed by a recorded voice saying the number had been disconnected.

"Try again. You probably misdialed."

She did with the same results and then stared at the phone with a puzzled expression. "I know I'm dialing the right number. It's the same one he's had for years. I'm sure of it."

Jake took the receiver from her. He'd never met her father. Talia had said Mr. Rivera was too old-fashioned to accept them living together without a commitment, so she'd kept the men in her life apart. "What's his name and where does he live?"

Another hesitation. Was she yanking his chain? Dialing the wrong number on purpose?

"Carlos Rivera. Raleigh, North Carolina."

Jake dialed information, gave the name and city to the operator and received a robotic number no-longer-in-service message. He disconnected. "Would he be listed under anything else?"

Biting her lip, Talia shook her head and winced.

"You should take the pills."

"I can't. I need to be here for Adam."

"I'll cover the kid."

"I— Thank you, but no."

"It's ridiculous to hurt when you don't have to. I'll get you some Tylenol." He cradled the handset, flung back the covers, swung his legs over the side of the mattress and stood.

Talia stumbled back a step. Her rounded eyes examined Jake from his shoulders to his abs, his hips and down his legs. Her lips parted and her chest rose. When her eyes found his again the hunger in the dark depths hit him like a lightning bolt.

She stood within touching distance in his moonlit bedroom and he ached for her. Electricity filled the air between them. Jake reminded himself of the kid behind him and Talia's previous fickle behavior. The combo curbed his urge to reach for her.

Besides, his hunger wasn't because he needed *her*. Any attractive, available, half-naked woman standing within inches of his bed would elicit the same reaction. He could use a good screw right now.

"You've seen me in underwear before, Talia. And out of it."

She swallowed and ducked her chin, but not before he saw the panic flickering to life in her eyes. She wrapped her arms around her ribs, lifting her breasts and drawing the thin cotton fabric taut across her beaded nipples. Her breasts looked larger than before. Had pregnancy changed her body?

What do you care?

"I wish I could remember," she whispered.

If she was faking her faulty memory, and he was certain she was, then she deserved an award for that convincing crack in her voice.

"I'll carry Adam back to bed. The pain pills are in my bathroom cabinet. Help yourself." He scooped up the boy and strode down the darkened hall toward the guest room. The kid was a lightweight, but also a dead weight. Adam didn't even twitch with all the commotion going on around him. Jake remembered his youngest brother and sister sleeping the same comatose way and squelched the memory. No point in looking back.

Jake laid the kid in the middle of the queen-size mattress and covered him. Talia joined him a few moments later. In the absence of a nightlight she had left the adjacent bathroom light on and the door ajar.

"I had to put him in a regular bed when he turned two because he kept climbing out of his crib."

The smile and the love in her voice yanked at a different kind of hunger Jake would just as soon not acknowledge. Had his mother ever cared that much? He couldn't recollect hearing her use that tone or being there to tuck them into bed. She and his father sure as hell hadn't fought to get him back after social services took him away. But his parents hadn't released him for adoption, either. Not that a preteen was high on anybody's wish list.

He looked over his shoulder at Talia. The slash of light behind her clearly outlined her slender figure in the thin gown. Her attire couldn't be called seductive by any stretch of the imagination, but the shadow of her curves jarred him awake below the waist. Intentional? Was she out to resurrect what she'd killed by walking out? Not gonna happen.

He snapped upright as the words she'd just spoken penetrated his lust. "How long ago was that?"

Her soft smile morphed into a frown. "I don't know."

"Aw c'mon, Talia." He couldn't mask his irritation.

Her brow puckered. "I want to remember. I do. But I can't."

"Try harder."

Grimacing, she lifted a hand to rub her temple. A full minute passed. She crossed the room to tuck the covers around her son and then slowly straightened. "Maybe I'll wake up tomorrow and remember everything. The doctor said it could happen that way."

Her wistful tone grated. If Jake had any luck at all, her "lost" memory would return. If not, he'd be stuck with her until he could reach her father and then put Talia and Adam on a train bound for home. As for the amnesia thing, he was a seeing-is-believing kind of guy, and he'd seen nothing to persuade him she wasn't faking the whole deal. But what did she hope to gain with this farce?

"I have to work tomorrow." He had a hell of a lot to do. His crew was good, but he was the one who kept the cogs turning, and his was the mug that had to be in front of the camera. He didn't make the big bucks by sitting back and letting fate play the cards. "You'll have to keep the rug rat quiet."

"I will."

"The doctor said you couldn't be left alone, so Monday, if you're still here, you'll have to go to the shop with me while we shoot."

"Shoot?" Alarm rounded her eyes and mouth.

"The show."

Looking puzzled, she shrugged and shook her head. The usual flinch followed, as if her head hurt every time she moved it.

"I was in Hollywood signing the contracts for the TV show when you left." No flicker of recognition betrayed her charade.

Was it possible this wasn't a hoax? Nah. Had to be. Amnesia was too hokey to be real.

He massaged the knot in his neck. He'd been flattered and excited when the producer had approached him four-and-a-half years ago. What had started as a simple request to design a car for a movie had evolved into an offer for Jake's own show after Crandall had toured Larson Ltd.'s facility. Discussing the pros and cons with Talia had helped Jake make the decision to accept, and that decision had changed his life. How could she have forgotten the hours they'd lain in the dark talking after making love?

"I'm sorry." Her nails dug into her upper arms. "We weren't married or engaged or anything, were we?"

"I don't do marriage."

"But we were...involved?"

"We were lovers. We lived together almost a year."

Her lashes fluttered. "Why did I leave?"

"You tell me."

She sighed. "I wish I could."

He fisted his hands and fought the urge to reach for her, to comfort her. *To shake her.* This amnesia business was getting old. "It didn't take you long to replace me."

His bitter words sent her gaze rocketing to the sleeping child and her lips mashed into a thin quivering line. She took a deep breath, squeezed her eyes shut and then whispered, "He—he's not yours then? I mean, I heard what you said about me not calling for four years, but..."

A hesitant question instead of an accusation. If she wanted to milk his assets, wouldn't she have gone with the latter? Or was she more devious than that? "He's not mine if he's two-and-a-half."

"I'm sorry. I had to ask. I can't believe I can't remember who—" She put a fist to her mouth, bowed her head and studied her curled toes with what looked like genuine distress. Her shoulders shook with a ragged inhalation and then squared. "I'm going to remember."

But she didn't look convinced. Either this was the best acting job south of Broadway or Talia really had lost a chunk of her life. At three in the morning he was too tired to make the distinction and too likely to make a mistake if he took her into his arms and offered the comfort she looked like she needed, because for some damned fool reason he still desired her.

"Get some sleep." He turned and headed back toward his room. The more walls between them, the better.

"Jake?" Her voice, barely above a whisper, stopped him at the door. "I'm sorry I can't remember us."

The hell of it? So was he. But he sucked up his regrets and reminded himself she'd replaced him easily enough.

"Don't be. I would never have married you or given you the kid you obviously adore." And he had no right to be irritated that she'd found someone else who would. "Be glad you left, Talia. I am."

Now who was lying?

CHAPTER THREE

JAKE AVOIDED his guests until lunchtime, but that didn't mean he didn't know where they were every second of Sunday morning.

Talia and Adam had played quietly indoors and out, but Jake's radar had honed in on her like a LoJack tracking device. Talia was a distraction. Just one more reason to get rid of her.

After lunch he carried the bag of personal effects he'd retrieved from Talia's car to his den. She perched on the edge of the sofa with a magazine—one containing a big spread on Larson Ltd. "Ready to go through this stuff?"

Talia nodded hesitantly as if she were afraid of what she might discover. Or maybe her head still hurt. She set aside the magazine. "Now's a good time. Adam's down for his nap. Maybe something will trigger my memory and we can…get out of your way."

He bit back a curse. "I don't mean to make you feel unwelcome, but this is a pretty hectic time. I'm trying to finish the show's season plus keep up with my regular workload. After we wrap on Friday I'll have some downtime. If you haven't remembered everything by then or heard from your father or a friend, I'll drive you and Adam home."

And he'd leave them there in the care of anyone other than himself.

"Friday is longer than the two days you offered."

He shrugged his tense shoulders. "You're here. Adam's happy. And I still don't like the idea of you in a hotel room."

Jake upended the bag, pouring everything on the coffee table. The bits and pieces of standard car junk, toys and snacks hadn't told him anything when he'd hastily searched them for names and addresses yesterday. But the navigation system buried beneath the tissue box offered possibilities. He'd been so rattled by Talia's unexpected return and the necessity of bringing her into his home he'd forgotten about it. He picked up the handheld device and hit the on switch. Nothing happened. The batteries were dead.

He pawed through her junk until he located the charger. Just his luck. She had a DC adapter, but no AC. "You keep searching for clues here. I'm going to plug this into my car."

"Why?"

"If you used your navigation system on your trip then I can find out where you were headed, and then I can contact whoever was expecting you." Better yet, he could take them there and dump them.

Problem solved...except for finding out why she'd left him.

He loped outside and hopped into his Escalade. The sooner he had answers, the sooner she'd be gone.

Jake had installed plenty of high-end GPS models on the cars he'd customized, but he wasn't familiar with this particular budget brand. It took him a few minutes to figure out how the gizmo worked. Once he did, the destination on the screen punched the air from his lungs and knocked him back in his seat.

His office address.

Talia had been on her way to see *him*.

But why?

His first thought went to Adam. But the kid couldn't be his. The hospital staff said so. Jake shoved the image of the boy aside. But it nagged him like a loose wire.

Could the doctors and nurses be wrong about the kid's age? Nah. They'd assured him that teeth were a pretty reliable indicator at that age.

Next he considered money, fame or whatever it was women wanted from men with both. He'd never had trouble finding women, but since the show had taken off he'd had more than his share of attention.

Was that why Talia had looked him up now? Had she seen the article in *USA Today* reporting Jake had just inked a new five-year deal?

He grappled for other reasons Talia would look him up and recalled the bruises on her face, shoulder and wrist and the cut on her cheek. A sick feeling entered his stomach, quickly followed by a surge of anger.

The hospital had assumed Talia's cuts and bruises had been caused by the car accident. But what if they hadn't? Could she have been fleeing an abusive relationship?

Whoa, man, you're jumping to some pretty wild conclusions.

But as far as he knew, Talia didn't have any family other than her father, and Jake had been around the block enough times to know the legal system wasn't foolproof in domestic abuse situations. Restraining orders were only as reliable as the one ordered to be restrained, and jackasses who hit women weren't known for their intelligence or law-abiding habits.

Would Talia have considered Jake a safe harbor?

He yanked the GPS cord from his power outlet and headed back into the house. He wanted answers and he wanted them now.

That nagging feeling made him detour up the back stairs to the boy's bedroom. In the dim sunlight seeping through the gap in the closed curtains he examined Adam's face. The kid was pure Talia in the shape of his eyes, nose and mouth. Even his eyebrows arched like hers. Sure, Jake had brown hair and eyes too, but his weren't the same shade as theirs, and his hair was stick-straight, not wavy.

Once in a while something Adam said or did reminded him of his youngest brother, Ricky. But that was just Adam's age.

For the first time Jake wished he had baby pictures of himself to confirm the boy wasn't his and put his mind at rest. But he had none. His parents hadn't taken many pictures and who knew where the ones they had taken were now?

No, Jake decided. The doctors had to be right about Adam's age and that meant the kid wasn't his. He sure as hell didn't want him to be. He jogged down the front stairs to confront Talia. She looked up from the sofa when he entered the den, and the lost look on her face told him she hadn't had any luck with the items from the car.

"None of this triggered anything. Not a person, not a place, not a thing to tell me where I was going or to whom."

"Me. You were coming to see me. My office address was programmed into your navigation system. Why?"

She gasped. "I—I don't know."

The confusion in her eyes combined with the color draining from her face took him aback. No one could fake that pallor. Which meant Talia wasn't lying about the amnesia.

Holy spit.

He crossed the room, sat beside her and grasped her chin, angling her face to inspect the cut and swelling on her cheekbone. A fist could have done this just as easily as an airbag deploying. He ought to know. He'd been punched around by other kids in foster care until he'd learned to fight back.

"The bruises and cuts, are they from your accident or before?"

Her brow puckered. "Before?"

He lowered his hand. "Talia, did someone hit you? A boyfriend? Adam's father? Your father?"

Her fingers flew to the surgical tape on her cheek. "I don't think so. I would remember that. Wouldn't I?" Her hand dropped to her lap and fisted. "Why can't I remember? Adam needs me to remember. If I can't, how can I keep him safe?"

The sharp edge of panic in her voice cut deep. Against his better judgment, Jake pulled her into his arms. "You are safe, and as long as you're here with me, nothing is going to happen to either of you."

Talia hugged his middle, fitting against him just like the old days. Her breasts pressed his chest, her thigh, his leg. Her head tucked beneath his chin and her scent filled his nostrils. Jake's body rumbled to life.

She'd always been physically affectionate, and it had been hard for him to adapt to her frequent hugs after a lifetime without them.

He hissed a breath through clenched teeth and peeled her off one inch at a time. It wasn't easy to do when every cell in his body wanted to cling and his mouth hungered for a taste of her. She might claim she wasn't able to remember how explosive they'd been together, but he hadn't been able to forget. God knows he'd tried.

He shot to his feet. He had to find a way to jar her memories. And the best way to do that was to go back to the beginning.

"I have to get back to work. Come and get me when Adam wakes up. We'll go to the park."

"I'VE BEEN to Tanyard Creek Park before." Talia's eyes didn't stray from Adam on the playground, but she could feel Jake's gaze on her profile as well as she could the hot, humid evening air.

"You remember?"

She turned her head. His assessing expression confirmed her suspicions. "No. But you're watching and waiting as if you expect me to. Did I come here often?"

He exhaled slowly. "We came together. You liked watching people play with their dogs."

She strained for something, *anything,* and found nothing. "I don't think I have a dog."

He shifted on his feet and angled his face toward Adam, who played happily in the sand with the toy truck Jake had retrieved from her wrecked car. Jake's tense muscles practically screamed frustration.

"What do you know?" she prompted, and grasped his bicep. His skin was hot to the touch beneath the cuff of his polo shirt. She let him go. "For pity's sake, Jake, I realize the doctor said to let me remember on my own, but please, tell me if you know something. Do you think I like living in a black hole?"

His gaze hit hers, direct and alert. "You told me your father was allergic to dogs."

She didn't remember, but it sounded...reasonable. A welcome breeze stirred her hair, cooling her overheated skin. She lifted her hair off her nape. "Maybe I'm on vacation. But if I am, I wasn't expecting us to be gone long."

Jake lifted his eyebrow in a silent question.

"There are only a few days' worth of clothing and toiletries for Adam and me in my suitcase."

The dappled shade on the opposite side of the clearing beckoned. A wisp of something too vague to see drifted like a ghost across her consciousness and then evaporated. Keeping an eye on Adam, she strolled around the edge of the play area. Jake followed. When she stopped at a picnic table his posture stiffened and his eyes narrowed.

She dragged her fingertips over the rough wood and sat on the bench. "Tell me why this spot drew me."

His nostrils flared and his pupils expanded. "We shared our first kiss here. At this table. After your office picnic."

Her breath stalled in her chest. She searched his face and dark eyes for answers. Why couldn't she remember? She closed her eyes and tried harder, but it was like trying to catch a cloud.

The bench depressed beneath her and then a warm mouth covered hers. Startled, she opened her eyes. Jake's face was so close to hers he was out of focus. His hands caught her waist, holding her in place while his lips brushed back and forth in slow, gentle sweeps.

Desire, hot, urgent, sensual and familiar, rolled through her. Kissing him felt good. Right. Her lashes drifted shut and a whimper of pleasure bubbled up her throat. She lifted her hand to touch his face, but Jake raised his head abruptly and stood before she made contact.

His gaze probed hers. "Remember now?"

His husky voice made her pulse race. Her lips tingled. But her mind was a blank movie screen—all white space. Disappointment weighted her shoulders. Why couldn't she retrieve memories of the two of them? Jake must have been important to her at one time. "No."

And then a sobering jolt of guilt erased the arousal. Did she even have the right to kiss him? "We can't do that again. Not until I know whether or not I'm committed to someone else."

Jake's eyes tracked her thumb's fidgety sweep over her bare ring finger. He expelled a rough breath.

"I'm not making a pass. I'm trying to prod your memory. Don't attach any significance to the kiss. It meant nothing."

To him, maybe. But to her it meant she'd willingly let go of something good. Why would she have done something so foolish?

JAKE LARSON might be fully clothed, but Talia saw him naked. Blame it on Sunday evening's kiss.

She wrapped her cold hands around her overheated middle and wished the memories of being his lover had stayed lost in the black hole of her brain. No such luck.

Almost as soon as she'd fallen asleep last night she'd started dreaming, and those Technicolor visions of being Jake's lover had been far too real to be fantasy. She'd awoken this morning hot and bothered, wet and breathless and aching. For Jake. Not a great way to start the week.

She could recall his taste, his scent, the textures of his skin and hair and tongue, and a multitude of other sensory details as vividly as if she'd climbed from his bed hours ago instead of the one in his guest room. She wiped damp palms against her hips.

Why, oh, why had she voluntarily left that passion behind? Had she come to Atlanta to rekindle their affair?

Shoving away the unwanted erotic thoughts, she focused on Jake through the wide office window overlooking the garage area. He looked confident and sexy and right at home in his khaki pants and black polo—apparently his show uniform. From what she could see on the six screens on the console beside her, the camera adored every line of his handsome face and tall, muscled frame, and audio only enhanced the resonance of his deep, magnetic voice.

Falling in love with him would have been all too easy,

and she must have loved him or she never would have shared his home or his bed. She knew that much about herself. Or thought she did. The rest…wouldn't come. She stifled a frustrated groan.

"Look, Mommy," Adam said for the umpteenth time. He stood on the leather sofa pushed up against the plate glass, his stubby finger pointing to yet another tool used in supercharging the car Jake worked on. Her son's wide-eyed gaze remained riveted on Jake, his crew and the assortment of cameramen moving around the hoisted coupe with the grace and timing of choreographed dancers.

A wisp of memory teased her, drifting across her brain like a specter. A blue car? But Jake stood beneath a red one. She tried to chase the murky thought, but it vanished.

"See that?"

"I see." She smoothed Adam's hair.

Her son loved anything automotive. But then what boy didn't? There was no genetic link to Jake's passion for cars, just as there was no connection in the similarity of Adam and Jake's hair color. She wished there was, if for no other reason than she hated being adrift. But that would mean she'd kept Jake from his son, and she couldn't bear knowing she'd done something so selfish.

"And cut," the guy beside her said into his microphone headset. "That was great, Jake. We'll break and finish up after lunch."

Jake looked at the window. Adam bounced up and down, waving frantically. Slowly Jake lifted his hand—a hand Talia now knew had touched her intimately, skillfully. As if he read her thoughts, Jake's gaze collided with hers and held. Her pulse and breathing quickened. Her skin tightened. She may have forgotten parts of her life, but she hadn't forgotten what sexual chemistry felt like. And Jake Larson evoked it in spades. She wished he didn't.

But regardless, she couldn't act on the attraction until she knew she wasn't committed to someone else. Did she have someone she loved and shared mornings with the way she had with Jake the past two days?

Adam's father, for example. Was she still involved with him? If so, why wasn't he searching for them? The police knew where to find her if anyone filed a missing-person report. But so far, the police hadn't come knocking. Even if she'd broken up with Adam's father, surely he'd want to keep tabs on his son?

Did he even know about Adam? He must. She wouldn't keep a secret like that. Not unless she had good reason. Like fearing for Adam's safety. She touched her wounded cheek. Could Jake be right? Had she fled an ugly relationship? She didn't think so.

And Adam hadn't asked for his father, not once, a niggling voice reminded her. Wasn't that unusual?

She had too many questions and so few answers.

Jake said something to the man beside him and then strode toward the office. The door opened. Adam scrambled off the sofa and across the room, where he held up his arms in a plea. After a second's hesitation, Jake picked him up and smiled at him.

Talia's heart stuttered. They looked so right together, which made her sudden urge to rip her son from Jake's arms all the more irrational. Apprehension knotted her stomach. What was her brain hiding? And why?

"Let's grab some lunch," Jake said.

"Kin I had 'nother peanut butter sammich?" Adam warbled.

"I don't know if they have peanut butter, kid."

Talia chuckled. "That's his generic phrase to describe anything between two pieces of bread. He'll eat other foods."

Jake's gaze sharpened and probed hers, that lone eyebrow lifting in question. Her breath caught when she realized she'd remembered something else. She waited for more to follow, but nothing did.

How could she remember Adam's food foibles but not his father?

"That's all I recall other than a flash of a blue car earlier." She wasn't about to tell Jake she'd remembered his talent in bed. Her entire body flushed and tingled.

"Your boss's car." Jake shoved open the office door and stalked outside toward his SUV.

Talia raced after him. The sweltering heat and high humidity instantly produced a sheen on her skin. "What do you mean? What boss? You know my boss?"

"Knew," he called over his shoulder as he leaned in and settled Adam in his car seat.

Talia experienced a strange urge to caress his behind. She shoved her hands behind her back. If her dreams were any indication, she'd once had the right to do exactly that to Jake and she'd been bold enough to.

He turned and caught her ogling. Her cheeks caught fire and his eyes narrowed suspiciously before taking in her short-sleeved apricot V-necked top and white linen pants in a slow, pulse-accelerating sweep.

"I knew your boss when you worked in Atlanta. You and I met when I customized his blue Ferrari. He was always in surgery. You handled most of my calls and even some test drives."

"I worked for a surgeon?"

"An orthopedic surgeon." A rapid tapping on the office window drew his attention. He tossed her the keys. "Start the engine and the air conditioning. I'll be right back."

She could cool the car. But what about her memories? Those were hotter than Georgia in July, and judging by Jake's expression, just as unwelcome as a heat wave.

"WHAT do you have?" Jake asked Martha, his office manager.

"I didn't find a phone number or address for Talia's father, but I found this on the Internet." Martha handed him a sheet fresh off the printer.

An obituary column from the Raleigh paper. For Carlos Rivera. Jake scanned the text until he reached the "survived by" part to make sure she had the right Rivera. His gut dropped like a two-ton jack, and he stared out the window at the woman in his car. Talia had been very close to her father and had called him at least twice a week during the time she'd shared Jake's condo.

"Did you show her this?"

"No. You said to give whatever I found to you."

Martha could find a sand flea on a mummy's butt. She was even better at locating obscure car parts.

"Good job." He laid the obit on the desk and dug in

his wallet for the business card the doctor had given him flipping open his cell phone. Jake dialed and reached voice mail. After identifying himself he said, "Talia Rivera's father died two weeks ago. Could be that's what she's blocking. I need to know how to break it to her."

He left his number and then looked at Martha. "I'm taking them to lunch and then the cell phone store to see if she can remember which provider she uses. I'll be back to finish up."

Jake strode to the car. He couldn't send Talia back to her father, but if he helped her replace her phone, then maybe one of her friends would call and take her and Adam off his hands.

He had to get rid of them. Because, as attracted as he might be to Talia Rivera, he lived by three firm, fast rules. He didn't do women with children. He didn't repeat his mistakes. And when someone left him he cut them loose. It was easier that way. What good were people who claimed they loved you if you couldn't count on them to stick around?

Like his family. Like his foster parents. Like Talia.

Jake considered last night's kiss in the park to be one of the flat-out dumbest things he'd ever done. Damned if it hadn't revived the craving he'd been certain Talia's cowardly decampment had cured.

He climbed into his SUV. Her scent and her welcoming smile hit him with a flashback of happier times—the nights she'd greeted him at his front door wearing a sinful piece of lingerie or better yet, nothing at all. His entry hall had seen almost as much action as his bedroom.

He crushed the images and debated telling Talia about her father, but the kid in his rearview mirror sealed his lips. Did Adam know his grandfather was dead? Could a two-year-old even fathom death? Probably not. Would Talia have a meltdown? She'd never been the type to get overly emotional before.

But then he'd never thought her the type to bail without explanation, either. Had he known her at all?

Jake's phone rang five minutes later as he opened the door to the restaurant. He checked the number. The doctor's. "Get us a table. I have to take this call."

He answered as soon as the heavy glass door closed between them. "How do I tell her?"

"You don't," the intern said. "The amnesia is a self-protective mechanism. Her body isn't able to handle whatever she's blocking. I can't stress enough that we need to let Talia's memories return spontaneously."

Not what he wanted to hear. "What if I tell her anyway?"

"I'm not sure what will happen. If you're correct and losing her father is what triggered this, then the shock could be traumatic. She could have a more serious breakdown. Has she remembered anything else?"

Frustrated, Jake scrubbed his jaw. "Bits and pieces. Small stuff."

"Then she's making progress. Try to be patient. If she doesn't have a significant amount of recovery before her clinic appointment in two weeks, I'll refer you to a colleague who can try hypnosis. He'll attempt to uncover the memories in a safe, protected setting. In the meantime, you can *gently* evoke memories of innocuous things by serving her favorite foods or buying her favorite flowers. But avoid the big hairy deals."

"Big hairy deals? Is that medical jargon?" Jake couldn't keep the sarcasm and irritation from his voice, and the kid-doc had the nerve to chuckle. "And how am I supposed to know the difference?"

"Go easy on her. Avoid anything that might be painful for her to recall. Focus on the good stuff. Page me if she has problems, but otherwise, take it easy and don't jeopardize her mental health by feeding her information she isn't ready to process."

The good stuff. There'd been a lot of that. Until she left.

The dial tone sounded before Jake could argue he had no intention of keeping Talia around for a couple of weeks. He sure as hell wasn't going to buy her flowers and give her the mistaken impression that he welcomed her back into his life. Maybe reminding her of the couple they used to be would jog her memory of why she'd left and whatever came afterward. But that's what he'd been doing with the trip to the park and that kiss. The one that shouldn't have happened.

He stared across the parking lot at his vehicle, his means of escape, and debated taking the easy way out. But there was a chance that something he'd done had driven Talia away and he wanted to know what it was. He also had her current safety to consider. He couldn't send her back into a hazardous situation, although now it looked less like domestic abuse and more as if she just didn't want to remember losing her father.

He strode inside, found Talia and Adam's table and sat

in an empty chair across from her. She pushed a glass in his direction. Lemonade. How could she remember something as unimportant as his drink preference and not remember her father had died?

The truth hovered on his lips. But as much as he'd cursed and hated Talia for dumping him in such a cowardly manner, he wouldn't risk her well-being. And he sure as hell didn't want to be responsible for her son's. Revealing the truth would have to wait.

But that didn't mean he wouldn't use the week ahead to nudge her memories along.

CHAPTER FOUR

TALIA STARED at the new cell phone on the tabletop and willed it to ring. It stubbornly remained silent.

Why hadn't her father or someone called? It was Monday. She was almost certain she had a job, but she couldn't remember where or for whom she worked. With only three days' worth of clothing in her suitcase, hadn't she expected to be at work today? But she hadn't shown up. Why hadn't someone called to check on her? Didn't she have any friends?

When panic threatened to choke her she tried to comfort herself with the knowledge that she was still making progress. Earlier, Jake had asked for the name of her cellular provider, and the answer had instantly rolled from her tongue. So had her cell number.

But the scanty random fragments weren't enough. She needed more and she needed it *now*.

From her makeshift desk in the corner of Martha's well-appointed domain, Talia glanced through the partially open door of Jake's private office to check on Adam and found him still napping on the black leather sofa. Her child could sleep anywhere. She knew that, but not when or with whom he'd been conceived.

Pushing that disturbing thought aside, she redirected her attention to the job Martha had given her—sorting Jake's mail into two categories: personal letters and requests for car makeovers. Talia knew it was busy work to keep her out of the way, but she didn't mind. It kept her from dwelling on the ether between her ears.

Sorting required reading and the explicit content of several of the personal letters made her blush and gave her indigestion.

A heavily scented letter signed with a red lipstick kiss made her grimace. Jake had quite a fan club. There were offers of sex, marriage proposals and requests for him to father children. And there were pictures. Pictures of scantily clad women who wanted Jake Larson—and not to work on their cars.

Was her stomach churning caused by jealousy? Jealousy implied she still had feelings for Jake beyond lust. If so, then why had she left him? Had he hurt her? His barely suppressed rage when he'd asked her if someone had hit her implied he'd never physically injure a woman, but had he hurt her emotionally? Had she believed leaving him would be less painful than staying with him?

Had Adam's father been a rebound romance?

She shook off her questions, turned to Martha and pointed to the growing stack of personal mail. "Will Jake answer all of these? Some of them are quite…interesting."

Translation: disgusting and desperate.

The office manager nodded. "Every letter gets a reply, but most will only get an autographed photo. Jake will decide who gets what."

Jake. It all came back to Jake. If not for him taking them in, where would she and Adam be right now? She owed him.

The window overlooking the garage drew Talia the way a fresh bloom does bees. Her gaze collided with Jake's and her pulse hiccupped. The call he'd received before lunch had bothered him. He'd been quiet and vigilant ever since, and there was a stiffness in his shoulders this afternoon that hadn't been there earlier.

Had the call been about her? Was that why he looked through the window every time the camera stopped rolling?

What had happened to them four years ago?

If she remembered nothing else before Jake drove her and Adam home on Saturday, she absolutely had to know that. Because the rapid beat of her heart and the warm flush beneath her skin each time their eyes met told her that no matter who or what had come between them, she'd never completely gotten over Jake Larson.

GET HER memory back and get her out of your space before you start breaking rules.

Jake eyed Talia as he loaded the last of the dinner dishes into the dishwasher. The hum of awareness arced between them as it had throughout dinner. His gaze drifted from her face to the curve of her breasts, her waist and hips. Hunger gnawed at him despite his full stomach.

He wanted her. Damn it.

He winched his thoughts back in line. How could he do what the doctor ordered and focus on the good stuff without remembering that one of the best parts of his and Talia's relationship had been the blistering hot anytime/anywhere sex?

In the twenty-eight hours since Sunday night's kiss he hadn't been able to think about anything else. But unless he broke all three of his rules, a return to the sheets with Talia wasn't in the cards.

He wasn't disappointed. *Liar.*

All right, he was. But he'd get over it.

"Did we prepare meals together in the past like we did tonight?" Talia stood in front of the sink with a cutting board in one hand and a soapy sponge in the other. She looked up at him through her thick lashes and the impact of her gaze siphoned the air from his lungs.

"Dinner. My condo kitchen was about a quarter the size of this one. We did a lot of bumping into each other." And the frequent contact had resulted in them postponing the meal to get naked on more than one occasion. She'd end up naked on the counter or the kitchen table. Hell, they'd even made love on his floor. She'd made him get on the bottom and he hadn't minded the cold tile one bit.

His pulse accelerated. Damn it. He reminded himself of the kid sleeping upstairs—a kid who belonged to someone else. It cooled his blood, but only marginally. "You liked to cook, and you were good at it."

She'd been good at a lot of things.

Like leaving, the voice in his head insisted.

Talia rinsed the cutting board, set it in the drain rack and lifted a chef's knife from the soapy water. She weighed it in her open palm. "This feels comfortable. Familiar."

Go easy on her, the doctor had said. But how could Jake take it easy and get what he needed? If she was blocking her father's death, then prompting her memories of them as a couple shouldn't cause a crisis.

"It ought to. You brought that knife with you the first time you cooked for me. The next day you and your kitchen utensils moved in." Because he hadn't wanted to waste time driving across town to her place when he could come home from work and take her straight to bed.

"Chinese food was your favorite because you claimed it was the only way you could get me to eat my veggies." They'd made beef and vegetable lo mien tonight.

The sponge stilled. Her fingers tightened around it and water streamed into the sink. She stared at the darkened window.

Jake leaned on the counter beside her. "Do you remember?"

A blush climbed her neck and stained her cheeks. The quickening rise and fall of her breasts drew Jake's gaze and his own respiratory rate increased. "Talia?"

She looked at him and the passion smoldering in her eyes knocked him sideways. His hunger swelled. It wasn't the only thing.

Don't do it.

He reached for her.

Don't do it.

Don't—

The familiar taste of her mouth welcomed him, as did the feel of her in his arms and the instantaneous lick of desire. Her lips were as soft and warm as ever, but the superficial kiss wasn't enough. Cradling her uninjured cheek, he plunged his tongue past her lips and delved deeper into the recesses of her mouth, into her slick, satiny heat.

He slid his fingers through her silky hair and gently tugged. Her head tipped back and her tongue twined with his. He vaguely registered dampness on his waist as her arms surrounded him, but he was more interested in the press of her soft flesh to his torso. His blood roared and need clawed through him. He buffed her spine, her waist, and cupped her bottom.

Talia's fingers dug into his back. She shifted restlessly and her belly brushed his groin. His head snapped back. He sucked a sharp breath as a bolt of desire ripped through him, making him grit his teeth. He stared into her flushed face. "How can you forget that?"

Her lids, slumberous and sexy, fluttered open. He couldn't resist another quick sip from her mouth, which only led to a second and a third. He struggled to rein himself in. It wasn't easy. It never had been with Talia.

She spread her palms on his chest and her warmth permeated the thin barrier of his shirt. "Last night I dreamed about…being with you. I remembered your bed and… and a shower, but not cooking dinner."

Snapshots of memories crowded his brain as if she'd called them forth. Memories of hot, wet, slippery sex, tangled sheets, pillows and covers tossed to the floor. His bed and shower had gotten a lot of use and not just the traditional sleeping/bathing variety.

Jake fisted his hands. He could be smart, walk away and gain nothing. Or he could gamble and hope acting on her memories prompted more, which could possibly result in getting her out of his house and exorcising a few of his own ghosts.

But he had rules for a reason, and breaking them could embroil him in something he wanted no part of.

Talia's eyes squeezed shut and the fingers on his chest fisted. "I hate this. I hate not knowing. I hate that I've forgotten the people and places that are important to me."

If she'd been playing the pity card he could have pushed her away. But all he heard was frustration and fear.

"You haven't forgotten Adam. He's the one who matters most." He dragged a knuckle along her uninjured cheek. His pulse throbbed low and heavy.

Aw, hell. He'd never been one to play it safe. "Let me help you remember the rest, Talia."

It took a second for his meaning to sink in and then her eyes widened and her lips parted. "What if…what if there's someone else? At home. Waiting for me."

Her question hit him like a fist in the gut. He'd never been a poacher and he didn't share his women. The idea of her with someone else—

You know she's been with someone else. She had his kid.

But no one had called her and she'd had no voice mails waiting on her cell phone account. "Do you believe there is?"

She briefly closed her eyes and then shook her head. "I don't think I could feel this much with you if I had someone special at home."

He had no explanation for the relief coursing through him, and he sure as hell didn't have the right to feel it.

"Talia, before we do this you need to know nothing has changed. I'm still not interested in marriage or children. Whether your memory returns or not, I'm taking you home the first chance I get. And I'm going to leave you there."

Leaving her first was the only way he could guarantee she wouldn't bail on him again.

SINCE HER brain wouldn't tell her what to do, Talia had to trust her body. Her racing heart, shortened breaths and the fizz of arousal bubbling through her veins told her she might find the answers she craved in Jake's arms.

She took a leap of faith. "I—I'm okay with whatever you can give me, Jake."

Jake traced the bruise on her left upper arm and then skimmed to the one on her wrist with a featherlight touch that plowed goose bumps to the surface. He lifted her hand and brushed a thumb across her empty ring finger. "I don't want to hurt you."

She raised her chin and met his gaze. He cared. No matter what he said, she could see the concern mingling with the desire in his eyes. And right now his caring meant more to her than anything. Jake might push her away with his words, but his protective actions drew her nearer.

"I won't let you hurt me." For Adam's sake, she couldn't afford to. But she needed her memory back and she was convinced Jake held the key. In his touch. In his kisses. In his lovemaking.

Before she could question the wisdom of her decision Jake's mouth covered hers. Though he cradled her waist and nape gently, the raw passion of his kiss held nothing back. His unleashed hunger bent her head back and exhumed an answering response from deep within her. Talia latched on to the familiarity of her response, hoping to uncover more.

When no new memories raced forward to greet her, she mapped his body with her hands, relearning the shape of his muscled chest, the rasp of his evening beard and the texture of his thick hair.

He abruptly lifted his head and glanced at their reflection in the uncurtained window and French doors overlooking his back deck. "Not here."

He laced his fingers through hers and towed her to the foyer and up the stairs. Each step multiplied her excitement. He didn't turn on a lamp in his bedroom and only the pale moonlight streaming through the windows illuminated the space.

By the time he stopped beside his wide bed and released her, she shook with anticipation. He reached for the hem of his shirt, fisting the fabric and then pulling it over his head in an impressive display of well-defined abs and corded shoulders and arms. Had he always been this muscular?

Talia fingered the top button of her shirt with an unsteady hand.

"Let me." His hands brushed hers aside, skimmed down her torso to tug her shirttails free. His palms slipped beneath the cotton to grip her waist. The contact burned her skin for several heart-pounding seconds before he released her and eased the bottom button free. He slowly worked his way up. Cool air and warm knuckles brushed over her, making her breath hitch with each touch. Finally, he nudged the fabric apart and eased it over her shoulders, being careful not to jar her tender left side.

Her bra wasn't anything special, just basic white cotton with a touch of lace, but that didn't stop Jake from devouring her with his eyes. Her breasts swelled on a shaky indrawn breath. Had she worn sexy lingerie for him in the past? Nothing in her suitcase was remotely alluring. Did she have tantalizing pieces in her drawer at home?

He tossed her shirt aside and hooked two fingers behind her waistband and reeled her closer. She removed her bra and dropped it. A flick of his thumb and a scrape of a zipper and her pants parted. He eased her pants and panties over her hips and knelt in front of her to remove her sneakers and pull her clothing over her ankles. She braced her arms on his wide shoulders and kneaded his supple skin. His breath dusted her belly, leaving a coating of heat in its wake, and the tickle of his spiky hair against her navel elicited a shiver of desire rather than laughter.

He sat back on his haunches and looked up at her. She felt no shyness, no urge to cover herself. Jake had seen her nude before. Touched her before. Made love to her before. And this felt right.

He rose slowly, his big hands loosening his belt as he backed into the shadows in the corner. The leather chair creaked as he sat and again when he bent to untie, unlace and remove his work boots. She could barely hear the swish of his laces over her pounding heart.

She dampened her dry lips and watched his swift, precise movements. Had they shared this ritual before? They'd lived together, so they must have.

When his boots were out of the way he stood and made quick work of shedding his khakis and underwear. The lean, muscled lines of his body mesmerized her. She must have seen him like this a hundred times, but tonight everything was new and different.

Maybe it was the light and shade cast by the moonlight or the lack of memories, but whatever it was, her fingertips tingled with the need to touch him, trace the dark line of hair bisecting his chest, stroke his thick length, tangle her fingers in the wiry curls at the base of his shaft and cup the tender flesh below. She ached to press herself flush against him, to feel his hair-roughened skin against the smoothness of hers.

He closed the distance between them and pulled her into his arms, granting her unspoken wish. His body blanketed her with heat and his mouth consumed hers. Her belly cradled his erection and his hard thighs flanked hers.

Willing to go wherever this ride took her, she held tight to his waist and kissed him back. And as much as she relished the present and the passion he ignited, she hoped his lovemaking would take her back to the past.

He nudged her toward the bed with the steady press of his hips and she went eagerly. He broke the kiss to sweep back the comforter. Talia climbed onto the cool sheets and scooted to the middle of the mattress without looking away from Jake's intense gaze.

He planted a knee on the bed between her legs. When

he leaned forward his erection nudged her intimately, making her core tighten. She arched her back and moved against him. Winding her arms around his torso, she pulled him forward. He planted a hand on either side of her head and lowered ever so slowly until he hovered just above her. She wanted more and tugged. His hot skin seared her.

He stopped an inch shy of her lips. "Remember?"

No!

"I'm trying," she whispered, not wanting to break the spell. But the sensations inundating her didn't allow room for memories.

"See if this works." His elbows bent. He captured a nipple between his teeth and tugged gently. The sharp not-quite-painful nip made her gasp, and then his mouth opened over her and he laved her with the hot, moist stroke of his tongue. The suction of his mouth cast a net of need deep within her, but it didn't drag any memories to the surface. She tangled her fingers in his short hair and whispered words of encouragement.

He shifted to her right side. His hand cupped her other breast, rolled her nipple and made her moan at the twist of sensation low in her abdomen before he caressed his way downward to trace her bikini line and below. He combed through her curls and found her slick flesh deftly, accurately.

The surety and swiftness with which he found her pleasure points attested he'd driven her wild with wanting before. He read her body like an old, familiar book, knowing exactly how to touch her and when to pause to leave her clinging breathlessly to the edge of release. Her hips lifted to meet each stroke, silently begging him to fill the emptiness he created and take her over. But Jake seemed determined to deny her.

When she thought she'd tear his hair out in frustration he rolled to his side and reached for the bedside table. He returned with a condom.

A condom. That didn't feel right. "Did we use condoms before?"

"No." One tightly ground out word. "You were on the pill."

Seconds later he'd sheathed himself and moved above her. At that moment her memory wasn't nearly as important as having him inside her. She opened her arms and legs in welcome and guided him home. His thick tip nudged her and then sank deep, deep enough to force his name from her lungs in a rush of air.

Talia smoothed her hands over his back, savoring his supple skin and shifting muscles. She cupped his bottom and pulled him back each time he withdrew. Her lips found his jaw, his neck, his shoulder. He smelled familiar, tasted familiar.

But the rest of her memories just wouldn't come.

She hugged him tighter and squeezed him with her internal muscles, trying to hold on, trying to reach her past and the peak before he left her again. As if he understood her struggle, Jake's tempo increased. He thrust faster, harder, deeper until Talia tumbled over and over in a breathless whirlwind of sensation.

Before she could recover, the muscles of his face strained. He stiffened, bowed his back and pulsed inside her with a muffled groan. Seconds later his lids lifted, and his gaze locked on hers. That dark brow arched, silently questioning.

Still winded, she reluctantly shook her head.

As an exercise in memory retrieval, making love had been almost a complete failure. But at the same time it had raised one very important question.

Had she ever stopped loving Jake Larson?

CHAPTER FIVE

MISTAKE. *Big* mistake.

Jake stared into the bathroom mirror. He hadn't exorcised any ghosts. But he had resurrected a few demons he'd just as soon not have riding his back.

He'd never wanted or trusted anybody as much as he had Talia. And she'd let him down. Trusting her again was a bad idea, and if sex hadn't prompted any of her memories, then he had no reason to repeat the exercise.

No matter how much he wanted to.

He was setting himself up for another fall. He had to get Talia home. The sooner the better. If he and his team put in a few extra hours there was a good chance they could wrap the show before Friday. And then he'd get her out of his house and out of his mind.

With that decided he returned to the bedroom and found her asleep in his bed. It had always been that way. Unless he'd kept her awake talking, Talia fell into a deep sleep after sex. Back then he'd jokingly called it her post-coital coma, and he'd lost count of the nights his arm had gone numb with her snoozing on his shoulder. He hadn't minded a single one.

He'd never been one to gab, but talking with Talia in

the darkness had seemed safe. Easy. Comfortable. He'd told her things he'd never told anyone else. A hell of a lot more than he'd ever told the counselors the foster care system had assigned to probe his brain.

She knew about his childhood, his overworked, overstressed parents, who no matter how hard they'd tried had never had enough time, energy or money for their kids. He'd told her about ending up in foster care, but not his guilt over how he and his siblings got there. He'd never told anybody that. And never would.

She knew he had two brothers and two sisters, all younger, whom he'd never seen again, and that he'd packed all of his belongings in a duffel bag and left Alabama the day he'd turned eighteen, heading for Mooresville, North Carolina. There he'd scraped up all the grants, scholarships and financial aid he could get to put himself through one of the best auto mechanic technical schools in the country. His next stop had been Atlanta, where he'd busted his knuckles for other shops before he'd saved enough to open his own.

By the time he'd met Talia he'd made a name for himself with his unique customizations and attention to detail. He couldn't think of one other person who knew as much about the real Jake Larson as she did, and she'd never appeared to judge him. She'd seemed to care more about the circumstances he'd made for himself rather than the ones he'd been born to and scraped his way out of.

He'd thought he'd found someone who accepted him flaws and all. That's why her disappearing act a couple of months after he'd spilled his guts had cut so deep.

Had her supposed acceptance been a lie?

He stood by the bed torn between reason, which told him to get the hell away from her, and the desire to get close to her warm, flushed, sex-scented skin again.

Get in and go to sleep?

Wake her and send her to her room?

Sleep on the sofa in his study?

He couldn't crash in a guest room because each of those was temporarily assigned to Talia and Adam.

He rolled his stiffening shoulders. Climbing between the sheets and holding her was trouble. No doubt about it. His resistance was already shot to hell. Waking her would lead to questions. Questions he didn't want to answer. The leather sofa would be cold. *Cold won't kill you.*

He yanked on his boxers and headed for the hall and almost tripped over Adam. The boy had his blanket fisted in one hand and a trembly bottom lip.

"What's up, kid?"

"I want Pawpaw," Adam said, and punctuated the words with a sniffle. The light seeping from the bathroom caught the gleam of tears on his cheeks.

Jake's heart constricted. It didn't take an Einstein to know the kid meant his grandfather. Jake didn't want to send him back to bed to cry himself to sleep alone, but he couldn't let Adam climb in bed with his naked mother, either. That kind of thing earned therapists the big bucks that paid for Jake to customize their cars.

Now what?

Behind him lay the woman who'd left him and in front of him stood the child she'd had with his replacement. He was stuck between the proverbial rock and a hard place.

But he couldn't walk away from those big, brown, tear-filled eyes. He held out his hand and Adam grabbed his fingers in a snapping-turtle grip. Jake led him back to the guest room, hoisted him onto the bed and tucked him in. He turned to go, but Adam's quivering lip stopped him.

Damn.

"Move over, kid." He'd stay with Adam until the child fell asleep. Jake settled on top of the comforter. Adam wiggled closer and coiled his little toothpick arms around Jake's bicep.

The trust in that gesture clamped a vice around Jake's chest. Kids were so damned innocent. They always put their trust in the wrong people.

He couldn't let Talia or her son come to depend on him. He'd only let them down.

WITH HER heart racing and a scream lodged in her throat, Talia jerked awake to shrieking metal and the jarring impact of her left side against the car door.

Her eyes flew open. Gulping air, she tried to get her bearings. She lay on her side facing an unfamiliar wall on a comfortable mattress and not in a crumpled car.

A dream. Tension drained in a slowly expelled breath. She'd only been dreaming about the accident, not reliving it, but the vividness of the details rattled her. She'd remembered she'd been driving and crying and that she'd reached for a tissue and then looked up and *crash!*

Why had she been crying?

The room slowly came into focus, illuminated by the first rays of sunrise. Jake's room. Jake's bed. She'd slept with him. Her already-pounding heart hammered even faster. Biting her lip, she eased upright. The covers slipped from her bare shoulders. She snatched the sheet up over her breasts and turned her head. The bed was empty.

She brushed a hand over his pillow. Cool. Wherever Jake had gone he'd been gone awhile. He used to sleep later.

She caught her breath and waited for more…but nada. No more memories followed.

Swallowing a frustrated groan, she scanned the room. Her clothing lay in a crumpled pile. And then her gaze landed on Jake's discarded shirt draped across the corner of the dresser. She scooted out of bed, snatched it up and pulled the navy polo he'd changed into before dinner over her head. His scent surrounded her, tweezing a memory just out of reach. She waited for an image to form, but all she got was a smudge of forest-green that made no sense at all. She smoothed the garment over her thighs.

Adam. She needed to check on Adam.

She quickly walked to his room and stopped dead in the doorway. Two dark heads occupied the pillows. Jake, in black knit boxer briefs, lay flat on his back on top of the comforter. Adam lay beside him, a tiny bump beneath the covers with one little hand clutched in Jake's and his beloved blanket clutched in the other.

Suffocating panic assailed her as she stared at the males in her life. She struggled to regulate her breathing. Why would the sight of Jake and Adam together evoke such a strong reaction? She couldn't come up with a reason for her panic other than the obvious fact that her son had needed her and she hadn't heard him, and, oh yeah, she'd been intimate with a man she couldn't remember. A man she might still have feelings for. Why else would she have been coming to see him?

More urgently, what should she do now? She wasn't equipped to face either of the bed's occupants until she figured out what last night meant and if it had been a mistake.

She must have gone terribly wrong somewhere. She'd left Jake, a man who seemed perfect in every way except for his stated aversion to marriage and children, and she'd had a child with someone else.

Just one more person she couldn't remember.

It's only been four days since the crash. Your memory will return.

She sighed and Jake's eyes opened, blinked, zeroed in on her. His gaze raked over her from her tangled hair to her toes curling in the carpet, and her heart skipped beats. He shifted, stilled and turned his head toward Adam. He slowly extricated himself from the boy and the bed.

She didn't remember him leaving his room. But then she'd always slept like the dead after making love. Another memory. But another useless one. Where was the stuff she needed to know? The important stuff?

Jake dipped his head to indicate they leave the room. Talia wanted to escape. She'd prefer to be alone to decode her dream. Did she still have feelings for Jake? Had she been coming to Atlanta to ask him to take her back?

If so, she was out of luck. Sex or no sex, he clearly didn't have the same feelings for her if he couldn't wait to vacate the bed he'd shared with her.

She followed him into the hall, her gaze riveted on the broad, muscled V of his back until he turned, offering an equally tasty view of his powerful chest. She licked her dry lips, but the gesture did nothing to dampen the desire flickering to wakefulness in the pit of her stomach.

"I'm sorry. I didn't hear Adam call."

"He didn't. I found him in the hall. He asked for his Pawpaw." An odd tension flavored Jake's voice and his watchful eyes never left hers.

"My father and Adam are very close. Dad watches Adam while I work. He's my day-care provider." She gasped at the memory. Where had that come from? Where was the rest?

Jake's eyes narrowed. His body stilled and those amazing pectorals and biceps bunched. "Remember anything else?"

"The wreck. I dreamed about it, and it was so real I—" She hugged her middle. "I remembered turning onto the exit ramp and taking my eyes off the road for a second. When I looked up the other car was right in front of me, coming down when it should have been going up. I swerved. But he swerved the same direction and...then it was too late. I—" A chill raced over her. "Oh. My inattention may have contributed to the accident. Adam could have been hurt and it would have been my fault."

She didn't realize she was shaking until Jake wrapped

his arms around her and pulled her against the hard wall of his chest. She leaned into him, resting her cheek on his warm flesh, soaking up his strength and stability until a prickle of awareness infiltrated her distress. He rested his jaw on her head in an embrace that felt as comfortable as it was familiar, and she wondered, not for the first time, why had she left this man when they had a connection this strong between them?

She tilted her head back to look at him. Several strands of her hair clung to his morning stubble. She lifted her hand to free them and savored the sensual rasp against her fingertips.

Jake released her abruptly. "The police report says it wasn't your fault. Let's get some coffee."

He sidestepped her and headed downstairs. As rebuffs went, that one hadn't been subtle. She considered detouring by her room to get dressed, but discarded the idea. His shirt covered her. She followed him to the kitchen. The man casually strolling through the house in his underwear cancelled any cooling effects the chilly tile might have had against her bare feet. She willed herself to pull her eyes away from his tight tush and cleared her throat. "I also had a flash of something green earlier…when I put on your shirt."

His hand, holding a scoop of coffee grounds over the basket, stilled. "My favorite shirt was green. It disappeared when you did."

Was she a thief along with who knew what else? "Did…did I take it?"

He shrugged, finished measuring and then shoved the carafe under the faucet.

"Why would I take your shirt?"

His jaw shifted. "If we weren't going to sleep, you used to wear my shirts after sex. You claimed you liked smelling like me—as if I hadn't stamped my scent all over you in bed. I wore the green one the last time we were together."

Was that why she'd reached for his shirt this morning? Out of habit? And was that why she felt so comfortable in his clothing? Had she taken his shirt as a reminder or by accident? Or had he simply lost it? "And if we were going to sleep?"

"You slept naked. We both did. Couldn't stand to have anything between us." Bitterness added a bite to the last phrase.

A frisson danced over her skin. "Did I take anything else?"

Seconds passed while he emptied the carafe into the reservoir. "No."

"I wish I remembered."

The coffeepot hissed to life. "All you need to remember is why you came looking for me and the name of someone who can look out for you when you get home. I'm going to get my shower. We leave for the shop in an hour."

Had she loved him enough to take his favorite shirt? Or was the disappearance merely coincidental? Would she find it when she got home?

Talia sank into a chair and dropped her head into her hands. She *had* to remember why she'd left Jake, but even more important, she had to figure out why she'd come back and why the prospect of seeing him again had made her cry.

A CASE OF déjà vu slammed Jake the second he entered the kitchen twenty minutes later.

He'd provided breakfast for his guests until today. Now Talia stood by the stove cooking. French toast by the smell of it. His favorite. He hadn't had it since she'd left. His mouth watered and his stomach rumbled.

His shirt covered her to midthigh. His gaze coasted down over her wiggling hips and bare legs to the toes tapping out a tune that only she heard.

Oh, yeah, big-time flashback and his body responded with a stepped-up pulse and a burst of heat—the way it always had.

In their past she'd usually been the first to fall asleep and the first to awaken. More often than not back then she'd had breakfast waiting when he stumbled into the kitchen. Some days he'd eaten it hot. Others he'd been so distracted by the chef's seductive private dancing that breakfast had burned or grown cold.

But that was back in the day when he'd thought they'd be together indefinitely. Not married. Just together. A couple for as long as it worked for each of them.

Now he knew better.

But knowing didn't dull the wanting or curb the urge to sneak up behind her and slide his hands beneath the interlock knit and stroke her nipples and damp center the way he used to. His fingers twitched.

A noise halted his forward momentum and yanked his attention to the breakfast nook. His desire ebbed. Adam sat on a stack of phone books at the table, doodling on a piece of paper and munching a banana.

For a second the feeling of rightness at having people in his kitchen enfolded Jake. Breakfast had been the one and only time growing up when his entire family had been in the same place. The one time when his childhood had seemed normal. Whatever the hell normal was.

He shoved the memory aside. This whole scene was a little too homey for comfort and made him want something he'd never risk. He'd had his shot at holding his family together and blown it. He wasn't going there again.

Adam looked up and chirped, "Mornin', Dake."

"Good morning, kid."

Adam slid out of the chair, crossed the room and grabbed Jake's fingers in his little hand. His sticky banana-covered hand.

Jake let himself be towed to the table.

"Sit here."

Jake sat. No reason not to. Adam scrambled back into his chair and started humming. Poor kid. Couldn't carry a tune in a bucket. One of these days somebody would tell him just how bad he sounded. Jake didn't envy him that humiliating moment. Jake had been in third grade when his school music teacher had asked him not to sing at the holiday pageant.

Talia came up behind him. Her silky soft hair brushed his temple as she leaned over his shoulder to put his plate in front of him. Her unique scent combined with the musky aroma of sex enfolded him and his body tightened. He fisted his hands against the urge to spear his fingers in her hair and tug her down for a kiss or into his lap—the way he would have four years ago.

Damn. He hadn't realized how much he'd missed having her around. Kind of ironic that he wanted to forget the past as much as she wanted to remember it.

"Thank you." He forced himself to stay seated when he wanted to get up and get the hell away from temptation.

"You're welcome. Cooking is the least I can do considering all you're doing for us." She set a second plate in front of Adam. The humming stopped and the kid dug in like the reigning champion at a pie-eating contest. "If you could watch him for a few minutes, I'll get dressed."

"Sure."

Talia not joining them was no surprise. Although she used to sit at the table and watch him eat, occasionally stealing a bite from his plate, she'd never been big on breakfast. She headed upstairs, leaving Jake alone with her son.

Her son. Jake still couldn't get over her turning to someone else so soon after leaving him. It left a bitter taste in his mouth and a burn in his gut.

While he ate, Jake studied the boy. Adam was so much like his mother it was eerie, and the more time Jake spent with the kid, the more of Talia he saw in him. If there was any sign of the boy's father in that little energetic package, then Jake didn't see it.

If Jake had been another type of man, Adam could have been his and not some stranger's. But that wasn't the case. Long ago he'd promised himself no ties. No dependents. No pain. And no regrets for what he couldn't change.

He shoved another forkful of French toast into his

mouth, but it did nothing to soothe the hunger pains gnawing at him.

Adam's big, sad, brown eyes looked up from his almost empty plate and nailed Jake. "Pawpaw gone to hebben."

Jake's gut twisted. He glanced over his shoulder to make sure Talia wasn't within hearing range. "Yes, he's gone. I'm sorry."

"He fall down and go to sleep."

Jake's indrawn breath whistled through his teeth. Had Adam been with his grandfather when Rivera had passed?

"Mommy cried and the am'lance came."

The doctor's warning not to force Talia's memories or face a possible breakdown might become an issue if Adam repeated his words in front of his mother. Was Adam old enough to understand if Jake asked him to keep the news to himself? Probably not. But Jake had to try—for Talia's sake.

"Let's not talk to Mommy about Pawpaw. She might cry again." Was that too much pressure to put on Adam? He had no clue. And then Jake realized how odd it was that he wanted to protect Talia when just days ago he couldn't wait to get rid of her.

Only because you don't want to risk her emotional stability and lengthen her stay. No other reason.

"Finish your breakfast, Adam. We're going to the shop."

"To work on cars?"

"Right."

"I draw'd it." Adam abandoned his empty plate,

picked up his crayon in one sticky hand and shoved the picture he'd been scribbling in Jake's direction with the other. But the irregularly shaped image on the page wasn't what caught Jake's attention.

Adam held his crayon in his left hand. His *left*.

The back of Jake's neck prickled as unconnected items suddenly coupled like train cars.

Jake was left-handed and his father and grandfather had been lefties.

Jake was tone deaf. Couldn't sing or hum in tune to save his life.

And then there were the times he'd thought Adam reminded him of Ricky at that age.

Two similarities were a coincidence. But three? Denial ricocheted through Jake's skull. But the doctors had said—

Could their guesstimate on Adam's age be off by six months?

Jake shoved his food away only half-eaten. The inferno in his gut had nothing to do with hunger.

He had to get Talia back to North Carolina where she could verify her son's birthdate.

Because her son might also be his.

"I'M SORRY to be taking you away from your show," Talia said to fill the tense silence in the dark car. In the hours since they'd left Atlanta, Jake had been tight-lipped and mostly silent.

"You're not. The torque wrench broke. We can't shoot anything else until the replacement comes in. That'll be Friday at the earliest."

"Do wrenches usually break that easily?"

She was beginning to think he wasn't going to answer when she saw his lips tighten in the headlights of an oncoming car. "They do if I drop them."

Jake had been in the middle of this morning's filming when the wrench had slipped from his hand and hit the floor. She'd known by the expressions on the faces of the men around him that something bad had happened. Seconds later Jake had stormed into the office and ordered Talia to grab her stuff. He'd said he was taking her home early. She'd thought he meant to his house, but the minute they'd arrived he'd ordered her to pack her and Adam's belongings. Within a half hour they'd hit the highway for North Carolina, stopping only for gas, lunch and potty breaks for Adam.

"Will this mess up your schedule much?"

"I build a week in for emergencies. When's his birthday?"

She blinked at the abrupt change in topic. "Whose?"

"Adam's."

She opened her mouth to answer. But the answer wasn't there. She was sure it had been on the tip of her tongue a second ago. "I—I don't remember."

"What time of the year?"

"I don't know."

"Hot or cold when you brought him home from the hospital?"

Why was he so insistent? "Jake, *I don't know.*"

"Is he mine?"

She gasped in surprise. But try as she might to make out Jake's expression, the dashboard lights didn't offer enough illumination. "You said he wasn't."

"Not if he's two and a half." His thumbs tapped the wheel. "He's left-handed and tone deaf."

So was Jake. He couldn't even whistle on key. Her heart thumped. *Hard.*

If Adam was Jake's son, then why had she left Jake? How could she deny father and son the opportunity to know each other? She couldn't believe she'd make such a heartless choice.

"I—we can check his birth certificate when we get home. We should be there soon. My exit is coming up."

How could she remember directions to her house and not her son's paternity?

Did she just not remember or did she really not know who'd fathered Adam? Had she been sleeping with more than one man? Had she cheated on Jake? The possibility made her stomach churn. What kind of person was she? She was almost afraid to find out.

Her dread only increased as they turned through the crape myrtles flanking the entrance to her neighborhood. Apprehension knotted her stomach and tightened her muscles. She glanced over the back of the seat at Adam, now slumped over in his car seat sound asleep. It was after nine, past his bedtime.

Would whatever they discovered change her son's life?

Jake found her street using his GPS—a built-in device far more sophisticated than Talia's portable one, but she'd come to hate the sultry voice giving instructions from the gadget. That disembodied tone was practically the only one talking in the car.

Her house came into view. The white picket fence

she'd painted this spring gleamed in the streetlights. Another memory. Little useless facts sprinkled down on her like a shower, when what she needed was a deluge of critical, significant information.

Jake pulled to a stop in her empty driveway. She didn't want to get out of the car. The now-familiar panic gripped her throat. Why?

"Get the door. I'll get Adam."

Jake's words prompted her out of statue mode. She wiped her sweating palms down her pant legs, dug her keys out of her purse and forced her feet to carry her up the sidewalk. The sensor light clicked on, illuminating her path. Her hand shook as she fitted the key into the lock and pushed open the door.

Apprehension crawled over her skin like ants as she flipped the light switch in the foyer and then the den. She turned a slow circle. The house was empty and silent, but everything looked and smelled familiar. She recognized the pictures on the walls, the quilt draped over the back of the sofa and even the orchids and peace lilies blooming on the bookshelf beside the fireplace.

But she didn't remember Adam's father. There was no sign of an adult male sharing her pastel-decorated space.

"Where do you want him?"

She swallowed to ease her dry mouth. Jake stood in her foyer with a still-sleeping Adam cradled in his arms. "His bedroom is upstairs at the end of the hall."

Jake didn't ask how she knew. He just climbed the stairs. Talia strolled through the first level of the house, turning on lights and waiting for something to click and erase the dark spots in her memory. She entered her kitchen with its white cabinets and spotted a folded newspaper on the table. Why hadn't she taken it out for recycling? She always took the paper out as soon as she finished reading it.

She crossed the room and reached for it. Her father's picture stared up at her from the page, stilling her hand. *The obituary page.*

Her father was dead.

Pain speared through her, quickly followed by grief, overwhelming, wrenching waves of grief. A sob rolled up from her chest. She mashed her fingers over her mouth to dam a second one. Her knees buckled, but she caught herself by grabbing the chair.

Memories came rushing back. Memories of going to his house after work to pick up Adam. Having to use her key to get in because her father and Adam hadn't greeted her on the porch the way they usually did. Finding Adam playing with his favorite toy truck on the floor beside her prostrate father.

Adam had looked up and scampered to her. "Pawpaw's takin' a nap," he'd said.

But Talia had known from her father's odd posture that he wasn't napping. She recalled her terror as she'd sprinted across the room to check for a pulse and hadn't found one. She'd rolled him over, ready to perform CPR, but he'd been gone too long. She'd tried anyway.

"Talia?"

She startled and numbly faced Jake. "He's dead. My father is dead. I called 911. But it was too late."

Sympathy etched lines between his eyes and beside his mouth. His hand grasped her shoulder in a gesture of support. "I'm sorry. I wanted to tell you, but the doctor said not to."

"My father is dead. And I *forgot*. How could I forget that?" And then his words sank in. "Wait. You knew?"

He lowered his hand. "Martha found the obit online Monday. The doctor thinks that's what you're blocking."

Struggling to make sense of the last few weeks, she turned away and hugged herself. Her breaths shuddered in and then back out. Her father was gone—probably instantly from a massive heart attack, the doctors had claimed.

It had been just the two of them ever since her mother had passed away when Talia was fifteen.

And then Adam had made it three.

And now it was back to two. Her and Adam.

And Jake? Was he part of the equation?

"Where's Adam's birth certificate?" Jake's tight voice interrupted her thoughts.

"I'll get it." With anxiety miring every step, she returned to the den, opened the cabinet and the fireproof safe it concealed. *You know where it is but not what it says?*

Her hands shook as she withdrew the folder containing all of Adam's important documents. She couldn't bear to look, but she forced herself.

Father: Jake Larson.

Her heart pounded in panic, in despair. A wave of dizziness swamped her. She stumbled toward the sofa and sank onto the cushion.

What had she done? How could she have kept Jake from knowing his son and her son from his father? What kind of monster was she to deny them both?

Or had she had a very good reason?

Damn her blasted missing memory anyway.

"Talia?" Jake closed the distance between them and plucked the birth certificate from her fingers. She heard his breath hiss. "You have my name on here, but if he's mine, why didn't you tell me you were pregnant when you left me?"

She heard the accusation and implication in his tone and she wanted to give him the answer. She needed to give him one. But she couldn't. "I don't know."

"You claimed you were on the pill. Was that a lie? You wanted kids. Did you deliberately get knocked up?"

She flinched. Could she have done something so heinous? Her mouth worked, but her brain didn't supply any answers and no words emerged.

"Or did you run because you couldn't face me and tell me you'd been with someone else? Maybe that jackass you worked for. He always had the hots for you. Despite his wife."

Her mouth dropped open in horror. Could she have had an affair with her *married* boss? She couldn't even picture his face.

"I—I can't believe I'd do that." But she didn't know. Not for sure.

Jake must have heard the doubt in her voice because his mouth thinned and his eyes hardened. "You knew my rules. No rings. No kids. No forever. Is Adam mine?" he repeated.

"I—" *Don't know.* She bit back the words. He had to be sick of hearing them. She was. A feeling of helplessness overwhelmed her. She shook her head. "I wish I could tell you what you want to know. What we both want to know."

He swore and stomped out of the house. The outside lights flicked on. But Jake didn't get in his car and drive off. He snapped open his cell phone, stabbed out a number and paced back and forth across her lawn like a caged lion while he talked.

She'd never seen Jake this furious. *That* much she knew for sure. Why wouldn't the rest come?

Because she was very afraid that what she didn't know could cost her the most important thing in her life. Her son.

CHAPTER SIX

"YOU NEED a DNA test," Jake's lawyer said over the cell phone.

"If she refuses?"

"Your name on the birth certificate is grounds enough to get a court order. It takes three to five business days to get the test results. That means you could know something before the weekend, but mostly likely it'll be early next week. First thing in the morning I'll find a lab near her place and set up an appointment for tomorrow, and then I'll call you with the time and location. Work for you?"

Less than a week, but it seemed like an eternity. "I'll make it work."

Jake pressed a fist to his stomach. The fast-food burger he'd eaten a couple of hours ago sat like motor sludge in his gut, and fury lit his veins. "If he's mine, where do we go from here?"

"Depends on whether you want to see the boy and how litigious you're willing to get. Has she made any demands yet?"

"No." Talia hadn't asked for anything. She'd even offered to buy his gas for driving them home.

"Do you think she'll hit you up for a chunk of back child support? She's seen your house. She has to have some idea of what you're worth now."

If she cared about his money she hadn't let on. He scanned her compact two-story house in the dark. The place looked well-maintained and it was in a decent neighborhood. If she was hurting for money it didn't show. "Hell if I know."

"What do you want out of this, Jake? Give me a target and I'll hit it."

"I wanted never to be a father. But if I am…" He dropped his head back and stared up at the dark starless sky. "I won't turn my back on any child of mine."

The way his parents had on him.

"First, let's find out if he's yours. Then we'll plan our attack. The fact that she's offered less than full disclosure to this point works in our favor."

Jake ended the call, retrieved Talia's suitcase from the Escalade and returned to the house. He dropped the luggage at the foot of the stairs and found her sitting in the den. She had a large book of some sort opened in her lap. A baby book, he realized as he approached.

"Adam was months behind in cutting most of his baby teeth. The pediatrician was so concerned he had X-rays taken. But my father said I was just as late getting mine." She looked up. Sadness turned down the corners of her mouth. "I didn't remember that on my own. I read it here in my notes. If my father's death is what I'm blocking, then why can't I remember the rest now that I know about Dad?"

"You'll have to ask your doctor."

"What if I never remember? What if this book is all I have of Adam's first three years?"

The emotional quaver in her voice, her vulnerability and her obvious pain dampened his anger, but only slightly. A trapped, backed-into-a-corner feeling took precedence. "I want a DNA test. My attorney is setting up one for tomorrow."

The little color remaining in her cheeks leeched away. "I understand why you don't trust me, but—"

"If you refuse I'll get a court order."

"I'm not refusing, Jake. But this doesn't have to get ugly."

"How can it not? You were pregnant when you left me. You either cheated on me or screwed me over by getting pregnant when I'd specifically told you I didn't want children."

Her spine snapped straight. "I didn't get pregnant by myself."

"Birth control was your issue. You wanted it that way. In fact, you insisted. You claimed stopping for a condom interrupted the romance and kept us from being as close as we could be."

Saying the words out loud made him wince at his stupidity. *Jeezuz.* Had she been setting him up the whole time? Given the way he felt about having kids, he'd been a damned fool to let someone else be in charge of birth control. He should have used a backup method. He had with anyone else. But like he'd said this morning, they'd wanted to be skin to skin with each other.

"No matter what the DNA test shows, I can't trust you, Talia."

The wounded look in her eyes made him feel as though he'd punted a puppy. But he'd only stated the facts.

"I can understand how you'd feel that way. And since I can't remember what happened I can't defend myself or offer an explanation. I'll show you to the guest room."

"I'll stay at a hotel."

She put the book on the coffee table and stood. The record of Adam's life both compelled and repulsed him. He wanted to look. And yet he didn't.

"There's no need. Besides, there aren't any close by. The bed's already made. The sheets are clean. I washed them before leaving for Atlanta." She hesitated and then added, "My father used to stay over quite often. He liked to be around to tuck Adam into bed."

Her eyes shut tightly and she inhaled a long, slow, not-quite-steady breath as if the memory were painful.

He reminded himself she'd just lost her father. For the second time. The urge to take her in his arms and comfort her almost overcame his good sense. He clenched his teeth and shoved his fists in his pockets.

"It's the room next to Adam's. I'll put clean towels in the hall bathroom for you."

If he had an ounce of gray matter between his ears he'd hit the road. "I'll get my bag out of the car."

He took five minutes to do a two-minute job. After retrieving his bag he stood on Talia's front porch, bracing himself before going back inside. The heavy summer-night air reeked of flowers. Not surprising since Talia had always been a plant fanatic. She'd filled his condo and the areas around his front and back doors with blooming plants. The plants had died from neglect after she'd left. His feelings should have done the same.

Why in the hell hadn't they?

Why did he still want her?

She'd lied. Either by omission or commission. And he could not let himself get suckered by those big brown eyes again.

"WHAT HAPPENS when this is…over?" Talia focused on the fingernails digging crescents into her palms rather than the familiar scenery passing outside her car window.

"Depends on the results." Jake's clipped words chilled her. He'd spent the night in her guest room, but he might as well have been back in Atlanta for all the distance between them. Breakfast had been strained. Only Adam had had an appetite.

Jake's anger showed in the hard angle of his freshly shaven jaw, his stiff shoulders and his more aggressive driving style. Not that he was being dangerous, but he accelerated faster than usual at each light, braked harder and turned a little sharper at each corner.

Worry over today had kept her from sleeping well last night, and this morning everything seemed to rub her raw nerves the wrong way. The tape over the cut on her face made her cheek itch. Her head hurt and nausea teased the edges of her consciousness. Any second now, she thought she might burst from the emotions roiling inside her.

To distract herself, she turned and looked at her son. Her world. She hadn't been able to hold Adam close enough this morning. He'd squirmed and squawked a protest until she'd had to let him go. He'd immediately run to Jake, who after a slight hesitation had lifted Adam, carried him to the car and strapped him into his car seat.

Now Adam sat in the back humming off-key, kicking his feet to his self-made music and totally oblivious to the tension between the adults in the car.

If she never remembered another thing, there was one fact she was absolutely certain of. She'd do anything, endure anything for her son. No matter how painful.

She blinked and turned back to Jake's profile. "I mean if he's yours, then what?"

"You'll move to Atlanta."

Test number one, apparently. "What about my job, my house, my—"

"If *your* son is *my* son, then he's going to grow up knowing his father. If you have a problem with that you'd better get an attorney."

The threat sent a tidal wave of panic through her that made it difficult to fill her lungs. Leaving her friends and a job she loved would be a sacrifice, but one she'd willingly make for Adam to have the opportunity to know Jake. She gasped as the realization sank in. She remembered her job at Adam's pediatrician's office, her friends and her coworkers.

"We'll move closer to you. That's best for Adam."

The stoplight turned green as they approached the intersection. Jake hit the gas. A car coming from the right did the same.

"Look out!" Talia screamed.

Jake threw an arm in front of her, holding her against the seat, and stomped the brake. The Escalade shuddered to a halt, and the car running the light whizzed by, missing their bumper by only inches. To add insult to injury the driver flipped them the bird and blew the horn even though *he* had broken the law.

Talia's heart pounded. She gasped for breath and twisted in her seat to check on Adam. He was fine and seemingly clueless about how close he'd come to being in his second auto accident in less than a week.

"Are you all right?" Jake lowered his arm.

She turned back to Jake, and in that instant, everything was as clear as if her memory had never been gone. Everything. Including the fact that she'd left Jake because she loved him.

Her heart leapt to her throat. "Pull over."

"Are you hurt?" Genuine concern filled his voice.

"No. But I remember. All of it."

"Our appointment—"

"We're only five minutes away. Please, Jake. I know why I left you. And why I came back."

A horn sounded behind them. Jake glared at the rearview mirror and put the SUV into motion. He drove to the next parking lot, turned in and stopped the car. He flicked the key and silenced the engine. Only Adam's humming filled the air.

"I had a stomach flu that I couldn't seem to shake."

His narrowed eyes never strayed from her face. "You never mentioned being sick."

"I didn't want to dampen your excitement. You were in talks with the TV show people." She swallowed to ease the sudden dryness of her mouth. "I went to the doctor. He ran a test and said I was pregnant. He thought I could have been just one of the two-percent-birth-control-pill-failure statistics. I'd known I was a little late, but I never suspected..." She shook her head.

"Why didn't you tell me?"

"I tried. I couldn't make myself come right out and say I was pregnant because I knew how you felt about marriage and children. So I hinted around."

His jaw shifted. "And I made my position clear. No kids. No rings. No commitment."

His adamancy had crushed her. "Yes, you did. But I wanted our baby, Jake. I was afraid you'd tell me to get rid of him, and I loved you so much I was even more afraid I'd let you talk me into it.... So I left."

He clenched his hands into white-knuckled fists. "You had no right to make that decision without me."

"No. I didn't. I realize that now. When I left I never intended to contact you again or ask for anything. But I remembered how miserable you'd been in the foster-care system, and I didn't want that for Adam. That's why I kept your name and picture in my wallet. If anything had ever happened to me, my attorney had instructions to contact you and explain the situation. He's been holding a letter from me to you, explaining how much I loved you and why I did what I did, but that I didn't want to force you to do the one thing you'd always sworn you'd never do. Become a parent."

"Why come after me now? Four years too late."

Too late? She hoped not.

"When my father died I realized that as much as losing him hurt, I was better off for having had him in my life. He was an amazing person and he taught me—and

Adam—so much." She closed her eyes and struggled with her grief. When she thought she could speak without her voice breaking, she looked into Jake's dark, wary eyes and willed him to understand.

"I wanted Adam to have that chance with you. How much or how little you want to be involved in his life is up to you. But he deserves to know you, Jake. And you need to know him. He's amazing. Not a day goes by that I don't love him more."

She glanced out the window as comprehension dawned. "It wasn't my father's death I was blocking. It was the prospect of losing my son. That's why I was crying when I took the exit on the way to your house. And I didn't see the oncoming car because I was digging in my purse for a tissue.

"Adam is all I h-have left. He's my heart, my soul, my reason for being, Jake." Tears burned her eyes and clogged her throat. She searched Jake's hard face, looking for some sign of understanding or forgiveness and found none.

What she'd feared the most could very well come true.

She could lose Adam. At the very least, she'd likely lose Jake again.

And now she knew she'd never stopped loving Jake Larson and she probably never would.

JAKE DIDN'T know what to think.

Should he believe Talia's story? It sounded plausible. But he had enough doubts to want to see the DNA results.

He was a seeing-is-believing kind of guy. He *needed* to see the results.

Mechanically he restarted the car and pulled back onto the road. His eyes kept drifting to the rearview mirror and the boy singing off-key in the backseat.

Is he mine?

And what if Adam *was* his? Jake had had few good examples of parenting and had no clue how to be a father. How could he guarantee he wouldn't fail the kid the way he had his brothers and sisters? What if he turned out to be neglectful like his parents or abusive like more than one of his foster families?

His heart banged like a knocking engine and his mouth dried. He'd never been afraid to take risks. But this one might be more than he could handle.

Thirty minutes and three cheeks swabs later Jake was back in Talia's driveway, clenching the steering wheel until his knuckles ached while Talia unbuckled Adam from his car seat. She turned the boy loose on the lawn. Jake couldn't peel his gaze from the bouncing, running, whooping child.

Adam had been more active and more talkative since waking this morning. And the stuff that came out of the kid's mouth had made Jake laugh out loud more than once.

Is he mine? The question reverberated in his head again.

Talia removed the car seat from the Escalade and set it beside the driveway. She closed the door and walked around to his side. He lowered the window.

"Aren't you coming in?"

"No." He couldn't bear to spend every waking moment over the next few days watching Adam and searching for some small piece of himself in the kid. If he stayed he would. No need to torture himself. The die was cast. Either he was or he wasn't Adam's father.

"But your bag—"

"Is in the back. I brought it out this morning."

Mistake number one: he should have had a vasectomy years ago. But the idea of anybody getting near his goods with a sharp instrument made him cringe.

Mistake number two: he'd let his guard down and trusted Talia.

She'd been young, just twenty-two, when they'd met, fresh out of college and so darned green he'd been afraid someone—like her idiot boss—would take advantage of her. Jake had been thirty-one, bitter and jaded and banged up by the school of hard knocks. He had to admit Talia's rose-colored-glasses outlook had been a big part of her appeal. That and the fact that she overheated his libido from the moment they'd met when she'd delivered her boss's car to his garage.

But she'd left him, pregnant with either his child or someone else's. Could he trust her?

Not a chance he was willing to take.

"I'm sorry I didn't tell you about Adam as soon as I knew. For what it's worth, my father begged me to. He thought you had the right to know."

Small comfort.

"Please give Adam the opportunity to know what a great father he has, Jake." Hugging her arms around her middle, she backed away from the car.

She wouldn't say he was great if she knew he was the reason his family had been torn apart.

The pain in her eyes ripped him wide open. He turned away to look through the windshield instead of at her. "Do you have someone to call who can check in on you and...Adam?"

Why in the hell was saying the kid's name suddenly so hard? But from the moment she'd told him Adam was his, everything had shifted. Even though he wasn't convinced she was telling the truth, waking up with the kid in his bed again this morning had been different. He must have wasted ten minutes lying there watching the kid breathe.

"I'll call one of my coworkers. They aren't expecting me back at work until next week. I took some time off to deal with my father's estate and get his house ready to put on the market. And I have to make temporary child-care arrangements and tell the office I'm not coming back for long if we're moving to Atlanta. But I'll let them know I'm home."

"Make a follow-up appointment with your doctor."

"I will."

She'd stolen from him, damn it. His peace of mind. His trust. Maybe even his kid. Why did he care about her safety? "You'll hear from me when the lab calls."

"They're supposed to call me, too," she stated unnecessarily. He knew that. "Goodbye, Jake."

He checked to make sure Adam was out of the way and then pulled out of the driveway. He didn't look back.

What was done was done and it couldn't be changed.

And soon he'd know if his greatest fear—becoming a parent—had become a reality. And if it had, he hoped he was man enough to do the job.

Having her memory back was both a blessing and a curse, Talia decided. Because along with the good came the bad.

She moved through the house by rote, cleaning up while Adam napped. She not only recalled and relived the memory of losing her father, she remembered how leaving Jake had torn her heart out. She'd cried the entire eight-hour drive to her father's house. When she'd arrived he'd taken one look at her face, opened his arms and offered her a place to stay for as long as she needed.

For months after returning to Raleigh she'd lived on edge, alternately praying and dreading that Jake would come after her. When she'd finally realized he wasn't coming and that any chance of a happy ending was merely a fantasy, her heart had died a little more.

She shouldn't have expected him to chase her. If nothing else, his late-night, post-lovemaking confessions had taught her that he had a thing about people abandoning him. His family. His foster parents. Her.

Luckily, she'd had their child growing inside her to distract her. For her baby's sake she'd glued the pieces of her heart back together, bought a house and gotten on with her life.

She returned to the den and spotted Adam's baby book on the coffee table where she'd left it last night. She'd filled the album with every memento she could cram between the overstuffed pages. Memories she held in her heart and in her head.

Memories Jake didn't have.

She recalled the way he'd stared at the book last night—as if he wanted to take a look inside the cover but was afraid to. The expression in his eyes had been classic Jake, the man she'd fallen in love with, the one who she suspected yearned to be connected to someone, but because of his unhappy years bouncing through foster care wouldn't allow it.

He'd warned her time and time again during their relationship not to count on him, that he wasn't the kind of man to stick around, but his actions had contradicted his words. He'd shown her he loved her in a dozen different ways. But his words had pushed her away.

And she'd paid attention to the wrong signals.

She caressed the baby book's embossed cover. She had her memories. But she now knew firsthand how empty the lack of them had left her, how unconnected and alone she'd felt.

She'd made a mistake by selfishly denying Jake the chance to see his son born, to see Adam's first years. She should have told Jake about her pregnancy and given him a chance to rise to the occasion. She didn't doubt he would have. Instead she'd taken the easy way out and run home to her daddy.

She could never give back those lost years, but she had it within her power to give Jake the connections he lacked.

And maybe, just maybe she could make him love Adam as much as she did.

CHAPTER SEVEN

"YOU OKAY, man?" Rich, Jake's assistant and right-hand man, asked as soon as the garage emptied for lunch Friday.

Hell, no. "Absolutely."

"You sure? I mean, first you dropped that torque wrench a couple of days ago. I've never known you to drop anything. Steadiest hands I've ever seen whether we're working on a clunker or a three-million-dollar sports car. And now you seem...I don't know...distracted since Talia came back. We've never had to do so many retakes in a shoot."

Jake's neck burned. The valid criticism about his lousy performance today hit home. He wasn't about to admit he'd dropped the fragile tool on purpose Tuesday so he'd have a legitimate excuse to shut down filming for a couple of days and drive to North Carolina and check out Adam's birthdate.

Nor would he admit he was distracted because he kept waiting for the cell phone clipped to his belt to vibrate. The lab had said they probably wouldn't have the results before Monday, but there was a chance they could come through today.

But he could use a sounding board. And Rich knew how to keep his mouth shut. He'd been with Jake since day one. He'd been the first employee hired after Jake had struck out on his own. And he'd known Talia before.

"Adam might be mine."

Bushy eyebrows hiked under the bill of Rich's *Larsonize This!* hat. "Is that good news or bad?"

Good question. "He's a great kid."

"Well, yeah, and his momma's never been hard on the eyes, either. But do you want him to be yours?"

Rich's comment gnawed at Jake's jealous bone. Stupid, because Talia wasn't his. Not anymore. Did he want Adam to be? "Doesn't matter what I want. He either is or he isn't."

"Hey, I'm just saying, it's clear as untinted glass you and Talia still have the hots for each other. You couldn't keep your eyes off the window when she was here. If you wanted to hook up with her, permanent-like, the kid could be yours no matter whose he is biologically. Y'know. You could adopt him or something."

The idea didn't make Jake flinch the way it would have a week ago. A knock on the door saved him from having to come up with an answer. The FedEx guy strolled in. "Package for you, Jake. You gotta sign for this one. Personally."

He received packages all the time. Martha usually signed for them. Some were car parts. Some were gifts of an odd variety from his more ardent female fans. He'd learned to be leery of deliveries that came when he hadn't ordered anything.

"Go eat lunch before the caterers pack up, Rich." Jake always had lunch catered on Fridays as a treat for his crew. He figured it was the least he could do since they were helping him juggle his dual careers, the TV show plus the customizing business.

He signed the electronic keypad and passed it back to Bob, his usual delivery guy, then accepted the box. "They probably have a killer dessert you can take with you if you swing by the canteen."

"I have to admit, I love it when you get packages on Friday. See ya next week, Jake."

Jake carried the box to the office to dump until later, but his gaze fell on the return address. Talia's. His feet and heart and lungs stalled. What could Talia be sending him?

He set the package down on a workbench and reached for a box cutter. One sweep of the blade slit the tape, but Jake hesitated. She couldn't have the results yet, so what was this? Bracing himself, he opened the flaps and folded back the bubble wrap.

His green polo shirt topped the pile.

Talia had taken his shirt when she left. It looked a little more faded than he remembered. Why had she kept it? Unless she hadn't lied about loving him. His heart pounded against his rib cage.

He lifted the shirt and set it aside. A note in Talia's curvy, girly script had been taped to the top of Adam's baby book.

> I'd like to share my memories with you. I've enclosed Adam's baby book and two photo albums so you can see your son grow up.
> Talia

Your son. Jake's chest tightened. His hands shook as he lifted out the book on top. His skin prickled. Looking at the books meant getting involved. Getting involved meant risking failure. And rejection.

He put the album back in the box and stepped away from the table. Turning on his heel, he hustled toward the canteen. Lunch might ease the burn in his belly.

Running, Larson?

He stopped halfway across the complex and looked back toward the garage. He stood between his present and his past. The past he and Talia had created. The one that wasn't going to go away just because he walked away.

He didn't need a DNA report to tell him Adam was his son. He'd seen the truth in Talia's eyes. A truth he'd been too afraid to believe.

He'd been telling himself all these years that he wasn't afraid to take risks, but he'd been afraid to take the biggest one of all. Letting himself care for someone else. Someone else who might leave him.

Fear of trying is the same as failing.

He'd never looked for his brothers and sisters because he'd been afraid of how their lives had turned out after he'd let them down. He hadn't wanted to know. He hadn't wanted to care.

But he did care, damn it. Twenty-five years later the repercussions of that night still haunted him, crippled him. He just hadn't been willing to own up to it.

Talia had left him.

Because you gave her no choice.

He'd told her in no uncertain terms that he'd never marry her and never give her children. He'd said if she wanted kids she'd better find some other sucker to buy into that happily-ever-after fairy tale.

Except for concealing her pregnancy she'd never been less than honest with him. He couldn't say he'd been the same with her. Or himself. Because while he'd been hurt and pissed off that she'd left him, he'd also been relieved, he realized with twenty-twenty hindsight.

Every night she'd fallen asleep in his arms, he'd wondered if it would be the last. He'd been waiting for her to abandon him from the day she'd moved in. Because everybody else had. But that wall he'd tried so hard to keep between them hadn't kept him from falling in lo—

Love. The realization staggered him. How could he have missed that he'd fallen in love with Talia five years ago?

He'd even built his monstrosity of a house with her in mind, based on a comment she'd made during their last discussion. *Don't you want more than this bachelor lifestyle? Don't you ever want to put down roots and build a home and a family?*

He'd made some asinine comment about liking that he could pack up and move if he got the itch. Looking back, he could see that was the moment he'd lost her. The disappointment on her face wasn't something he'd ever forget.

Had he pushed her away?

No doubt about it. Because he hadn't liked the feeling of waiting for the bad news to hit.

Oh, hell. Now what?

Continue to run like a coward? Or scrounge up the guts to face his fears and risk getting hurt?

Talia closed the door behind the real-estate agent Saturday afternoon and headed to the kitchen to bake cookies for Adam's afternoon snack. He'd be hungry when he awoke from his nap.

She had to move forward. That meant meeting Jake halfway—more than halfway if necessary. She'd put her father's house and her own on the market today and asked the agent to refer her to a colleague in Atlanta. The lab hadn't called yet, but Talia didn't need to wait for the test results to know she and Adam would be moving.

The doorbell rang. Believing the agent must have forgotten something, Talia returned to the foyer and opened the door. Jake, wearing his favorite green shirt, the one she'd slept in so many nights, stood on her welcome mat.

She gasped and put a hand over her racing heart. "Jake."

"I want to be a part of Adam's life and I want another chance with you. I don't know how to be a father, but I'll learn. You can teach me."

Hope inflated her chest like a balloon.

"I want to marry you and adopt him and be the family you wanted. I'm not afraid to try anymore." He raked a hand through his hair, making the short strands stand in spikes. "Well, hell, yes, I am, but I'm going to do this. And do it right."

Her eyebrows shot up at his vehemence, but happiness filled her heart. In the past she would have just said yes and done whatever Jake asked. And that was why she'd run four years ago. She'd known she wasn't strong enough to stand up to him. But now she was. She had to think of Adam.

"You're going to have to explain this about-face. Come in."

He swept past her, trailing a wave of summer air and a trace of his cologne. She followed him into the den. He kept his back to her with his hands shoved in his pockets and his shoulders stiff.

"I'm the reason my family split up," he said without looking at her. "My parents were at work. They each worked two jobs to keep a roof over our heads and food on the table. I was in charge. My brothers were fighting. Wrestling, like they always did. One went through the storm door."

He paused and Talia wanted to go to him, to wrap her arms around him, but before she could turn thought into action, she remembered that in the past Jake had only opened up to her under the cover of darkness. In bed. After making love.

She stayed put, giving him his space.

"Billy cut his wrist. The blood was spurting out. The girls were screaming and Ricky started howling. Billy was crying because he thought he was going to die. So did I. I couldn't stop the bleeding. I had to call 911. The ambulance came. And then the cops came. They took all of us. And that was it. We were never a family again. Because I wasn't doing my job. I was in charge. I should have stopped their fighting."

The pain in his voice made her eyes burn and her throat clog. He turned then and the agony on his face winded her. "I let them down, Talia. But I won't let you and Adam down."

"I know you won't." That he'd carried this burden so long made her want to cry. "Jake, you were only eleven."

"My parents trusted me. And my brothers and sisters counted on me. When I saw my mother in court, she screamed, 'How could you let this happen?' as they carried us away. She blamed me. My father wouldn't even look at me."

She went to him then and grabbed his biceps. The muscles bunched rock-hard beneath her fingers. "They failed. You didn't. You were a child. Your parents had no right to put that much responsibility on you, then blame you for their neglect."

"They were doing all they could. I needed to do my share."

She cradled his face in her hands. "You kept your brother alive. That's what matters."

He took a deep breath. "There's something else you need to know. I bounced between foster homes because, according to the shrinks, I couldn't bond. I'm going to have to work at this. At us."

Her eyes burned with unshed tears. "Trust has to be earned, Jake. The people who took you in didn't keep you long enough to earn yours. But I will."

She rose on tiptoe and pressed her lips to his. His arms went around her, hugging so tightly she could barely breathe. He opened his mouth and deepened the kiss, plunging his tongue into her mouth and stroking, consuming with an edge of desperation.

Talia reveled in his hunger and her own need rose to meet his. When he finally lifted his head, she sank down onto her heels. "I never stopped loving you, Jake."

The love and tenderness in his smile tilted her world. "Then marry me. I don't want to miss any more of Adam's life. And next time we make a baby," his hand painted a warm swath across her belly, "I'll be there for every milestone."

"You don't want to wait for the paternity test results?"

"Don't need 'em."

That statement proved Jake had come a long way from the scared boy he'd been. "Then yes, Jake, I'll marry you and make a family with you."

"Dake!" Adam shrieked from the door and pelted across the room.

Jake bent and scooped him up. "We already did. We already made a family."

HQN™
We *are* romance™

How can he keep his eye on the ball when she's in view?

From *New York Times* bestselling author

carly phillips

Available in July!

Just one short season ago, major-league center fielder John Roper had it all. But this hot property's lucky streak has run out. Now it's up to him, and Hot Zone publicist Amy Stone, to get his life back on track. Amy finds it's easier said than done. With a crazed fan playing stalker and Roper's refusal to put his own needs first, she's starting to think that life in the fast lane isn't all it's cracked up to be. But when the two retreat to a secluded lodge, the sexy center fielder throws Amy a curveball—one she never saw coming....

Hot Property

www.HQNBooks.com

HQN™
We *are* romance™

Is there anything sweeter than a first love?

From *New York Times* bestselling author

SUSAN MALLERY

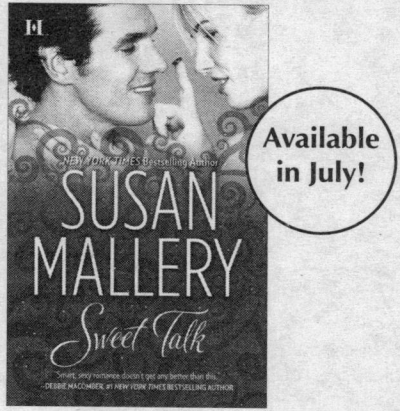

Available in July!

Twenty-eight-year-old Claire Keyes has never had a boyfriend. But falling in love now tops her to-do list. Ambitious? Maybe. But a girl's gotta dream, and sexy Wyatt is a dream come true. Although he keeps telling himself that he and Claire are entirely different, he lights up hotter than a bakery oven whenever Claire is near. If this keeps up she just might sweet-talk him into her bed…and into her life for good.

Sweet Talk

www.HQNBooks.com

HQN™
We *are* romance™

He can bear any pain but the thought of losing her...

From *New York Times* bestselling author

Gena Showalter

Bound by the demon of pain, Reyes is forbidden to know pleasure. Yet he craves Danika Ford, and will do anything to claim her—even defy the gods. For months Danika has eluded the immortal warriors who seek to destroy her and her family. But her dreams are haunted by Reyes's searing touch, even if a future together would bring death to all they hold dear....

The Darkest Pleasure

Catch the final installment of the sexy Lords of the Underworld paranormal series!

In stores this July!

www.HQNBooks.com

HQN™

We *are* romance™

He's getting under her skin...in more ways than one.

From *New York Times* bestselling author

Susan Andersen

Jane thought nothing could make her lose her cool. But she blows a gasket the night she meets the contractor restoring the Wolcott mansion. Devlin Kavanagh's rugged sex appeal may buckle her knees, but she won't tolerate theatrics from someone hired to work on the house she has just inherited.

Dev could renovate the mansion in his sleep. But ever since Jane spotted him jet-lagged, she's been on his case. Yet there's something about her. Jane hides behind conservative clothes and a frosty manner, but her seductive blue eyes and leopard-print heels hint at a woman just dying to cut loose!

Cutting Loose

Catch this sexy new title in stores this August!

www.HQNBooks.com

HQN™
We *are* romance™

From *New York Times* bestselling author

JOAN JOHNSTON

The Virgin Groom
He was every kid's idol, every man's envy, every woman's fantasy. And then Mac Macready's fiancée dumped him, and his future was looking mighty uncertain. And the most shocking thing of all was that the only woman who could save him was notorious Jewel Whitelaw....

The Substitute Groom
He'd taught his best friend's girl how to kiss—and never forgotten the touch of Jennifer Wright's lips. And now that Huck couldn't marry Jenny, Colt Whitelaw vowed to make the ultimate sacrifice. But first Colt needed to convince Jenny this was right—so he drew her close once more....

Catch these two compelling classic stories today!

www.HQNBooks.com

REQUEST YOUR FREE BOOKS!
2 FREE NOVELS PLUS 2
FREE GIFTS!

HARLEQUIN ROMANCE®

From the Heart, For the Heart

YES! Please send me 2 FREE Harlequin Romance® novels and my 2 FREE gifts (gifts are worth about $10). After receiving them, if I don't wish to receive any more books, I can return the shipping statement marked "cancel". If I don't cancel, I will receive 4 brand-new novels every month and be billed just $3.32 per book in the U.S. or $3.80 per book in Canada, plus 25¢ shipping and handling per book and applicable taxes, if any*. That's a savings of over 15% off the cover price! I understand that accepting the 2 free books and gifts places me under no obligation to buy anything. I can always return a shipment and cancel at any time. Even if I never buy another book, the two free books and gifts are mine to keep forever.

114 HDN ERQW 314 HDN ERQ9

Name	(PLEASE PRINT)	
Address		Apt. #
City	State/Prov.	Zip/Postal Code

Signature (if under 18, a parent or guardian must sign)

Mail to the Harlequin Reader Service:
IN U.S.A.: P.O. Box 1867, Buffalo, NY 14240-1867
IN CANADA: P.O. Box 609, Fort Erie, Ontario L2A 5X3

Not valid to current subscribers of Harlequin Romance books.

Want to try two free books from another line?
Call 1-800-873-8635 or visit www.morefreebooks.com.

* Terms and prices subject to change without notice. N.Y. residents add applicable sales tax. Canadian residents will be charged applicable provincial taxes and GST. Offer not valid in Quebec. This offer is limited to one order per household. All orders subject to approval. Credit or debit balances in a customer's account(s) may be offset by any other outstanding balance owed by or to the customer. Please allow 4 to 6 weeks for delivery. Offer available while quantities last.

Your Privacy: Harlequin Books is committed to protecting your privacy. Our Privacy Policy is available online at www.eHarlequin.com or upon request from the Reader Service. From time to time we make our lists of customers available to reputable third parties who may have a product or service of interest to you. If you would prefer we not share your name and address, please check here. ☐

From #1 *New York Times* bestselling author

Nora Roberts

Combine three handsome, stubbornly single young men and a meddling MacGregor grandfather for an uproarious tale of teasing, temptation and romantic torture, all the way to the altar!

The MacGregor Grooms

Don't miss these classic tales, in stores now!

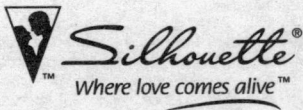

Visit Silhouette Books at www.eHarlequin.com